LIES IN THE SNOW

An Agent Victoria Heslin Thriller - 10
JENIFER RUFF

Greyt Companion Press

LIES IN THE SNOW

An Agent Victoria Heslin Thriller, Book 10

Copyright © 2025 Greyt Companion Press

Print ISBN: 978-1-954447-40-0

Ebook ISBN: 978-1-954447-39-4

Written by Jenifer Ruff

Cover design by Damonza

ALSO BY JENIFER RUFF

The Agent Victoria Heslin Thriller Series

THE FBI & CDC Thriller Series

The Brooke Walton Series

Psychological Thrillers

THE AGENT VICTORIA THRILLER SERIES

LIES IN THE SNOW is the tenth book in an award-winning series of standalone suspense novels featuring FBI Agent Victoria Heslin. A list of those books and others by Jenifer Ruff is included in this novel.

ONE

Just pretend everything is normal, I tell myself. Pretend you're not living an enormous lie that's going to end badly. That's all I need to do for now. A few more days of this won't hurt anyone.

The wind batters the windows of Black Ridge Lodge. Thick flakes of snow intertwine in a blur of white mixed with the holiday lights. Ten inches had fallen around the resort since morning. The snow covers ski tracks and fills boot prints, wiping away all evidence of guests and staff moving around outside.

If only a snowfall could do the same for me. Erase my past and the mess I've made. Shivering, I turn away from the window, searching for Steve amongst the other guests.

He's coming my way, smiling. When he reaches me, he slips his arm around my waist,

"Did you miss me, Anna?"

"Of course."

After we kiss, I brush my finger over the corner of his mouth where a smudge of my red lipstick remains.

"They're talking about whiteout conditions for tomorrow. We might be stuck inside." He raises his eyebrows in a suggestive way.

Leaning into him, I inhale his custom cologne, a smell I love because it's uniquely his. No one else will ever wear that exact scent. "Sounds wonderful."

Another kiss. I look up at him and lose myself in his eyes. They're a perfect match for his blue cashmere sweater.

At fifty-five, with silver hair at his temples, Steve is handsome and fitter than most men in their twenties. But it's his personality that hooked me. He wasn't what I had expected. He's a successful business person, so I'd prepared for arrogance and entitlement. Instead, he's patient and attentive. I've never had a relationship like this.

I push my black braided bracelets down my arm and rotate my right hand in a slow circle. It still aches from the unexpected fall I took this morning. Deep powder covered the moguls. I didn't see one coming until it was too late. It had been a long time since I took a spill that stole my breath and made me wonder if I was going to come out of it alive. Luckily, the only lingering pain is in my wrist.

Steve reaches for my hand. "Is that still bothering you? If it is, we should have it looked at."

"It's just sore, not sprained." I love that he cares. He doesn't want me to hurt or be uncomfortable. Despite the pain, I won't seek medical treatment. It's best we stay under the radar as much as possible.

I'm playing a dangerous high-stakes game with a lot to lose, but it's worth the risk. Being with Steve is exciting *and* comfortable. The fact that we both love to ski is a bonus.

At a nearby table, a woman with long red hair frowns at her male companion and says, "That guy from ski patrol has worked here six seasons and says he's never seen this much snow." She picks a thread off her teal sweater and flicks it into the air. "We should leave tomorrow morning before the next storm."

He shakes his head. "Are you kidding? I'm not bailing out now. The powder's going to be incredible."

"They'll shut down everything if it gets worse." Her voice climbs higher. "The entire mountain, Jason. And if the roads are too dangerous to trave l..." She taps her nails against the wooden table in rapid succession. "I can't miss my appointment on Monday."

They aren't the only couple bickering about whether to cut their trip short. Half of the guests in the lobby sound ready to bolt because of the storm. After working for three months in Alaska, a little Colorado snow doesn't terrify me. How bad could this storm be?

"I wouldn't mind more time together," I whisper to Steve in my most seductive voice. At the moment, I'm content to stay forever.

Unfortunately, several obstacles stand in the way of a happy future for Steve and me. Obstacles that are tough to ignore. We've been careful, but what if someone followed us here?

My phone vibrates in my pocket, but I ignore it.

His thumb caresses my neck. "You seem occupied."

I force a smile. "Just thinking about us." I'm not lying.

I let things go too far, but I couldn't prevent what happened. Falling for him. It's too late to change things now. I've fallen hard. We're having an incredible time at Black Ridge.

I have to tell him. Have to explain... but not yet. I wrap my arms around his solid frame and enjoy the soothing sensation of his fingers gliding through the length of my long brown hair.

Across the lodge, guys with ruddy complexions enter the building through the main door. I pull away from Steve. As they stomp snow from their boots, I scan their faces before I can relax again. Beside me, Steve is doing the same thing. Can any relationship withstand this stress, the constant need to look over our shoulders?

"Let's head to the bar." He motions to the other side of the lodge, waiting for me to go first.

Reluctance keeps me from moving away from the window. I want to stay suspended in this peaceful, perfect moment where everything seems wonderful and possible. I know it can't last. Everything I touch eventually breaks. The longer happiness continues, the more devastating the wreck-age.

TWO

Inside the lounge, at a table by the fireplace, Victoria Heslin observed the couple by the windows. The brunette woman turned her hand in a circular movement, fidgeting with her black bracelets while an older man in a blue sweater whispered words that made her smile. They held each other close, unbothered by the storm raging outside.

Unlike them, Victoria couldn't ignore what was happening beyond the glass. She willed herself to act as if it was just a normal day of flurries at Black Ridge Resort, but when the wind rattled the tall windows, her jaw clenched, causing a dull ache to spread across her temples.

People experienced things differently, through the lenses of personal knowledge. Dark memories and terror shaped Victoria's perspective on storms like this. She knew firsthand what incessant cold and snow could do, what they took and destroyed. She would never forget. Some people saw the snow as beautiful and magical. Victoria saw danger approaching.

Checking her phone for weather updates had become a compulsion. Her thumb hovered over the refresh button, though each temperature drop triggered a sense of dread. This trip was supposed to be a reset. Four days without chasing criminals or completing the massive amount of paperwork her job required, away from the occasionally exciting but usually mundane and tedious work that had consumed the last decade of her life. Time to relax without scanning every room for threats, though she was probably going to do that out of habit, anyway.

Ned had asked her not to check work emails. "Let's just be present," he'd said.

She'd promised him she could do it. She hoped she was right.

Her fiancé needed the break, too. News got around that he gave away as much care as he charged for at the veterinary clinic they owned. The appointments never stopped. Besides working long hours, he got up before dawn to run, swim, or bike. They didn't see each other as often as they wanted. Like most people, they could use a few more hours each day for things they wanted to do versus things they had to do. This trip was their chance to slow down, relax, and enjoy each other's company. Victoria had been looking forward to it. But the snowstorm changed everything. She had a powerful urge to leave Black Ridge while conditions were still okay.

The couple she'd been watching turned around. Holding hands, they left the window and moved across the room. They crossed paths with Ned, who was on his way back from the bar. He walked with a half-smile on his face, and the calm confidence she'd fallen in love with several years ago.

Setting a craft beer and a steaming mug of spiked hot chocolate on the table, he touched her shoulder. "How are you doing? Wishing we were on a tropical island?"

She laughed, though he was only partly joking. "Kind of. I'm just trying to keep my head in the right space."

"Same." He leaned around the table to give her a kiss. "We can leave. Your brother would understand."

Victoria wrapped her hands around the warm mug. Part of her wanted to take Ned up on his offer, but leaving meant letting fear control her decisions. She didn't want to live that way. "I know we can go, but I'm okay. I'm sure everything will be fine."

That was a lie. She wasn't sure.

Her brother had invited them to Black Ridge Resort, promising great skiing and family time. The weather was fine when they'd committed.

They hadn't known what was coming, and then it was too late to back out. The last weather report used the words "historic" and "unprecedented" for the approaching storms.

She glanced at her watch, hoping her brother might wrap up his workday any minute, since it was already coming up on 8:30 p.m. Visiting with Alex would give Victoria a focus besides the weather. She looked forward to catching up with him.

She sipped her cocoa, then closed her eyes for a few heartbeats. They were safe, surrounded by all the comforts of a luxury ski resort. Ned was with her. Her brother was here, and her sister-in-law would arrive shortly. Victoria needed to relax and appreciate it.

"Excuse me."

She snapped her eyes open to find someone staring at her. The woman was in her mid-forties with a waterfall of copper-red hair, styled despite the weather, and a wreath pendant clipped on her teal sweater.

"I'm sorry to bother you, but my husband insisted you were the woman from that plane crash. The one in the Arctic. I told him he was being ridiculous, but... Oh my goodness." The woman's wide eyes moved to Victoria's hands with their missing fingertips, her most unusual feature. "You are her, aren't you? Victoria Heslin. You were with your boyfriend when your plane went down, right?" The redhead's eyes darted to Ned.

"That's us." Ned's tone carried a protective edge. "Victoria is my fiancée now."

"Oh. Congratulations. That's wonderful." She eyed him up and down. "Aren't you both worried about being here in this snowstorm? After what you went through?" She arched her thin eyebrows and twisted her mouth.

Victoria hated attention. Besides that, this woman had just touched on the fears Victoria had been trying to ignore about the snowstorm. She set her mug down and clasped her hands together so her shortened fingers were no longer on display. "My brother works here. Ski patrol. He's outside doing avalanche control work as we speak."

"Well, that's good to know." The woman tossed her hair over her shoulder. "I'm Maura, and I hate to run now that we've met, but Jason and I have a table waiting. I couldn't leave without settling our little debate. He was convinced you were Victoria Heslin, and I guess he was right." Her grin stretched from ear to ear. "I'm sure we'll see each other around."

"Have a nice evening." Victoria's response was genuine but brief, the kind that acknowledged friendliness without encouraging more social interaction. She'd learned to perfect that balance over the years, preferring to observe people from a distance rather than becoming part of their vacation stories.

When Maura left, Victoria scanned the large room, taking everything in. An elementary-school-aged boy and a girl with a reindeer on her sweater couldn't sit still. The boy pointed out the door.

"Mom, can we go use the hot chocolate and coffee machines in the lobby? Please?" he asked, bouncing in his chair as his sister nodded in agreement.

A group of laughing twenty-somethings clinked their beer mugs together. Two older couples spoke in concerned tones about whether they should have left yesterday. Victoria noted the exits and which people in the room looked capable of handling a crisis. Ingrained habits. Survival habits.

Relax, she told herself.

Against the far wall, two male bartenders worked behind the counter. One flipped a bottle of vodka end-over-end before pouring the liquor into a glass, all the while chatting with customers. Despite his showmanship, Victoria's attention snagged on something else.

The couple she'd seen snuggling by the windows now stood at the end of the bar. Victoria recognized the man's blue sweater and the woman's silver one with a distinctive black design around the neck. The entire vibe between the two had changed. Gone was the intimacy she'd witnessed earlier. The man's shoulders were rigid as he gripped his phone. Whatever he was saying made the woman wince.

When she reached for her companion's arm, he pulled away as if her touch hurt him. Keeping his distance, he threw cash on the bar, spun around, and stalked toward the exit.

The woman didn't follow. She watched him leave with a crestfallen expression, as if she'd just lost an argument that mattered. She rotated her wrist. The movement was faster now. More of a nervous gesture than an absentminded one.

This was exactly what Ned meant. Victoria couldn't help surveying and analyzing, minding other people's business without meaning to. Her radar for suspicious behavior never stopped working.

Her phone buzzed, pulling her attention away from the scene.

A text from her brother: *I'm finally done for the day. Can you meet me at my office?*

Excited, Victoria showed Ned her screen. "Alex is back. We can go see him now."

As they finished their drinks and prepared to leave, Victoria took one more look toward the bar. The brunette in the silver sweater remained there alone, looking around with one hand over her heart. Maybe the couple had quarreled about the storm. One wanted to escape the weather, and the other wanted to stay. But it looked like more than just that.

THREE

Ned and Victoria crossed the resort's lobby, headed toward Alex's office. Fireplace reflections danced across hundreds of glass ornaments on the enormous Christmas tree. Nearby, two men lounged in deep armchairs. The one with the crew cut kept glancing up from his phone to watch guests pass by.

Holiday piano music drifted through the air but did nothing to drown out the insistent wail of the wind just beyond the walls. Fortunately, the resort's buildings were interconnected. No one had to go outside to reach the guest wings on the upper levels, or the locker rooms, the gym, and the medical area on the lower floor. Only the spa and yoga studio were in a separate building.

At an elaborate coffee machine that occupied an entire counter, the boy and girl from the restaurant had found their entertainment. The stainless-steel machine featured a digital display with dozens of illuminated buttons for every drink from espresso to hot chocolate to caramel macchiatos. They giggled as they created different combinations, took a sip, then dumped them into the trash and started again.

Behind the marble guest services desk, two employees wearing matching blazers with snowflake pins on their lapels maintained professional smiles. Thomas, according to his brass nametag, looked to be in his early thirties. He kept glancing at the children by the coffee machines, and his smile faltered each time their wasteful game brought a squeal of delight. Rosalie, a woman with smooth dark skin, a little older than college-aged, remained focused on the guest in front of her, somehow tuning out the children.

Ned led Victoria down a corridor lined with framed photographs of Black Ridge in every season. The summer photos showed mountain bikers navigating rocky trails and wildflower-dotted meadows. Fall brought images of hikers trekking through aspen groves. In the winter scenes, skiers carved through fresh powder. The spring photos captured the same slopes, but the people wore short sleeves under brilliant blue skies. One look at the images reminded Victoria why her adventure-loving brother loved it here.

Halfway down the hall, they stopped outside a door labeled *ALEX HESLIN, SKI PATROL MANAGER*.

Beside his door was a framed photo of the current ski patrol. Eight men and three women, with Alex in the center.

Victoria heard her brother speaking in clipped sentences about 'unstable snow.'

She knocked, and he responded, "Come on in."

At six feet two, Alex was an inch taller than Ned. Both men were lean and muscular from their love of sports and the outdoors.

Standing in front of a mounted map of the ski trails, Alex slid a hand-held radio into a holder at his hip. He wore ski pants with the navy sweater Victoria had given him last year.

"You're wearing my Christmas gift." She couldn't hide her smile.

He glanced down at his chest, then smiled back. "Yeah. It's a good one." He turned back for one last glance at the map. Victoria caught his worried expression, the tightness around his eyes and mouth.

"Everything okay? You seem stressed."

Before he answered, a dog greeted them, tail wagging as she trotted over to investigate. She had smoky brown fur with distinctive white markings across her face and chest.

"This is Elspeth." Alex's voice warmed as his dog worked the room, sniffing Ned's boots, then Victoria's.

Victoria took a knee, extending her hand for Elspeth to smell before scratching behind her ears. "Finally, we get to meet. Alex has told me so much about you."

"Part German Shepherd, part Coonhound," Alex explained as Ned joined Victoria on the floor, letting Elspeth investigate his jacket pockets. "Rescued her as a puppy. She's been doing search and rescue work with me for almost two years now."

Elspeth seemed to approve of both visitors, leaning into Victoria's scratches and sniffing Ned's pockets.

"I knew the three of you would hit it off." Alex picked up a container of beef jerky from his desk. "Elspeth is amazing. She's trained to detect carbon dioxide under the snow. She can do the work of twenty people in a fraction of the time." He removed a strip of jerky and screwed the cap back in place. "Without her, we'd be pushing probes through the snow, which takes forever, and we don't have that kind of time. We have fifteen minutes if we're lucky. With an avalanche rescue, timing is everything."

Victoria watched her brother's hands moving as he spoke. He possessed the same restless energy she did. He needed to stay busy, especially during a crisis. They'd always been alike in that way.

Elspeth stood at attention, riveted by Alex's every move. After she got her treat, she returned to her bed in the corner.

"Nice office," Ned said, settling into a chair.

One wall of the office featured a large window overlooking the widest slope and the main chair lift, barely visible in the snow and darkness.

The furniture was dark leather and mahogany, like pieces from a Ralph Lauren catalog. So different from the contemporary furnishings in the lodge and guest rooms.

"When they modernized the guest wings, they moved the old furnishings into the administrative offices," Alex explained. "It's a major upgrade from what I used to have, and it helps. When I have to deal with guests who think our rules don't apply to them, this space gives me some credibility."

Victoria smiled. "You deserve that respect regardless of your furniture. If people only knew how critical your job is."

The office shelves held an array of rescue equipment: first-aid kits, ropes and carabiners, probe poles, harnesses, pulleys, and space blankets. Proof that ski patrol's mission included saving lives.

Alex sat and opened a takeout box from the resort's grill. "Hope you don't mind if I eat. This is the first real food I've had since breakfast. Just protein bars and coffee all day."

Victoria's protective instincts flared. It was after eight o'clock, and he'd been working outside all day. As his older sister, the one who'd helped raise him after their mother died, she didn't enjoy seeing him push himself this hard.

"I'm sorry I've been so busy, and especially about the weather," Alex said between bites of his burger. "And I have bad news. Minka can't come tonight. The storms messed up all the flights. She got out of court early, but her flight was delayed again. Even if her plane takes off, she'll land too late to drive here safely. She'll have to stay at our condo."

"That's disappointing. But we'll see her tomorrow." Victoria looked forward to spending time with Minka, especially since she suspected and hoped Alex and Minka had brought everyone together to share some exciting news.

"The timing of these storms couldn't be worse." Alex leaned back in his chair until the front legs lifted off the floor—a habit since childhood, always balancing on the edge and pushing limits. A quarter inch too far back, and the chair would topple.

Victoria shrugged. "You can't control Mother Nature."

"If only." Alex hovered precariously. "Would be a lot easier than mitigating her tantrums. We've had a fantastic season until this weekend."

Ned tilted his head in a questioning gesture. "I figured a ski resort would love all this snow."

Alex's chair dropped forward with a thud. "There can be too much of a good thing, and this right here is what that looks like." He pointed out the window. "We'll get a brief lull, then another storm hits tomorrow afternoon. The next front is supposed to be worse. Strong winds and whiteout conditions. Take my advice and hit the upper trails tomorrow morning while they're still open."

His radio buzzed with static before a voice broke through: "Alex, it's Corey. I've got new readings for the ridgelines above the access road. Not our territory, but the data is concerning."

"Send them to me." Alex's expression darkened as he stared toward the window once again. A muscle twitched along his jaw.

"Everything okay?" Ned asked.

Alex's smile looked forced. "Just part of the job. Conditions can change fast in a storm."

Seeing the way he gripped his radio and the sudden tension radiating through his body was like looking in a mirror. Victoria had been trying to control the same stress responses all day.

Whatever he was dealing with, it wasn't routine. Unlike the rest of them, Alex couldn't worry about the storm from the safety of the lodge. He had to work in it and make life-or-death decisions regarding the dangers it posed. Her brother carried the weight of everyone's safety on his shoulders.

FOUR

Alex turned on his computer and pulled up a topographical map of the area. Colored overlays and numbers changed in real time, showing snow depth and wind direction. He zoomed in on one area. His frown deepened.

"With all this snow, is visibility the main issue?" Ned asked.

Alex kept studying the screen. "Most ski areas worry about visibility, but we have bigger problems. We've got avalanche-prone areas. Heavy snowfall and sustained winds create the perfect conditions for avalanches. It's ski patrol's job to prevent them."

He grabbed his radio again. "Hey, team. This is Alex. I'm moving tomorrow's schedule up by an hour. We need to check every ridgeline before visibility drops. Fuel up, and I'll see you all bright and early. I'll have assignments ready for you then. It's going to be a long day."

Ned shifted in his seat. "How do you prevent avalanches?"

"On the main slopes with lots of traffic, skiers compact the snow and stabilize it just by skiing. On the less-used backcountry trails where snow stays loose and deep, we ski the trails ourselves. We use cutting techniques, digging in with our edges to reduce the buildup." Alex pointed at the red-circled areas on his wall map. "For all the areas we can't reach on skis—the areas above the slopes—we trigger controlled slides with explosives."

"Do you use dynamite?" Ned asked.

"Pentolite." Alex glanced at a locked steel cabinet in the corner. "The key to keeping the slopes safe is triggering small slides to move the snow before nature triggers big ones."

"Sounds risky," Ned said.

Alex laughed. "Only if you don't know what you're doing. Or if you stand in the wrong place at the wrong time."

"Is there any chance we can watch you work while we're here?" Ned asked.

Ned loved to learn, and he was always up for an adventure. But Victoria suspected he was also trying to bond with her brother. Understanding Alex meant understanding an essential part of her.

She and Alex were similar in so many ways. They were both introverts who preferred hiking on mountain trails to lunches and charity galas. They'd grown up wealthy but chose hands-on careers, earning respect rather than relying on inheritance. They dressed up and socialized only when family obligations required it.

The tragedy of their mother's death brought them together. They needed each other, their father needed them, and grief was a strong bond. Years later, their adult lives on opposite sides of the country pulled them apart. Alex retreated to the Colorado mountains, while Victoria threw herself into FBI work in the D.C. area. But now, especially since Alex had married and settled down with Minka, Victoria wanted more. She wanted holiday gatherings where they weren't practically strangers catching up with major life events. She wanted them to be close again.

"Most of tomorrow's work will be off the main trails," Alex told Ned. "How's your skiing?"

Victoria rubbed her calves, a little sore from earlier. "We got some runs in after we arrived. I was pleasantly surprised by Ned's skill. He can handle whatever you throw at him."

Ned grinned. "First time skiing with your sister. I didn't know how good she was."

Alex's smile was the first genuine one she'd seen from him all evening. "She grew up on the slopes. We were both on the high school ski team. And as you've probably figured out by now, Victoria excels at everything she does."

"That's not true." Victoria laughed. "But I like that you think so."

Alex turned to Ned. "If you want to come with me tomorrow, you're welcome. My team starts at daybreak, but since you're on vacation..."

"Ned never sleeps late," Victoria said. "He'll probably want to go for a run first thing."

"Not in this weather," Ned answered.

"Does nine a.m. work for you?" Alex asked. "I'll text you the meeting point."

"Sounds good," Ned answered.

Victoria rubbed the back of her neck. "Since Minka isn't coming tonight, I think I'll turn in early. I'm already wiped out."

Alex wasn't listening. His attention had returned to his computer screen. Deep lines formed across his brow.

Elspeth lifted her head, and seconds later, heavy footsteps approached down the hallway.

A man in ski patrol gear stopped in the doorway. Broad-shouldered, late twenties, with thick blond hair swept across his forehead. "Hey, Alex. Wanted to see if you were still here."

"Meet Jordan Deery," Alex said. "He's one of our best patrollers. Former military. There's no one I trust more on this mountain. And this is my sister Victoria and her fiancé, Dr. Ned Patterson, although at this rate, they might just be permanently engaged."

"Nice to meet you both." Jordan delivered firm handshakes. "Alex has told me a lot about you."

"Where are you from originally?" Victoria asked.

"Wyoming." He covered a yawn. "Sorry about that."

"Rough night?" Alex asked with a grin. "I forgot to ask how things worked out with the blonde you were chatting up last night."

Jordan looked away, embarrassed. "She was chatting me up."

With an amused smile, Alex said, "Jordan's our resident heartthrob."

Alex's teasing implied Jordan was a bit of a womanizer, but Alex respected him and valued his friendship, so Victoria wouldn't let that bother her.

Alex clapped his hand on Jordan's shoulder and gave him a serious look. "I'm glad you're here. We have to update Peter." He signaled for Elspeth, then turned to Ned and Victoria. "Sorry. Duty calls. I'll see you both in the morning."

Alex headed down the hallway, leaving them in his office. Victoria caught pieces of his conversation: "...calling the sheriff..." " ... imminent..." "...we need to block..."

"That's not even our territory," Jordan said clearly.

As the voices faded, Ned grabbed his coat. "Ready to head back?"

Victoria nodded. "He's really worried. And Alex doesn't rattle easily."

"This is his job. He knows these mountains better than anyone."

True, but as Victoria followed Ned out of her brother's office, she sensed his concerns were bigger than routine avalanche control.

Tomorrow morning, she planned to gain a better understanding of what he was dealing with. Maybe she could help instead of worrying from the sidelines. She could be the supportive sister he'd always relied on, and she'd have a way to channel the anxiety building in her chest every time the wind shrieked.

FIVE

Ned hovered his key card over the sensor. "After you." He pushed their door open and stepped aside.

Victoria kicked off her boots and moved to the windows. Earlier in the day, the view offered an endless expanse of snow-covered forest. Now, only blackness and her reflection stared back at her as she pulled the curtains shut.

As Ned used the bathroom, she changed into a long-sleeved Georgetown T-shirt she'd bought freshman year of college. It was soft from years of washing, several sizes too big, and her favorite thing to sleep in.

When he emerged, she smelled their mint toothpaste as he leaned down to kiss her. "Don't fall asleep without me. I'll be right out," she said, slipping past him into the bathroom.

As she washed her face and brushed her teeth, every creak and groan of the building made her wince. It sounded as if the storm was testing the resort's structure. She hurried through her routine, eager to get into bed.

When she returned, Ned was already under the covers, propped up on one elbow. "Come here. I saw you rubbing your calves earlier. Let me help."

Victoria stretched out on the bed. Ned massaged the tight muscles in her calves. "That feels amazing." She sighed as the tension released. "Your turn after this."

After a few minutes, they traded positions, and Victoria returned the favor, working the knots from his thighs. They talked about the day—the best runs, Alex's obvious stress, Minka's delayed arrival.

Ned pulled her close, his arm around her shoulders. She nestled against his chest, tracing lazy circles over his heart.

"You know what Alex said earlier about me being good at everything?"

"Yeah?" His fingers combed gently through her hair.

"I don't like that. Makes me sound insufferable. I know I'm not good at relaxing. And I'm sorry about that. I should be better at just being present with you instead of always thinking about work or what might go wrong."

"You don't need to over-analyze the comment." He kissed the top of her head. "You want to know what I think when I look at you? Besides that you're so beautiful."

She tilted her face up to meet his eyes. "What?"

"That you choose to put your life on the line every day to protect people. That's pretty amazing. And tonight, I saw someone who's a little nervous about whether her brother will like her fiancé."

"I'm not nervous about you two liking each other. I know you will. You already do. I just want..." She paused, trying to articulate the sentiment. "I want us to feel close again. Alex and I, we've been more like polite strangers these past few years."

"Well, don't worry. He's already accepted me. I can tell."

"How?"

"He invited me to go with him tomorrow."

She huffed through her smile. "Um, you kind of invited yourself."

"True, but he agreed. Plus, that joke about us being permanently engaged. He wouldn't tease if he didn't think I was sticking around." Ned reached over to turn off the bedside lamp. "Besides, we have something in common that's really important to both of us."

"The fitness stuff?"

"More important. We both love and admire you."

Victoria's response was a kiss that said everything she felt but couldn't quite articulate—gratitude, love, and the comfort of being with someone who truly knew her.

Later, when they were ready to sleep, her head rested on his chest. The familiar rhythm of his heartbeat beneath her ear was more soothing than any sound machine.

"More snow coming tomorrow afternoon," he murmured, his hand tracing slow patterns on her back.

"But the morning looks clear?"

"Yeah. Alex will get his break."

Victoria drifted off, warm and safe in Ned's arms as the storm battered the building, scraping across the roof like a predator testing for weakness.

Sometime later, Ned's sudden movement jolted her awake. He was sitting up, head tilted, listening. The room was dark except for the faint glow from the digital clock.

"Did you hear that?"

"No. I didn't hear anything. What is it?"

"Like a roaring sound. Far away but..." He stopped mid-sentence, still listening.

Victoria held her breath. A door opened and closed somewhere down the hall. "Thunder?"

"Maybe." Ned remained tense and uncertain beside her.

Finally, he relaxed back into the pillows, and his breathing deepened.

Victoria's mind wouldn't quiet. She tried to convince herself it was just the stress of travel, of wanting everything to go well with Alex and Minka, of being somewhere new, but it was mainly the snowstorm.

Eventually, she fell asleep again, unaware that the weather had already delivered its first dangerous blow.

Victoria's internal alarm jolted her awake in the pre-dawn darkness. Something was wrong. She remembered Ned waking her during the night. He'd heard strange sounds in the distance. The details were fuzzy now.

She reached across the bed and found his warm shoulder. Still there. But the wrongness persisted, a familiar prickle of unease she couldn't ignore.

Slipping out of bed, she walked to the window in her socks, pulled back the curtains, and gasped.

Massive pine trees at least a century old lay shattered across the snow. Giant branches hung at unnatural angles, torn from their trunks by the sheer weight of accumulated snow and ice. Yesterday's healthy forest was now a graveyard of splintered wood and debris.

Ned stirred behind her.

"You have to see this," she whispered.

He joined her at the window, wrapping his arms around her waist. "Whoa. Looks like the apocalypse hit."

The trees on the ground had endured decades of winter weather but couldn't withstand yesterday's conditions. What else had the storm ravaged during the night? She considered what Alex had told them. Heavy snow also meant avalanche danger.

After a quick workout of pushups and sit-ups, they showered, dressed, and headed downstairs. The elevator doors opened to a noisy, chaotic scene in the lobby. People surrounded the front desk. Fragments of conversation stood out. "...can't get through..." "...blocked..." "...don't know how lon g..."

Another group of guests hovered outside the restaurant. At first, Victoria thought they were waiting on tables, but there were plenty of empty tables inside.

A resort employee with "Bella" on her name tag hurried over with menus. "Sorry for the delay. We're short-staffed everywhere today and doing the best we can." Her smile was strained.

"Why?" Victoria asked. "What's going on?"

"A lot of our people can't get in because of the avalanche."

"Avalanche? Where? When did it happen?" Victoria's worried thoughts went to Alex. Was he okay?

"Last night. A bit after 10:30. There was a massive slide about half a mile away, maybe farther. It blocked the access road in multiple places."

Ned turned to Victoria. "That must be what I heard."

"Some people heard the rumble. Others felt it." Bella shrugged. "Different areas of the resort, different... I don't know, acoustics or whatever. But most people are finding out when they come downstairs to get breakfast."

Victoria felt a stab of guilt. How could she have slept through it? "How bad are we talking?"

"Road's impassable. Nobody's getting in or out until the crews can clear it, and with another storm coming, it won't be soon. But hey, you came to ski, right? The slopes are safe. Our ski patrol monitors them day and night. We've got a break in the weather. And we've got plenty of food. Not the full menu, of course. Eggs get delivered every morning, so we'll run out of those before the end of breakfast, but nobody's going to starve. Follow me, I'll get you seated."

Victoria fought the urge to demand information. "Is everyone okay? I mean, was anyone hurt?" she asked as she and Ned followed Bella through the restaurant.

Bella shook her head. "No. Our ski patrol realized there might be a problem and put up barricades to close the road before the slide. It's not resort property, not supposed to be our responsibility, but they were paying attention. Who knows what might have happened if they weren't?" She stopped at a table by the window. "I'll be back soon with coffee."

The red-haired woman, Maura, approached them. She'd pulled her long hair into a messy updo. "Can you believe this nightmare?" she asked. "I told Jason we should have left yesterday. Did he listen? Of course not. Now we're held captive like prisoners. They're saying crews can't even start until they're sure there won't be more slides. We could be stuck here for a week."

A familiar sense of dread crept up Victoria's spine. She wasn't sure how much of what Maura said was fact and how much was rumor. Once people fully realized they were trapped, their nerves could unravel at a frantic pace.

A server dropped a tray of glasses nearby. The crash of shattering glass cut through the dining room like a gunshot. Conversations stopped. Heads turned. The young server stared down at the mess, her face flushed with embarrassment and stress.

Victoria's phone pinged with a text from Alex.

Change of plans. Can't meet. Half my team can't get here. Dealing with avalanche response.

Victoria tapped keys as fast as she could. *What about Minka? Did she make it in?*

She tapped her foot under the table as she stared at her phone, waiting for Alex's reply. It never came.

The overhead speakers emitted a quick buzzing sound, then a man's voice filled the dining room.

"Good morning, guests. This is Peter Stanhook, the manager here at Black Ridge. As you may have heard, an avalanche occurred late last night on the access road leading to the resort. The road is blocked, which means for the time being, we're unable to leave the property. However, I want to address any safety concerns. The slide occurred on a different mountain face than our ski trails. Our slopes remain safe, and we continue to monitor them. We'll provide updates as we receive information about when the road will open again. Thank you for your patience and understanding."

The announcement did little to ease the tension in the room. Anxious murmurs continued as guests processed the information.

Bella returned with coffee and took their order.

Victoria blew out a breath and looked around, surveying the dining room. To her left, a mother coaxed her daughter to eat a few more bites of pancake.

The little girl set her fork down. "Mommy, what's an avalanche?"

"It's when a lot of snow slides down a mountain all at once, like a giant wave."

"Like a snow waterfall?"

"Yes, exactly, sweetie."

"How does it happen?"

Her mother glanced at her husband before answering. "When there's too much snow in certain places, the snow just lets go."

The father leaned forward. "It won't happen here. The resort is safe."

At the next table, an older man delivered bad news to his companions. "Don't bother calling about flights. Everything's getting canceled. Airlines won't even discuss rebooking."

The woman with him wrung her hands. "I only packed four days of medication. What if we're stuck longer than that?"

Most of these people had probably faced nothing worse than a delayed flight or a power outage. They weren't prepared for a complete loss of control.

Growing up wealthy hadn't shielded Victoria and Alex from trauma. Their mother's abduction and death had shattered any illusions of safety. It's what drove Victoria to join the FBI. Since then, several situations had shown her that in a disaster, humans often became the biggest threats. She'd seen panic spread like wildfire, transforming rational people into desperate ones. Civilization was thinner than most people believed. They'd soon see the cracks.

Ned looked out the window at a world of white. "I should call the clinic and let them know I might not be back when I said I would. Find out if Dr. Harris can stay longer, if it comes to that, or if Melissa should start canceling my patients."

"Let's find out what we're dealing with first. All we have right now is secondhand information."

"You want to drive out to the avalanche site?"

"Yes. I need to see how bad it is. We can't just sit here waiting for updates."

"Fair enough. Let's go look after we eat."

When their food arrived, Victoria took a few bites of toast. Her appetite was gone. That's what happened when she got nervous. She sipped her coffee and waited while Ned devoured his breakfast.

Soon after leaving the restaurant, they were in their rented Tahoe SUV, driving toward the only route down the mountain to see if they were truly trapped.

SIX

Resort workers had plowed the road all the way to the blockage a half
mile away from the resort.

Ned and Victoria weren't the only ones who wanted to see the damage
for themselves.

Cars, SUVs, and trucks crowded the lookout point, engines still ticking
in the frigid air. Just beyond the parking area, a barricade of sawhorses,
orange cones, and cement blocks stretched across the access road. Victoria
imagined Alex, Jordan, and the rest of the patrol team hauling those roadblocks into position after they left her last night. Their job never ended.

Victoria pulled her jacket tighter as she and Ned joined the crowd gathered at the barricade's edge. The wind wailed through the mountain pass,
carrying the occasional crack of settling snow from the debris field. Almost
everyone had their phone out, capturing the shocking scale of devastation.
Victoria recognized the energy in the crowd. Not the morbid curiosity
people felt watching disasters on the news, but raw fear and anger. Mental
inventories of everything now threatened or lost. Mouths hung open. No
one could look away.

The avalanche had plowed a massive channel down the mountain, at
least a hundred yards wide, tearing down everything in its path and creating
an impenetrable barrier between the resort and the outside world.

Enormous trees yanked from their roots now jutted from the snow
alongside boulders like the inner guts of a gaping wound. A dislodged
pine tree clung to the mountainside at an impossible angle. The chaotic

jumble of destruction covered the road, making it appear as one with the mountain, as if no road had ever existed there at all. A "Danger Falling Rock" sign protruded at an odd angle through a towering drift of snow.

Victoria scanned the crowd dynamics. A middle-aged couple took photos. The father from the restaurant wrapped a protective arm around his daughter. The group of twenty-somethings from last night shook their heads in awe, taking selfies with the destruction. People processed crises differently. Some would become problems.

A thump emanated from somewhere around them.

Someone gasped. "What was that?"

A low rumble rolled through the air. Everyone looked up as loose snow streamed down from the ridge above. Those with good survival instincts stepped back. Others pressed closer to get a better view. The crowd became dead silent until the sound faded, and the snow stopped moving.

Victoria couldn't help replaying the frightening facts in her mind. If the accumulated snow atop the mountains moved again the way it had last night, every person out here would be at its mercy, as helpless as insects in its path.

The thought triggered a lightheaded spell and a spike of nausea in her empty stomach. She bent forward, hands on her thighs, forcing herself to take deep breaths.

"Victoria? Hey, are you okay?" Ned's voice seemed to come from far away, but his hand was on her back. He positioned himself to block the crowd's view, shielding her moment of vulnerability.

"I'm okay," she managed, though her voice sounded strange in her ears. "Just give me a second." She kept her head down and her eyes closed, waiting for the dizzying sensation to pass. *Pull yourself together. You're fine. You're safe.*

Ned stayed close. "Take your time."

When Victoria straightened, she felt shaky but in control. The worst had passed. Ned gave her a questioning look, and she nodded to let him know she was okay.

A man in a Black Ridge ski patrol jacket was addressing the anxious crowd, assuring them that despite the avalanche here, the slopes were safe, for now. His name tag read "Tom," and though his voice remained steady, he kept his eyes on the ridge above the debris field, as if he was afraid to look away. "Avalanches are always a risk along this road when we get this much snow... but everything is fine back at the resort. There's no danger of a slide there."

"With all this damage, how did power lines and cell service survive?" Ned asked.

"Power lines don't follow the same path as the access road. They have a more direct route. Cell towers never get placed in avalanche zones, so we're okay there, too."

Victoria welcomed that news. They couldn't leave, but as long as they had communication, they weren't cut off from the world.

A young man with no hat and a crew cut asked, "How long before they can start clearing?"

"Depends on the weather," Tom explained. "The city won't bring its equipment until the snow is stable. The slide blocked two locations, and they'll need to clear the lower blockage first before they can reach this section. Everyone should go back to the resort. It's safe there."

"Another storm's coming this afternoon," someone grumbled. The speaker pushed forward. It was Maura, with her red hair under a turquoise cap. "How do you know there's nobody buried under all that?"

"We closed the road." Tom pointed to the barricade in front of them.

"Closed by those things?" Maura eyed the sawhorses with disgust. "Anyone desperate enough to leave could have moved those."

As Victoria studied the immense field of debris, another question came to her. Had there been roadblocks on both sides of the slide zone?

Minka! The thought hit her like ice water. Minka could have been driving through when the mountain let go.

With her imagination running into the darkest possibilities, Victoria gripped her phone and pressed the contact for her sister-in-law. Each ring felt eternal.

"Victoria?"

"Yes, hi." Victoria choked down a sob.

"Please tell me you're all okay," Minka's voice was sharp with worry.

"Yes, everyone here is fine, as far as we know."

"Oh, good. I've been glued to the news since Alex texted me about the avalanche. How blocked is it? Are we talking a few hours or days?"

"Days. We're looking at it now." Victoria searched for words to describe the devastation. "It's a gigantic mess. Like the mountain swallowed up the road."

"I'm so sorry you got caught up in this. This isn't what we imagined when we invited you."

"It's not your fault. Things happen. But I am worried about Alex."

"You and me both. Without his full crew, he'll try to do everything himself. That man thinks he's invincible. During a snowstorm last winter, he worked thirty-six hours straight until he literally collapsed."

"I'll keep an eye on him," Victoria promised. "And I'll try to get updates on the clearing timeline."

"I've already got calls in to the county supervisor and the state transportation department. I'll get answers as soon as they know." As sweet as Minka was, her conviction reminded Victoria why opposing counsel feared her in court.

The crowd at the barricade had thinned. The initial shock was wearing off, replaced by the practical reality of their situation. People were returning to their cars, some making calls to manage the logistics of staying at the resort longer than they'd planned.

"I should let you go," Minka said. "Stay safe. And thank you for looking out for Alex. Love you."

"Love you, too. We'll see you soon."

As Victoria stared out at the barrier of snow and debris, soon couldn't come fast enough.

SEVEN

"There's nothing we can do about this," Ned told Victoria as they stared at the blockage. "The weather is holding for now, and the slopes are open. Let's drive back to the resort and ski. The fresh air and exercise will help make things seem better."

An hour later, Victoria and Ned sat close together on the chairlift, their gloved hands intertwined. Ned had convinced her that the slopes were safe. They wouldn't be open otherwise. But things didn't seem better yet. Suspended in the air with no shelter from the elements, the biting wind cut through every layer. Victoria's fingers grew cold despite her gloves.

Below them, a small boy in a green jacket snowplowed across the trail. As they watched, he lost his balance and plopped onto his backside. A second later, he popped up with the resilience only children possess.

"Not ideal conditions for beginners," Ned said. "Though all the powder makes for softer landings."

Victoria continued to track the boy's progress. "It's so much better to learn as a child. Lower center of gravity, but more importantly, they have no fear. Children don't analyze potential disasters the way we do. They don't worry about broken bones, head injuries, and torn ligaments. They just go."

"It's settled then." He lifted their hands and smiled. "When we have children, we'll have them skiing before they can walk."

Ned's comment about children lingered in her mind. This might be a good time to discuss their future together, but the storm and the avalanche had stretched her nerves thin.

"Strange the way we're acting like children now," she said instead. "Ignoring what happened, what could still happen, and entertaining ourselves on the slopes."

"What else can we do? Panic? Sit in our room and stare at the walls? This is the best thing for everyone's sanity. And we don't have a lot of time before the next storm hits."

"You're right." But even as she agreed, Victoria gazed at the clouds gathering on the western horizon, her mind conjuring terrible scenarios: food shortages, power failures, medical emergencies, the possibility of another avalanche when the next storm hit.

"You're doing it again." Ned squeezed her hand. "I can almost hear the gears turning in your head. Try to relax."

"I can't help thinking about what could go wrong. Prevention is better than dealing with the aftermath."

"It's not on you. Not this time. You're just along for the ride. Try to enjoy it."

That made her laugh out loud until her thoughts circled back to her concerns. The storm appeared to be moving faster than the weather service had predicted yesterday.

"Tips up!" The lift operator's voice jolted her back to the present.

When they got off the lift, a ski patrol member was holding a large trail closure sign. With a skating motion, Ned and Victoria headed over to find out if it was Alex.

He spotted them and snapped a crisp salute, followed by an overhead wave.

Victoria grinned and saluted back, waving her pole overhead.

"What was that about?" Ned asked.

"A family salute we did as kids. Our mother taught us. It's just silly."

Alex waited for them to reach him. "Hey, you guys. Sorry to bail on you this morning, Ned. We've got five patrollers covering what normally takes ten, and the five of us were up all night. The rest of our team is stuck on the other side of that avalanche field. Same with Minka. She didn't make it here. She's at our condo."

Victoria raised her goggles and felt her eyes water in the wind. "I know. I talked to her earlier."

"Unbelievable timing." Alex repositioned the sign in his grip. "This is not how I pictured this weekend going. Didn't think you'd get stuck here."

Ned gestured to the sign: DANGER. THIS TRAIL IS CLOSED. "You're about to close a run?"

"Unfortunately, yes." Alex huffed. "Honestly, I think these signs draw idiots like magnets. Yesterday, some kid skied right past one I'd just posted. I took off after him, and he made things worse by going off-trail and cruising through the trees. He's lucky neither of us got killed."

"What happened to him?" Ned asked.

"When we got to the bottom, I kicked him out. Can't have people endangering others. It's not the first time it's happened. I've dealt with situations just like it, but I've never been that angry. My hands were actually shaking. I think the older I get, the more I realize how much I have to lose."

Victoria smiled. "We were just discussing risk analysis on our way here. I'm glad you appreciate the inherent dangers of your job, Alex. We don't want anything to happen to you."

"I could say the same, Tori. That hothead I chased was reckless, but he wasn't a serial killer or a cartel member."

"Good point." Ned balanced on his board, arms crossed. "Anyway, how do you decide when to close trails?"

"Risk assessment." Alex checked his watch. "Increased fall rates on certain runs, poor visibility near cliffs, and wind gusts over fifty miles per hour." His radio crackled, interrupting their conversation.

"Hey, Alex, it's Tom. I'm in the equipment garage. One of our snowmobiles was left out, and the keys are missing. They're not in the ignition, not on the key hooks, nowhere."

Alex frowned. "Which machine?"

"The new Polaris. I asked everyone on patrol. No one admits to using it. I don't know how anyone would get into the garage to get the keys. With the road blocked, thought I should mention it. Someone might try to get home some other way."

"That would be suicide," Alex said. "There's no safe way down the mountain right now, period. Make sure the equipment garage stays locked."

Alex ended the transmission. "Last thing we need is a guest trying to leave and getting themselves killed. Sorry. What was I saying? Oh, right. Avalanche zones are my primary concern now. We close any zones that could hurt people before it gets to that point."

His radio hissed on again.

"Alex, Sam here. I'm at Top Ridge Station. Clocking gusts at forty-eight miles per hour at the summit, and they're getting stronger. Now they're calling for two to three more feet of snow by morning."

Alex frowned. "We might have to shut down everything sooner than planned. I'll assess the situation and make the call within the hour."

Shut everything. Victoria repeated the words in her head. No skiing meant no distractions, just sitting in the lodge watching the storm close in around them. She forced herself to breathe normally.

"Can we help you?" Ned asked.

Alex waved to a group of snowboarders. "Thanks for offering, but I brought you guys here for a vacation. The way things are moving, the slopes might all be closed by afternoon. Enjoy them while you still can."

Victoria remembered her promise to Minka. While Alex looked after everyone at the resort, she needed to make sure he didn't work himself to death. "Take a fifteen-minute break and grab a healthy meal. Talk to us."

"I have to get this thing posted." He lifted the sign. "Then I've got a list of zones to check before conditions deteriorate."

"Come on, Alex. We came all this way to see you." Victoria didn't want to guilt-trip him, but if that's what it took to get him to slow down for five minutes, she'd do it. If he ran himself into the ground, he wouldn't be of help to anyone. "Just a quick coffee."

Alex studied her face, then smiled. "Did Minka recruit you to watch out for me?"

"Maybe," Victoria admitted. "And I'm glad you have a partner who loves you and worries."

"Fine. Ten minutes max. I'm actually starving. Fair warning though, my radio won't stop, and I can't ignore calls. Let me post the sign first, then we'll get some food."

Victoria and Ned skied with Alex to the top of a black diamond run. As he planted the closure sign in the center of the trail entrance, making it impossible to miss, he got another transmission.

"Alex, it's Jordan. I'm in the woods along Red Fox Trail, and I need you up here. Now."

Alex frowned again. "Didn't we close that trail already?"

"Yeah. We did."

"Then what's the situation?"

"I'd rather not explain over the radio. Can you come?"

"I can be there in twenty minutes."

"You'll spot me from the chairlift," Jordan said. "Just get here as soon as you can."

The call ended with a squelching sound, leaving an uncomfortable silence.

Alex looked between Victoria and Ned. "I need to see what that's about. I promise I'll meet you later. We'll have dinner together. Like I said, ski while you still can."

Before either of them could respond, Alex pushed off down the slope, carving swift turns as he headed toward the chairlift that would take him to Red Fox Trail.

Victoria watched him disappear into the distance, an uneasy feeling settling in her stomach. When people were reluctant to explain themselves over the radio, it usually meant terrible news.

EIGHT

Victoria fought her way down Blue Spruce Run, her skis disappearing into powder so deep she could barely control her descent. The snow clung to her equipment. Her quads screamed with effort as she tried to keep her ski tips from diving under the surface. Along the trail, pine trees sagged, looking almost defeated, and branches bowed under the weight of yesterday's snow.

With so many trails closed, a steady stream of skiers and snowboarders wove around each other on the remaining runs. Victoria stayed hyperalert, anticipating others' movements. Unlike Alex, she'd never been a speed demon, except during races with a clear course in front of her. She enjoyed taking her time, the sensation of balance and control, making each turn deliberate and smooth.

Despite the conditions, Victoria found a rhythm. The deep powder demanded complete focus and technique. When she finally came to a stop, snow spraying in an arc, she felt the satisfaction that came from conquering a challenging effort.

Ned carved to a halt beside her, in front of the West Face Lodge. They'd visited there for a bathroom break and a snack yesterday afternoon. Less than twenty-four hours ago, when they had no idea an avalanche would cage them in.

Victoria pushed her goggles up and stepped out of her bindings.

Ned stacked their equipment in the rack as the first snowflakes began falling, hours ahead of yesterday's forecast.

"Here we go again." Victoria brushed snow from her jacket. Each flake felt like a countdown ticking toward complete loss of control.

Ned held the door for two teenage boys heading out, their faces flushed with excitement.

"Hawk, this is so sick!" one exclaimed. "It's snowing again!"

His friend Hawk, sporting a spiky purple mohawk and earmuffs, grinned as he held up his neon orange phone. "My account is blowing up. If only we could get an actual avalanche on film."

Ned smiled through gritted teeth. "Let's hope we don't have another one."

Hawk looked back over his shoulder. "Are you kidding? Getting stuck here is the coolest thing that's ever happened to me! This content is gold!"

Victoria watched them clomp through the snow, their adolescent invincibility intact. She wasn't sure what to think of their ability to see adventure and opportunity rather than looming danger.

Inside the lodge, nearly every table was occupied. People hunched over phones, no doubt searching for updates about the avalanche, road clearing progress, or the approaching storm.

"Restroom." Victoria motioned toward the back.

Ned pointed to the cafeteria line. "I'll get the food."

"Soup, please. Anything with vegetables. And grilled cheese," she called back.

After using the facilities, Victoria claimed a table and opened the security app for her house to check on her greyhounds. They lay scattered around the rooms, napping, which is what they did most of the day. Only Oliver was missing. She found him on a backyard camera, running, then making an abrupt stop to sniff. The temperature in Virginia was fifty degrees, and the sun was shining over the Blue Ridge Mountains in a blue sky. She couldn't help missing home.

An announcement came over the intercom, cutting through the dining room chatter.

"Attention guests: Due to deteriorating weather, we are closing all upper slopes and upper lifts effective immediately. All skiers and snowboarders need to head down to the lower mountain. We will continue monitoring conditions and aim to keep the lower slopes open for your enjoyment as long as safely possible. Thank you for your cooperation."

Protests rose around them, followed by the scraping of chairs as people gathered their gear to leave.

"We have to get to the top before they close the lifts," someone said, causing Victoria to roll her eyes skyward and think of what Alex had said about rules not applying.

Ned appeared minutes later, carrying a tray of food. "Did you hear that?"

"Hard to miss." Victoria opened her soup container and found it half full compared to yesterday's portions.

Ned's sandwich looked anemic, with wilted lettuce and thin fillings.

Her phone screen lit up next to her tray.

"Oh, it's Alex. Maybe he's free to join us." She answered the call, pressing the phone to her ear. "Hey, can you meet us now?"

"Victoria?" Wind roared in the background, making him hard to hear. "Are you still on the mountain?"

"Yeah, we're at West Face Lodge. I can order for you."

"I can't meet you. But can you come up here? To Red Fox Trail."

Alex's tone made Victoria sit straighter. He was twenty-nine, but in that moment, she heard her twelve-year-old brother and the same fearful uncertainty from when kidnappers took their mother, and the family didn't know if she'd ever come home.

"What's wrong?" Victoria asked, catching Ned's questioning look and shaking her head.

"We have a situation up here."

The simple words chilled her. "What kind of situation?"

"I need you to look at something. Might be a crime scene."

Victoria's hand tightened around her phone. "On the slopes?"

"Near one, to the side. In the woods. The general manager already called the county, but they can't get through. I told them you're here, and that you're an FBI special agent and you've handled pretty much everything. I hope you don't mind."

Ned was watching her. She felt removed from the buzz of people around them as she slipped into the focused state that came with her work.

"That's fine, Alex. I don't mind. What are we dealing with? Is it a skiing accident?" She kept her voice low so that no one beyond her table could hear.

"Doesn't look like it. The woman has no ski equipment. She's not dressed for the mountain at all. Can you have a look?"

Victoria turned to the windows and the falling snow. Red Fox Trail ran down the back of the mountain. She'd skied it only once before. To get there, she'd have to go back to the top. "The upper lifts aren't running."

"We'll fire up lift J for you. It's the closest to West Face Lodge. Can you come now?"

She met Ned's gaze across the table. "Give us ten minutes to get to the lift."

Finished with the call, she pushed her tray aside, then reconsidered and grabbed the remaining bread. No telling when she'd eat again.

"What's happening?" Ned asked, retrieving her dropped glove from under the table.

"A potential crime scene. Alex was pretty vague."

"I'm coming with you."

Victoria nodded. Ned's medical background could be valuable, and she wanted him with her.

Her concern stemmed from the fact that Alex was an experienced para-medic with a long history of rescues. During his seven years on mountain patrol, he'd seen almost everything, including compound fractures with broken bones jutting out of limbs. He'd orchestrated avalanche rescues and tragic recoveries. Just last winter, a snowboarder without a helmet hit a tree and suffered a traumatic brain injury. Alex kept the kid alive with a trauma kit until the medical helicopter arrived. The neurosurgeon who operated claimed the snowboarder wouldn't have survived without Alex's intervention.

Despite all Alex had witnessed, whatever he'd found up on the mountain had him shaken.

NINE

A stocky man with snow in his beard exited the station as Ned and Victoria approached lift J.

"You're Alex's sister?" he shouted.

"Yes."

"Patrol radioed about you." He gestured toward the mountain peak, now shrouded in gray. "You know where you're headed? Sam's Gully down the back side to Red Fox Trail. Powder's waist-deep up there right now, and once you commit to that route, there's no turning back. You sure you can handle it?"

Victoria nodded, adrenaline already sharpening her focus, as Ned answered, "We're good."

"You'll see closure signs at the top of the trails. Just ski around them. Alex says you can't miss him from the lift. I'll shut this thing down the second you're off. Can't risk keeping it running in these conditions." The man retreated into his hut, slamming the door against the wind.

The lift jerked, then shot forward, scooping them into the air. Victoria kept one hand wrapped around the safety bar. Beside her, Ned tucked his chin as snow slid down his goggles. In front and behind, empty chairs swayed with an unsettling creak of metal.

This ride up was already more miserable than the last and triggered more memories she'd fought to suppress. The heart-stopping terror of Flight 745 going down, spiraling toward a frozen wasteland below. Days of sub-zero temperatures and questioning whether living through the crash was a blessing or a curse. She'd sworn never to experience that helplessness again. Yet here they were—imprisoned by one storm, with another blizzard approaching, cut off from the outside world.

She pressed her lips together with determination to keep her worries under control. Entirely different circumstances, she told herself. No one was lost. They had everything they needed and more. If anyone required serious medical attention, a helicopter could reach them. At least for now. But if conditions worsened... The mohawk kid might welcome the attention that would come with that, but she didn't.

Visibility dropped as they climbed higher. The skiers below became ghostly smears of color in the swirling white. A solid wall of gray clouds pressed in from all sides.

The ride seemed to take forever. Near the top, the lift leveled out, and Victoria spotted flashes of red in the woods between trails. Two men in ski patrol jackets stood out against the white landscape. A dog with Elspeth's coloring moved between the figures. An empty rescue sled lay abandoned in the snow nearby.

One man waved his arm overhead. Not their childhood salute, but she could tell it was Alex. She raised her pole in response.

After another five minutes of slow-moving ascent, they were at the top. The powder on Sam's Gully required every ounce of Victoria's skill to navigate. By the time they reached the Red Fox connector and maneuvered around the closure sign, her legs were tired.

Alex broke away from the trees as they came down the slope. Behind him, Elspeth bounded through the snow like a deer, wearing boots to protect her feet.

"Thanks for coming." The wind muffled his voice. "She's in there."

"What are we looking at?" Victoria asked now that she and her brother were face-to-face.

"A woman. Mid-to-late twenties. No skis or snowboard. She's wearing street clothes under a jacket. Jeans. Regular boots. There's an empty champagne bottle beside her."

"Is she alive?"

Alex crossed his arms. "Definitely not."

"Obvious signs of trauma?"

"Can't tell. She's frozen solid, and we haven't moved anything. Didn't want to contaminate the scene in case it's not an accident."

At the tree line, where the open trail became a maze of snow-laden conifers, they removed their skis and followed existing tracks through the snow. The effort of post-holing through deep drifts had Victoria breathing hard.

"We flagged a perimeter." Alex pointed to colored markers outlining a wide area around the scene. Large ski boot prints and small dog tracks crisscrossed the area. The contamination was unavoidable given the circumstances.

The other ski patrol member partially blocked Victoria's view of the body, standing with his back turned away from the scene.

"Jordan?" Victoria asked, remembering who had called Alex earlier. She couldn't see the man's face under a balaclava and goggles, but from his size, he appeared to be the same man she'd met last night in Alex's office.

"Yeah. Thanks for coming up here to look at this." Jordan stood rigidly upright, his ski poles gripped in one hand. "I didn't touch anything."

Victoria nodded, then lowered her gaze for her first look at the body.

TEN

Victoria removed a glove and searched for a pulse on the dead woman's neck. The cold bit at her exposed fingers, and as expected, nothing stirred beneath the frozen skin. She quickly pulled her glove back on.

Brown hair splayed out around the victim's head like a dark halo against the white ground. Fresh powder covered the corpse, though not enough to bury her, which meant she'd arrived there after yesterday's heaviest snowfall. The woman lay on her back, arms extended at slight angles from her body, legs spread in a shallow V—almost as if she'd been making a snow angel before death claimed her. Her eyes were open, lips parted. Her form had created a perfect impression in the snow. She hadn't moved since arriving at that spot.

A dark green bottle of champagne rested beside her. Nearby, a pile of frozen, lumpy vomit stained the snow.

Jordan looked down at the pile of vomit. "Uh, that was me. I found her, and, uh, I didn't have time to get away before... before that happened."

Military training usually meant exposure to trauma, blood, and death. Yet Jordan had gotten ill at a crime scene. Either he'd lied about his military experience, or this body had affected him more than it should have. She made a mental note to ask Alex about Jordan's background later.

"How did you find her?" Victoria asked as a powerful gust ripped through the trees. Clumps of white powder fell from the branches, landing on her shoulders with soft thuds she felt through her jacket.

"I noticed her when I was doing a routine sweep. Would have seen her earlier if the ski patrol wasn't spread thin today. There aren't enough of us to monitor the trails like we need to. Wasn't expecting this." He averted his gaze and looked up at the stalled chairlift and the chairs swinging in small, jerky movements over the ski slope.

Victoria crouched closer to the body, her knees sinking into the snow as she took in the details. Even in death, with ice crystals coating her eyelashes, eyebrows, and skin, the figure was striking. She had a rare chameleon-like beauty. Her features were elegant but not defining, the kind of face that makeup artists and photographers loved because it could become anything. Depending on her choices, she could probably look unremarkable and plain, or, with the right styling, transform into a supermodel on a magazine cover.

The victim wore jeans, now stiff with ice. Not dressed for skiing or trekking around outside on a mountain. So what was she doing here?

Ned stood over the corpse, examining it without flinching. "I don't see any obvious wounds or injuries."

"Neither do I."

Victoria removed her glove again to search the victim's coat and pants pockets. She came up with nothing. No wallet. No ID. No phone.

She stood and scanned the immediate area, her eyes tracking the disturbed white surface and the distance to the nearest ski trail. The cold made her nose run, and she pressed a tissue against it. "You searched a broader area?"

"Yeah, we looked around," Alex answered. "I brought Elspeth to make sure there wasn't anyone else up here. Someone who might still be alive. Elspeth didn't signal. Other than that, since she was dead, we didn't move her or touch anything. Wanted to wait for you, you know, just in case."

She turned to Jordan. "When you got here, did you see any tracks besides the ones you made?"

"No. Any tracks got covered by the time I arrived."

They'd already contaminated the scene. Two men, a dog, and now, her and Ned. Too many people, but unavoidable under the circumstances.

"You said the champagne bottle was empty." Victoria studied the way it sat in the snow. She didn't see the cork anywhere.

Jordan held up both hands. "I didn't touch anything," he said again. "Just saw it was open. Not sealed. That's all I meant."

Victoria looked from the body to the chairlift overhead, calculating trajectories and possibilities. The chairs were still swinging, empty and ghostlike in the storm. Had the victim fallen? Been pushed? Or did she come up here on her own?

The nearest groomed trail was at least ten yards away through deep powder that had been difficult for her and Ned to navigate on skis. How had a woman in street clothes and suede boots intended for city streets made it this far?

"You guys have already done everything I would have. We should get her down the mountain before the storm worsens."

"Uh, should you maybe check her wrists, see if she has one of those ID bracelets?" Jordan suggested.

"ID bracelets?" Victoria asked, wondering why he would pose that question. Adult women rarely wore jewelry with their names on them.

"You know, the kind that has medical information," he added.

The question struck her as oddly specific. Sometimes, people who made unsolicited suggestions were trying to redirect the investigation.

Jordan's balaclava and goggles concealed his face, but not his body language. He shifted from foot to foot, unable to stand still. People fidgeted in the cold, but also when they had something to hide.

"We can do that when we get her inside." Victoria finally looked away from him.

The wind continued to pick up. The temperature kept dropping. Soon, the weather would make any investigation impossible.

"So, we should move her onto the stretcher now?" Jordan sounded eager to be done with the scene and get out of the cold. Probably wanted to brush his teeth too, after spilling the contents of his stomach earlier.

"Yes, move her to the stretcher." Victoria picked up the bottle with her gloved hands. She could tell by its weight that it was empty.

There was nothing more they could do on the mountain. A young woman was dead and frozen. It might have been an accident. A tragic mistake. But as Victoria took a last look at the strange remote location, the victim with no ID and inappropriate clothing, her instincts told her otherwise.

ELEVEN

Victoria skied down the slope alongside Ned, planting her poles with each turn. In front, Alex and Jordan guided the stretcher-sled with the covered corpse between them. Elspeth bounded along the packed trail the sled created.

The descent took longer than expected. The stretcher-sled was unwieldy in the deepening snow, requiring frequent stops to reposition their grip and navigate around other skiers. During the stops, Jordan couldn't stop fidgeting with his hands.

As they descended, the storm intensified. Wind drove snowflakes horizontally, creating a snowy veil that blurred the massive lodge ahead. Their tracks were already filling with fresh snow.

The shrouded body attracted attention. The addition of Elspeth racing through the snow in her boots turned the scene into a full spectacle. Skiers did double-takes as the patrol team passed. Some pointed at the stretcher, others at Elspeth. For Victoria, the sight of the body was a stark reminder that no one was invincible. For others, the whole procession seemed like entertainment. Two snowboarders—the kid with the mohawk and his friend—slowed to follow, filming on their phones.

"This is gold!" Hawk shouted.

"Hey! Have some respect," Ned yelled back, echoing Victoria's thoughts.

As they approached the base area, skiers pointed in their direction. Word was spreading. A dozen people had gathered near the lodge entrance, phones already out and recording.

Bits of overheard conversation made Victoria cringe. "...fell from the chairlift..." "...blood everywhere..." "...an avalanche on a back trail, that's why the dog is with them..."

None of it was correct, and that was troubling. False information could multiply at an alarming rate and create panic. That was the last thing they needed at a resort where they were all confined with no way out.

"Please step back," Victoria instructed as Alex and Jordan transferred the stretcher to a waiting gurney. The crowd shuffled back mere inches, phones still recording.

In their winter gear and after being out in the cold, the lodge's warmth felt stifling. As they wheeled the gurney past holiday decorations, a cheerful holiday song played over the sound system. Not the right soundtrack for their grim procession.

Conversations died as guests stopped whatever they were doing to stare at the covered body. Some gawked from a distance, giving the patrollers room to pass. A few moved closer, firing questions at Alex and Jordan.

Victoria watched everyone's reactions. Who seemed too curious? Who looked nervous rather than shocked?

As the elevator doors opened with a mechanical ding, Alex's radio came on.

"Alex, it's Corey. Still need a patrol team member to assess the East trails and Smoke's Ridge before this blizzard hits. I can't be everywhere at once."

"Copy," Alex responded, maneuvering his end of the gurney with one hand. "Jordan and I are dealing with a situation in the lodge, but one of us will check those areas as soon as we can."

"Why are you indoors when we need everyone out here?" Corey asked, his frustration clear.

Alex gave the gurney a final push to position it inside. "Like I said, we'll be out there soon." He ended the transmission and slid his radio back into the strap at his hip.

"You're not going to tell them?" Jordan asked, voice low.

"Not over the radio," Alex replied. "The team doesn't need distractions right now."

Victoria approved of her brother's discretion, though it was only a matter of time before everyone at Black Ridge knew a woman had died there.

On the lower floor of the lodge, the air was warm but stale, carrying the acrid smell of old coffee. When they reached the medical area, a man in a suit—early fifties, with an athletic build and salt-and-pepper hair—paced while wearing wireless earbuds. He stopped mid-stride when he saw them.

"This is Peter Stanhook, our general manager," Alex said. "Peter, meet my sister, FBI Special Agent Victoria Heslin, and Dr. Ned Patterson, her fiancé."

Peter's eyes drifted to the covered body, then back to Victoria. "Thank God you're here," he said, his voice hoarse. "This is a serious problem."

TWELVE

"Hello." The manager walked toward them, the tap of his dress shoes echoing in the medical bay. He extended a damp hand to shake theirs. Dark circles ringed his eyes as if he hadn't slept last night and had dealt with multiple crises before this one. "I've contacted the county sheriff, but they can't reach us. No one from law enforcement can get through."

"The police aren't coming?" Jordan asked.

Peter shook his head, and that slow movement captured hours of frustration. "The access road isn't the only casualty of yesterday's storm. They're dealing with a slew of emergencies and expect problems to multiply overnight. They might not reach us for days. Meanwhile, we need to know what happened to this poor woman sooner rather than later. We need answers about her death." He turned to Victoria, desperation creeping into his voice. "Do you think you can help us?"

The deceased had lost her life under unusual circumstances. They needed to understand how she had died. Every moment of waiting jeopardized the investigation, and the longer they waited, the more rumors spread. For those reasons, Victoria didn't want to put off the investigation either, but she had to follow the proper procedures. "I need to speak with the sheriff first. I'm not going to overstep jurisdictional boundaries."

Peter's phone rang. He glanced at it, then answered with a clipped, "Thomas? What is it?" After listening, fingers pressed against his temple, he said, "Tell everyone there's no need to worry; everyone is safe. I'll provide updates once we have some actual information." He hung up and ran a hand through his disheveled hair. "Guest services is getting bombarded. First with avalanche questions. Now this."

His phone chimed with a notification. Then again. He stared at it, and his skin turned ashen. He turned the screen to show them a video of their procession down the mountain: Elspeth bounding down the slope behind the covered stretcher. It had thousands of views already.

Before anyone could comment, static from Alex's radio cut through the tension.

"Corey here. We need another controlled slide for the ridge above Spruce Pine before it goes, but a few trails below it are still open."

"Close them," Alex said without hesitation. "Now." He lowered the radio and addressed the group. "We were working on that ridge this morning. It wasn't enough. We're short-staffed on the most critical of all days. Jordan and I have to get back out there."

"Yes, go. Both of you." Peter wrung his hands. "Safety is priority one, but we need to keep the trails open for as long as possible. People need to keep busy."

Alex lifted his chin. "I'll keep the slopes open if they're safe. That's my job." He embraced Victoria, then clasped Ned's shoulder. "Thank you for your help up there."

Alex was headed back out into the storm because people depended on him. He and Jordan had lives to protect. But Jordan's reactions at the crime scene nagged at her, and she couldn't wait.

"Alex, hold on a minute."

He paused, Elspeth at his heel, and turned back. "What is it?"

She glanced at Jordan, who was already out the door, and lowered her voice. "Jordan found the body?"

Her brother's expression shifted, becoming more guarded. "Why are you asking?"

"I saw his reaction. His body language when we were in the woods, the way he—"

"Victoria." Alex cut her off, his voice firm but not unkind. "I don't know what you think you saw, but if you're questioning Jordan's character, I assure you I trust him with my life. He's my closest friend here."

The conviction in her brother's voice was absolute. Victoria nodded, realizing she'd pushed as far as she should for the moment. "Okay. I just wanted to ask."

"Jordan's a good man. He was shaken up by finding the body. Anyone would be. But I've worked with him for three years. I know his character. He's a bit of a player, but he's honest about it, and he's never crossed any lines that matter."

"Okay, thanks. Be safe." She gave him a quick hug.

Her brother's loyalty was admirable, but people close to us could still hide secrets.

THIRTEEN

As Alex and Jordan headed back into the storm, Peter turned to Victoria, anxiety radiating from every pore. "So, once you talk to the sheriff, could you help us determine what happened? Before people assume the worst."

Victoria wondered what his definition of "the worst" might be. Murder? Negligence? More bad publicity? "Yes," she answered. "I can begin once I get authorization."

Peter made the call to the sheriff, then placed his phone down. They crowded around the small screen, staring at a man in his sixties wearing a cowboy hat. Behind him, an operations center buzzed with crisis activity. Dispatchers with radio consoles barked coordinates into headsets. Wall-mounted screens displaying weather radar in flashing bursts of color and the constant backdrop of ringing phones painted a picture of a region under siege.

"I can only spare a few minutes." The sheriff spoke without looking at the camera. "What's your status?"

Peter was all business. "Sheriff Wilson, this is the FBI agent I mentioned. Victoria Heslin."

The sheriff turned toward his camera then, tired eyes with pouches beneath them. "Agent Heslin. I know who you are, and it's an honor to meet you, though I wish it were under better circumstances. I understand you're at Black Ridge, and you've recovered a body under suspicious circumstances."

"That's correct," Victoria answered. "A deceased female, mid-twenties to early thirties, found in the woods next to a ski trail."

"Cause of death?"

"Undetermined, pending examination."

He was quiet for several seconds, his weathered face thoughtful. "How confident are you in your preliminary assessment? Any chance it was a tragic accident?"

Victoria outlined the key factors: the victim's inappropriate clothing, lack of identification, and the remote location.

"Under normal circumstances, I'd have my people up there in an hour. But with three counties declaring emergencies and the National Guard activated..." He rubbed his jaw. "If I involve the FBI and this turns out to be an accidental death, I'll have paperwork for months. But if it's homicide and I delay..."

He looked directly into the camera. "Agent Heslin, I'm requesting FBI assistance under emergency circumstances. You have full authority to investigate until my people can reach the scene."

He leaned closer, his face filling the screen. "Keep me informed."

Victoria glanced at Ned, who nodded almost imperceptibly. "I can conduct initial assessments and keep you informed."

"Excellent," Sheriff Wilson said. "Peter, if this is a homicide, having an FBI agent on scene might be everyone's best chance of containing the situation."

As the call ended, Victoria felt the weight of responsibility settling on her shoulders. If this were a murder, the killer might be confined with them, hidden among the staff and guests, probably watching every move they made.

She looked at the covered body, then at Peter's anxious face. Time to find out what they were dealing with.

On the count of three, Ned and Peter transferred the body from the gurney to a medical examination table.

Peter removed his suit jacket and rolled up his sleeves. He flexed his fingers as if trying to shake off an unpleasant sensation. "I can't believe we're the ones doing this. This table is meant for injuries and altitude sickness, not autopsies."

"No one is doing an autopsy here," Victoria corrected, removing her coat. "Just a straightforward external examination."

Despite a lack of proper equipment and a forensic team, the fundamentals remained the same: observe, document, analyze.

"Have you examined a dead body before?" Peter asked.

"She knows what she's doing," Ned answered before Victoria could respond. "Victoria has attended more autopsies than most doctors. She led the task force that caught the Numbers Killer in D.C. a few years ago."

Peter's eyes widened. "The female spree killer? I remember that case. That was you?"

Ned nodded. "And the missing college student in Cancun. Avery Jennings. Victoria represented the FBI in that investigation."

"Hell of a resume." Peter whistled as he paced to the window. "We've had deaths here before. Heart attacks, strokes, a fatal injury, but nothing this strange." He wrung his hands. "God, I need that road opened. Wasn't our responsibility, by the way. The city owns that section of the road." He reached into his pocket and shook two white pills into his palm. "Aspirin," he explained, swallowing them dry. "Between the avalanche, the social media nightmare, and now this, I've got a massive headache. And we still have another storm to deal with today." He shook the bottle. "Want some?"

"No, thanks," Ned and Victoria both replied.

She needed to ensure they documented everything properly. If this woman was a victim of foul play, as Victoria suspected, they had to be thorough. Every piece of evidence mattered. Mistakes didn't stand up in court.

Her ski boots clomped loudly on the tile floor as she moved around the table.

"I'll get our regular shoes from the locker room," Ned said. "Be right back."

Peter maintained his distance from the body. "I wish we already knew what happened."

"Let's see if we can figure that out," Victoria said. "Can you record everything? It'll protect all of us from a legal perspective."

Peter readied his phone's camera.

The woman on the table wore designer jeans, suede boots, a winter coat, and black leather gloves. Perfect attire for the lodge after skiing, but inappropriate for being outside on a snow-covered mountain.

While Peter filmed, Victoria searched the woman's pockets once more but still found nothing. The victim was someone's daughter, or wife, or a young mother. Did they have any idea she was dead?

Ned returned carrying both pairs of shoes.

"Thank you." Victoria sat on a bench to change out of her ski boots. "I need to collect evidence related to a possible sexual assault. It's standard procedure for any unexplained female death, and evidence could degrade over the next few days."

"You think she was assaulted?" Peter asked, his face going pale.

"I'm not sure yet. Normally, a nurse would do an exam, but I don't have that training." Victoria paused, considering her options. "What I can do is take some external samples. If there was sexual contact, DNA evidence might be present on her underwear or inner thighs. It's not ideal, but it's better than losing evidence while we wait for the access road to open." She looked around the small space. "Do you have cotton swabs? And evidence bags or small containers?"

Peter pointed to a row of cabinets.

"Do you have fingerprinting supplies?"

"I don't think so. Why would we?"

"Ink pad?" Victoria scanned the medical room's surfaces.

"There's one at the front desk," Peter offered.

"I'll need that and some clean white paper. Copy paper works."

"I'll get those items," Peter said, answering his phone on the way out.

Victoria and Ned searched the cabinets without speaking.

Outside, the howling wind was a constant reminder of the storm. The medical bay's fluorescent lights flickered, and shadows danced across the shelves.

She located a digital thermometer while Ned found swab sticks.

Peter returned. "More videos are going viral. Corporate's going to want answers I don't have." He looked at Victoria desperately. "How long before we know what killed her?"

"She can't answer that yet." Ned's voice held an edge that wasn't there before. "It takes time to do this properly, and she's just getting started."

Peter handed over the requested supplies. "Will these work?"

"Yes, thanks." Victoria accepted the inkpad and paper. Wearing latex gloves, she removed the victim's right glove, revealing unpainted nails. The frozen fingers were stiff, more like a mannequin's hand than a human one. Victoria pressed each digit against the ink pad, then transferred the prints to paper.

Peter watched from several feet away, arms crossed over his chest. "This is..." He looked away when Victoria manipulated the corpse's arm to get a better angle. "Sorry, I'm not usually squeamish, but this is just... I don't know. Disturbing."

Victoria completed the full set of prints, labeling each one. "These aren't perfect, but they're usable for identification if that becomes necessary."

When she lifted the victim's wrist to photograph her bracelets, something beneath the jewelry caught her eye. She slid the bands up, revealing a small tattoo on the inside of the woman's wrist. A crude star with uneven lines.

"Prison ink," Victoria said.

Ned looked closer. "You're sure?"

"Definitely. It's crude work. The inmates have little choice. Other inmates do the tattooing. Every facility has a version of this." She photographed the tattoo before letting the bracelet strands fall back into place.

"She doesn't look like someone who served time," Ned observed.

"Could have been white-collar crime. A short sentence. We'll find out when I run her prints. That's the good news. If she has a record, her prints will be in the system."

She placed the makeshift fingerprint cards in a plastic bag and moved on, reaching for the victim's jacket zipper. She pulled, and what she found underneath sent a chill through her body.

FOURTEEN

Victoria stared down at Jane Doe's sweater. One she recognized. Black and silver with a distinctive knitted neckline pattern. A two-inch tear marred the material along the left side, as if it had caught on a sharp object.

She'd seen an identical sweater yesterday on the woman who rotated her wrist and bracelets in a compulsive gesture.

Victoria's gaze dropped to the black bracelets on the victim's wrist again. Five separate strands of onyx beads connected by silver links.

Similar age. Similar build. Brown hair. The sweater and the bracelets.

Victoria studied the deceased's face, trying to match the features with the images in her memory. She recalled the shocked look on the woman's face when her companion left after what appeared to be an argument at the bar.

What had happened between last night and this morning?

An ache spread across Victoria's chest. The victim had been right there. Close enough to help. If Victoria had approached her, offered even a simple, "Are you okay?"—would this person still be breathing?

Stay objective. Gather all the evidence. Theorize later. The mantra felt hollow now, considering what she hadn't done yesterday.

Victoria documented the statistics: approximately twenty-seven years old, five-feet-seven inches tall, around one-hundred-thirty pounds, brown hair, brown eyes.

She searched for features like scars, additional tattoos, and birthmarks, and found none. She checked for defensive wounds and signs of a struggle, anything that might show how this person had died. Beside her, Ned conducted his own assessment. Neither found obvious signs of trauma.

Victoria turned the body over and lifted the sweater, revealing a long scrape across the lower back.

Ned bent over for a better look. "She might have fallen onto a sharp object. Or got dragged over one. I'm leaning toward dragged."

Victoria took another photograph of the injury. "We only document the facts."

"How did she die?" Peter asked. "Do you know yet if she was murdered?"

Victoria looked to Ned, who shook his head. "There's no obvious cause of death," he said. "No petechial hemorrhaging in the eyes, so probably not strangulation. Hypothermia seems most likely, but something's not adding up."

"What do you mean?" Peter asked.

"I studied the subject after our ordeal in Greenland." Ned looked at Victoria, then gestured to the deceased. "When people die of hypothermia, they go through predictable stages. First comes confusion and disorientation. They make poor decisions, wander off trails. Then they undress."

"When they're freezing?" Peter looked skeptical.

"As hypothermia progresses, people feel overheated. They usually remove their clothes, even in freezing temperatures. It seems irrational, but it's a documented phenomenon in most hypothermia deaths. There's usually burrowing behavior too," Ned continued. "In the final stages, hypothermic victims seek small, enclosed spaces. They crawl under bushes, into doorways, anywhere that feels protective. It's an instinctive response."

"But we found her in the open," Victoria said. "No attempt at shelter, no removed clothing."

Ned nodded. "If she succumbed to hypothermia, she either died quickly, which is rare, or she was already unconscious when exposed to the cold."

Peter frowned. "That champagne costs three hundred dollars a bottle. People don't drop that kind of money unless they're celebrating a special occasion. Maybe she got drunk, thought it'd be fun to hit the slopes, and passed out up there? I mean, it's horrible either way, but preferable to the alternative... a murder."

"It's possible," Victoria said. The victim might have been celebrating, but people rarely celebrated with expensive champagne alone. And the woman at the bar didn't look like she was in a celebratory mood.

Victoria checked the victim's clothing labels for names or initials and found nothing.

She lifted the victim's foot for another look. "Her boots are too small for her feet." Victoria pointed to the deep pressure marks where the toes had pushed against the front. "Size seven and a half boots, but her feet are probably a size larger."

Ned frowned. "Who wears boots that don't fit?"

"A woman who cares more about style than comfort? Or someone borrowing a friend's shoes?" Victoria suggested. "I don't know."

Later, after collecting swabs from the victim's fingernails, inner thighs, and underwear, Victoria stepped back from the table, satisfied she'd done all she could. She turned to Peter. "We need a cold, secure place to store the body. Thawing might reveal additional bruising, but it will also speed up decomposition. Best to keep her frozen until a forensic team can take over."

"There's a walk-in freezer in the service area." Peter scowled. "If guests discover we're storing a body next to their dinner ingredients, our reviews will tank. But we'll rope off a section. On the bright side, it won't be a problem since our regular deliveries have stopped until the roads open."

Victoria gathered the evidence bags she'd created. "Can you secure the room?"

"I'll ensure it stays safe. You have my word."

"All right," she said, though she wanted to inspect the location herself. "We'll help transport the body."

"I appreciate that. Everyone's working multiple jobs today." He sighed. "What a complete disaster."

"Ready?" Ned positioned himself at one end of the exam table. On his count, they transferred the corpse back onto the gurney, covered it with a clean sheet, and wheeled it toward the storage area.

Victoria followed, carrying the DNA swabs and champagne bottle in separate sealed bags. She mentally sorted through everything they still needed to discover. So many questions demanded answers. Most pressing: who was their Jane Doe? What had led to her death? And was someone else responsible?

Her thoughts kept returning to the couple she'd seen last night, and their heated argument at the bar. She needed to find that man right away.

FIFTEEN

Apparently, two ski patrol guys rolled a gurney with a dead person through the lobby not too long ago. I missed it. Now I need to hang around a bit to find out what people are saying and what they've seen.

Large flakes of snow pelt the lobby windows as I study the choices on the elaborate coffee machine, the type of amenity that tries to justify Black Ridge's exorbitant resort rates.

I select three shots of dark espresso and wait while the machine clicks and whirs, frowning at large splatters of coffee and hot chocolate on the counter. Around me, guests track snow across the tile floors as they shed layers of winter clothing, leaving widening pools of slush and salt stains that no one bothers to mop. I guess there aren't enough cleaning people to deal with our mess, thanks to that avalanche.

I prepare my coffee and toss the empty sugar packets and stirrer atop the nearest trash bin. It's overflowing with discarded cups and pastry wrappers. Coffee in hand, I move past the giant Christmas tree into the shadowed alcove on the far side of the gas fireplace, where I can observe without being noticed. Word of the dead body spread fast. Even from the corner, I can hear the concerns and complaints at the check-in desk, where Thomas and Rosalie are trying to reassure people that everything is fine.

To find more information, I turn to social media. The first video tagging Black Ridge has a profile picture of the kid with the purple mohawk. He's impossible not to notice around here. The hair, obviously, and he's obsessed with recording and posting every hour of his day.

His shaky clip, blurred with falling snow, shows ski patrol with a stretcher between them. A beige-gray sheet covers a body from end to end, making it clear the person isn't breathing. Beneath the video, the caption includes #DeathatBlackRidge.

Not the ideal hashtag, but I can use the clip.

I select a phone contact and open the message string with "Grandma Gigi," then type a message.

I'm still at Black Ridge Resort because of the avalanche, but my friend left early. Weather getting rough. Miss you.

After forwarding the message with the downloaded clip, I get a response right away.

Sorry to hear that your friend left. Drive safe. I'm making banana bread with chocolate chips. Can't wait to see you soon.

Good. Now they know. Or at least they know what I *want* them to think happened.

After deleting both messages, I slip the phone back into my pocket.

I'm just another concerned guest waiting for the road to open, hoping to leave before all hell breaks loose.

But some of us know there are bigger problems than being shut in at a resort.

Some of us know exactly who was lying on that stretcher, and why.

SIXTEEN

Peter had insisted they stop at the registration desk on their way to his office. "I need to do damage control," he'd said. "Rosalie and Thomas are drowning in questions they can't answer."

Rosalie had removed her blazer and now wore a Black Ridge logo shirt. She reorganized a stack of papers that didn't need organizing, keeping her hands occupied as Maura and her husband demanded information. When Peter approached, she excused herself and hurried to the end of the counter.

"Almost everyone is asking about the body Alex and Jordan found." She sounded on edge, trying to stay professional. "First, they thought there was another avalanche. Now people are saying it was a murder. I don't have any information. I don't know what to tell them."

Peter pressed his hand against his forehead, frowning as Hawk and his friend slowly circled the overflowing trash bins and filmed the unsightly scene. Rather than answer Rosalie, Peter made a phone call. "Marjorie. Please have the trash in the lobby emptied right away. Thank you." He hung up and said to no one in particular, "The PR nightmare keeps growing."

Rosalie kept her back to the guests. "I saw Jordan and Alex rush back out. What's going on?"

Victoria stepped forward. "Hi, I'm Victoria Heslin. Alex's sister. I'm with the FBI, and I'm leading the investigation."

"I'm Rosalie." She tapped her name badge. "I'm an intern from Cornell's Hotel Management program."

Despite everything, Victoria almost smiled. "You're getting excellent crisis management experience. You could write an interesting case study about all of this."

"Oh, for sure. But for now? What do I tell people?"

"Say law enforcement is investigating. If pressed, add that out of respect for privacy, we can't release any details until we've notified the family."

"That sounds right," Peter agreed. "Emphasize that guest safety remains our priority."

Victoria wanted to offer reassurance that guests had nothing to worry about, but making promises she couldn't keep would only create bigger problems later. She lowered her voice. "Has anyone claimed to know the deceased or reported a woman missing?" She was thinking specifically of the man with the blue sweater from the bar.

"No, nothing like that." Rosalie shook her head. "Everyone's speculating, but no one has solid information. So it *is* a woman? But you really don't know who she is?"

"She's not an employee," Peter said. "We confirmed with this morning's phone chain that none of our staff are missing. At this point, we're not sure if she's a registered guest. Please notify me ASAP if anyone claims to know the woman or what happened."

Rosalie straightened her posture. "Got it."

Peter's phone rang, and he turned away from the desk. "What? You can't be serious. We have no other way out of here." His voice rose before he caught himself, glancing around at the nearby guests. "Yes, I'm well aware of the forecast. It's causing more trouble than you can imagine... Fine, just keep me updated."

He disconnected with an angry huff and motioned for Victoria and Ned to follow. "Let's head to my office."

Peter remained silent until they reached the administrative corridor. "That last phone call was the county. They're pulling the road crews. They barely got started clearing the blockage a few miles away, but now they're worried about more avalanches. We're on our own here for at least another forty-eight hours."

Victoria understood the delay. With another storm building, the county couldn't risk lives or equipment. But she didn't like it. The longer they remained isolated, the worse conditions would become, and the more likely people were to panic. Not to mention that forty-eight hours was an eternity in a homicide investigation. Evidence would deteriorate, memories would fade or become contaminated, and if there was a killer among them, he or she had more time to plan next moves.

They entered Peter's spacious office, where a Christmas tree with a skiing motif filled one corner of the room. On the back wall, tall windows overlooked the slopes. People were still skiing the trail they'd come down with the stretcher.

"You told Rosalie the woman isn't an employee," Victoria said.

"That's right. After the avalanche, HR used our phone chain to contact all our employees. We had to make sure everyone was safe, and they are. They're home or they're here now trying to cover for those who couldn't make it in. But they're all accounted for."

"What about guests?" Ned asked.

"We're still working through that list. It's not as easy as you might think." Peter moved to his desk, shoulders sagging under the weight of everything he needed to do.

"I hope to find out who she is when I run her prints," Victoria said. "I'd also like a copy of your occupancy report. The guest list with room numbers and check-in dates."

"We print it daily as standard procedure." Peter lifted a stack of paper from the top folder on his desk.

"Can you spare an employee to work with us?" Victoria asked. "Someone who knows everything about how the resort runs."

Peter rubbed his bloodshot eyes. "That would be your brother. He knows this place and the mountains better than anyone else. Honestly, he could run the resort if he were willing to spend more time at a desk instead of outside. He's your best bet, but I can't spare him long. Not in this weather."

"Glad to hear he's valued."

They exchanged phone numbers, and Peter handed over the requested occupancy report.

Anticipating the possibility of a power loss with the approaching storm, she asked for writing materials. When Peter offered her a notebook and pens, she requested a pencil as well.

He gave her an odd look but retrieved one from his desk drawer.

"Once we identify her, I'll have to notify her family, won't I?" Peter drummed his fingers in a quick pattern over his desk. "Or will you handle that?"

At the dread in his voice, Victoria looked up from the guest list. "If her family is here, I can speak with them. You can come with me to represent Black Ridge."

She'd delivered devastating news many times. Those notifications were a terrible but necessary part of her job. She handled the communications with empathy and compassion. Having received life-changing news herself, she understood the weight of those moments when someone's entire world shifted forever. "We'll handle it together."

Peter's phone alerted him again, vibrating against the wooden desk like an angry insect. When he glanced at the device, one eye twitched with a nervous blink. "It's Bob. My only maintenance guy on the property. Might be about our generators."

"Is there a problem?" Ned asked.

"The backup systems failed last week's inspection. A company was supposed to repair them today, but thanks to the avalanche, they can't get here." Still standing, Peter took the call, shifting his weight from side to side as he listened. Seconds later, he said, "On my way," then pocketed his phone.

"It's worse than we thought," he said, grabbing a winter coat from the back of his chair. "If we lose our main power supply before the backup systems get repaired..." He didn't finish the sentence, but they all understood. No power meant no heat, no lights, no communication.

"My office is yours. Whatever resources we have are at your disposal." Peter paused at the door. "Please figure out what happened."

As the door closed, Ned watched Victoria with a slight smile that seemed odd given their circumstances.

"What?" she asked.

"Nothing."

"Then why are you looking at me like that?"

"Just watching you work."

She looked up at him and sighed. "I'm sorry about all this. Who would have thought a ski vacation could go so wrong?"

He laughed. "We have a history of this." Then he turned serious again. "Don't apologize. We need to focus and figure out what happened to that poor woman."

Even after all they'd endured together, his unwavering support still amazed her. Victoria appreciated his use of "we." This wouldn't be the first time he'd assisted her during an investigation. They'd worked together when Ned's best friend went missing right before his own wedding. Ned had also helped her investigate when their neighbor disappeared. He lacked Victoria's profiling background, but he was exceptionally perceptive about human behavior.

She looked down at the guest list, then back at the windows where snow continued to fall like a white curtain hiding everything behind it.

"Let's get to Alex's office." Victoria gathered her things, her mind already racing through the questions she needed to ask. "We have work to do."

SEVENTEEN

Victoria moved through the lobby, noting the trash bins were still overflowing, and a throng of guests remained clustered around the front desk, waiting to speak with Thomas and Rosalie.

This wasn't the vacation any of them had planned. She and Ned should be relaxing with Alex and Minka, not investigating a suspicious death. No one had asked for any of this. The storm, the avalanche, potential generator issues—all of it was out of her control. But the investigation presented an opportunity to do what she knew how to do, to get her through an otherwise chaotic situation. For the sake of the deceased and justice, the investigation would proceed one step at a time in a methodical, thorough manner.

They entered Alex's office and sat in the worn leather chairs.

Victoria scooted to the front edge of her seat. "We need to identify our victim. That's our priority."

The trail was still warm but growing colder by the minute, just like the world outside the lodge.

Victoria's phone showed two bars. Barely enough signal strength. The FBI app loaded slowly, stalling twice before finally accepting the victim's photos and prints.

"The connection is terrible," she muttered, watching the upload crawl to forty-three percent before stalling. They were losing precious time to technical issues.

"Storm's affecting the cell towers," Ned said.

She tried again. On the third attempt, the system connected. Finally, she had photos and fingerprints running in the FBI's identification systems.

Footsteps pounded down the hallway, making Victoria and Ned look up. Alex burst through the door, Elspeth at his heels, both covered in snow. "Visibility's down to ten feet," he announced, not bothering with greetings. "Had to abort two separate avalanche assessments. It's getting dangerous out there. A slide missed Jordan by about twenty yards."

He pulled off his gloves and dragged a hand through his wet hair. His radio squawked, and he turned the volume down without looking. "I've got about ten minutes before I have to get back out there. Have you identified her?"

"Still working on it," Ned answered. "Victoria thinks the woman has a prison record, so her fingerprints will be in the FBI database."

Alex raised his eyebrows. "But no one has come forward? No spouse, friend, nobody?"

"Not yet," Ned answered. "Strange, right?"

"Yes. Most guests don't travel alone, especially the women." Alex filled Elspeth's bowl from a container of dog food, then collapsed behind his desk. "This reminds me of what happened at the lake house that time."

Victoria nodded, remembering the mysterious drowning victim at their family's lake house. No one claimed to know who she was, but someone was lying.

She checked her phone. The FBI databases had finished processing, and the results were not what she expected.

"No match for the victim's photo or the prints," she told Ned, frowning at the screen.

Ned tilted his head the way he did when he was confused. "But you said her prints would be in the system."

Victoria could only stare at the results, as if expecting them to change. She'd been so confident. The tattoo had looked like the rough prison artwork she'd seen before. "I was sure that tattoo was done in an institutional setting."

"Maybe it wasn't prison?" Ned suggested. "Just amateur work someone did at home?"

Victoria shook her head, doubt creeping in. It wasn't the first time evidence didn't match her initial assessment, but she'd felt so certain. Maybe she hadn't done a good enough job collecting the prints.

Alex looked between them. "If she doesn't have a record, how are you going to figure out who she is?"

Victoria forced herself to refocus, pushing aside the unsettling feeling of being wrong about something she'd considered obvious. "I might have a shortcut," she said, watching Elspeth scarf down her food. "I think I saw her last night. At the bar."

Alex jerked his head around. "You saw the victim alive?"

"If it's the same woman," Victoria said. "She was with an older man wearing a blue sweater. They had an argument. I'm not certain it's her, though." Especially since she'd just been wrong about the tattoo. "I'm only sure about the sweater. It might have been a popular item this season. Maybe the resort's boutique carries it, and other people at Black Ridge have the same one. I need to see the bar security footage from last night to know more."

"I can get that." Alex turned on his computer. The login screen appeared, disappeared, and then froze entirely. On his third try, he could enter his access codes.

Finished with her food, Elspeth settled into her bed, watching them work.

Victoria moved behind Alex's desk. "I need to see the video from around eight-thirty, right before you sent me a message last night."

Alex tapped the keyboard to access the monitoring system. A loading symbol circled on the screen. The footage eventually appeared, grainy but clear enough. "There. That's from the camera on the bar."

Alex scrolled to the correct timestamp. The camera had captured one side of the room, from a distance, showing a couple at the left end of the bar. The man in the blue sweater faced the camera; the woman was visible only from behind and briefly in profile. Everything seemed to be fine with them until the man took out his phone. What he saw there changed his demeanor. The tense interaction lasted less than a minute. When he threw money onto the counter and stormed out, the timestamp read 8:32 p.m. The woman remained, watching him leave while rotating black bracelets around her wrist. Bracelets that looked exactly like the victim's.

"That argument might be the reason our Jane Doe ended up dead last night," Ned said.

"Can you email me what we just watched?" Victoria asked.

Alex tried. The transfer started, then stalled.

When the security video finally hit her phone, she played it again, comparing what she could see of the woman's profile with the victim's features.

In the clip, the bartender approached the brunette woman from the other side of the counter. He pocketed the money her companion had left. Their brief exchange was inaudible.

Victoria hit pause.

Ned pointed to the man on the screen. "He stormed out. Hours later, she's dead."

Victoria stared at the image, a knot growing larger in her stomach. "I should have approached her after the argument. Just asked if she was okay."

"You couldn't have known," Ned said.

"I'm trained to notice when people are in distress."

"Maybe they weren't even traveling together," Alex suggested. "They could have met here for the first time. It happens. People hook up for a vacation fling, then decide they made a mistake."

"I don't think that's the case," Victoria answered. "I noticed them earlier. They had their arms around each other. They weren't strangers then, and they have an established intimacy to be arguing the way they are."

"Then why hasn't he come forward to say she's missing?" Alex asked.

Ned shrugged. "Maybe something happened to him, too."

A desperate voice came from Alex's radio, interrupting their conversation. "Alex, need you at—"

Alex turned the volume down. "I took Elspeth back to where we found the victim. We swept the area in the woods around Red Fox Trail again, just in case. We didn't find anyone else."

The radio squawk persisted. Alex sighed, pressing the button. "Give me five more minutes, Corey." He turned to Ned and Victoria. "If the mystery man's also frozen somewhere, he's not anywhere near the slopes, or we would have spotted him by now."

Victoria wasn't convinced. The mountain had countless trails and remote areas. It was a vast territory to search.

The lights flickered, dimmed, then surged bright enough to make them squint.

Alex grimaced. "That's not good."

The faltering power was particularly unsettling now that they knew the generators were in trouble.

Victoria moved toward Elspeth's corner. She crouched beside the sleeping dog and stroked her fur as she spoke to her brother. "Do you know the bartender?"

"His name is Matthew Ruckus. Worked here for three seasons. He doesn't live on-site. He has an apartment in Deer Valley with his dog. His shift ends when the bar closes at one a.m., so he didn't go home last night. He'd have gotten stranded here. He's probably working now."

"Let's go talk to him."

Before leaving, Victoria watched the security footage one more time. In the video, the woman's head turned left, then right, scanning the room. She checked over her shoulder twice before disappearing from the frame.

Victoria paused the clip of the woman's last backward glance. Her eyes were wide, her mouth open. She knew she was in danger, and she was afraid.

EIGHTEEN

Yesterday

"Ready to go back to our room, Anna?"

"As soon as we finish these." I lean against the bar, savoring my drink. "Two more nights isn't nearly enough," I murmur, holding Steve's gaze as I trail my fingers down his neck and onto his shoulder.

His phone buzzes. He sets down his scotch and pulls the device from his pocket. As he stares at the screen, his expression changes into one I hardly recognize. His blue eyes widen, then narrow, face scrunching into a deep frown.

"Is it work? A problem with one of your big projects?"

He keeps scrolling as if he hasn't heard me, except now he's glaring.

When I touch his arm, he jerks away like I've burned him.

My knees go weak. I grip my glass harder. Is this the moment I've been dreading? When all the lies come crashing down and ruin everything? If so, it's too soon. I'm not ready.

Steve steps back, increasing the distance between us. He sets his phone on the bar, then slides it toward me. "What is this?" His voice is sharp and demanding.

I don't want to look, but I have to. Still, I hesitate before picking up his phone.

The first message stuns me. *She's a liar. She isn't who you think she is.*

A wave of nausea hits, but I don't look away. The message came from an unknown number. Photos follow. Images of Steve and me together. I'm wearing the same cream sweater and scarf I skied in yesterday. The huge Christmas tree in the resort's lobby is visible in the background.

I scroll through more photos of us over the last few weeks. We're laughing, touching, kissing. All moments I thought were private. All taken from a distance with a zoom lens.

It gets worse. There are more photos of just me. Photos from another life that Steve knows nothing about. Photos I didn't know anyone else possessed. In one, another man has his arm around my waist in a restaurant. In the next, I'm exiting a house in the suburbs, heading to a Mercedes SUV in a circular driveway.

Gripping the bar to keep from swaying, I summon the courage to meet Steve's gaze. He glares, but I don't look away, though I'm dying to disappear through the floor and make this moment end.

"What is this?" he asks in a voice and tone I've never heard from him.

I can handle an angry man, one who turns red-faced, shouting with clenched fists. If Steve had yelled or struck me, righteous indignation could have taken over, allowing me to walk away knowing he was like all the others. Smart and powerful, but also violent and narcissistic. Not worth my guilt or sympathy.

But Steve maintains perfect control.

"Wow," he says. "You really fooled me."

"I was going to tell you. Please, give me a chance to explain."

He speaks over me. "Is everything about you a lie?"

"My feelings for you are real. Everything we have is real." The words tear out of me because they're true, perhaps the only true things I've said in months. I reach for him again.

"Don't," he warns, voice still sharp and steady. "Don't touch me."

He opens his wallet and tosses cash onto the bar. "Whatever you're doing, you're a fool if you think you'll get away with it. Don't come near me again."

He has every right to be angry as he walks away with long strides and perfect posture. I scan the room. People are chatting incessantly about the storm, ordering drinks, getting drunk, worrying, laughing. No one is looking at me. No one noticed our tense exchange.

I grab my drink and drain it. If only I'd told him sooner. If I'd confessed and tried to explain the whole messy truth before he discovered it himself. Maybe he would have understood.

An awful ache spreads through my chest. It hurts in a way I didn't understand was possible. Somewhere along the way, I'd started planning a real life with him. I'd actually let myself imagine a future where I'd take care of him when he got old. The kind where I could wake up every morning and not have to remember which version of myself I was supposed to be. We'd spend his final years in a small chateau in Italy, or maybe a beachfront property in Portugal. Somewhere beautiful, quiet, and secluded, where the past couldn't find us.

Maybe I'm delusional, but I believed it could happen. I thought we could disappear together and start fresh. Maybe we still can. He just needs time to calm down. I think about the Dom Pérignon chilling in our room. Steve's surprise for tonight. "To celebrate us," he'd said when he bought it. I'd almost told him everything then, but I didn't. But now... I could open it, remind him of why we're so good together, and try to forget what just happened.

Then I picture Steve's face from a minute ago, before he left me alone here. His expression contained a mixture of pity and disgust. He'd pulled away as if he couldn't stand me. He's a proud man, and I lied to him.

"Can I get you anything else?" The bartender appears, dropping his gaze to my empty glass. His nametag reads Matthew. Late twenties, with kind eyes. The look he gives me suggests he witnessed some of my exchange with Steve.

"I'm fine."

"Rough night?" he asks.

"I told you I'm fine."

My phone chimes. Another photo. This one shows me from thirty seconds ago with an empty glass in my hand and a shocked expression on my face. My blood turns to ice. Someone is watching me right now, close enough to capture every detail. I whirl around, scanning the crowded lodge. The photographer could be anyone. That couple sharing dessert? The group of women taking selfies? The guy staring at his phone? I don't recognize any of them.

I stumble away from the bar, my legs unsteady. The crowd feels like a vise closing in around me.

The elevator can't come fast enough. I keep looking over my shoulder. My finger stabs the button repeatedly. The doors finally close, and I lean against the wall, gasping for air. When I look up, I catch my reflection in the polished metal—flushed skin, brown hair, blue eyes, the silver and black ski sweater I bought specifically for this trip. Everything I'm wearing is new, chosen for the woman I wanted to become. She's now in danger because someone sent those photos.

NINETEEN

Behind the bar, Matthew Ruckus rubbed his eyes with the back of his wrist before reaching for a bottle of tequila. He mixed a drink without an ounce of the theatrical flair Victoria had witnessed last night. No perfectly timed bottle flips or smooth moves. Just a sweat-stained shirt and an air of exhaustion.

A young woman with a pixie cut and tattoos on her arms and neck worked beside him. She spoke to him while holding two bottles. Matthew responded with a curt nod toward the one in her right hand.

Alex waved to get Matthew's attention.

Matthew filled two draft beers and set them on the counter. He pocketed a tip before heading over.

"How are you holding up?" Alex asked over the noise of the patrons.

Matthew shrugged. "Peter put me up in a room with two other guys who got stranded last night. Got my neighbor to walk and feed my dog until we can leave. Josie's helping me out today. She's having to learn as she goes. People are still drinking. Tipping... not so much. I guess they're mad about being stuck here. You?"

"More concerned about the snow than usual." Alex gestured to Victoria. "This is my sister, Special Agent Victoria Heslin, and this guy will be my brother-in-law someday soon—Ned Patterson. They're visiting from Virginia."

Ned offered his easy smile while Victoria said hello.

"Hey, nice to meet you." Matthew wiped his palms on his apron before turning back to the next customer.

"Matthew, hold on." Alex raised his arm to get the bartender's attention again. "Could we talk privately?"

Matthew tugged at his collar, eyes moving from Alex to the customers waiting for drinks. "To be honest, I'm kind of busy, as you can see. Am I in some kind of trouble?"

Alex smiled. "No trouble. This isn't about you. It's about a guest. It's important."

Matthew seemed to consider Alex's request. "Okay, give me a minute." He filled two more drink orders, then wiped his hands on his apron again. The bar showed no signs of slowing. Matthew was stalling.

Finally, he gestured for them to follow him behind the bar.

Alex lifted a section of the counter, and they slipped through a nearly hidden door next to the liquor shelves. They entered a quiet break area with a couch, chairs, an old coffee machine, and a wall-mounted television. The Weather Channel played with the volume muted. Red and purple storm warnings blanketed the map while a meteorologist traced the storm's path. The scroll at the bottom warned of "blizzard conditions" and "widespread power outages."

Matthew stared at the screen, arms folded across his chest. "The storm is going to be more powerful than they thought."

"Unfortunately," Alex said. "So, Victoria and Ned are helping the police with an incident."

"Does it have to do with the body Jordan found?"

"Yes, and we need your help." Victoria made eye contact. "I imagine you see a lot from behind the bar. You might have seen or overheard conversations that could help us."

"Look, I just serve drinks. I try to stay out of people's business. Management doesn't like staff who get involved with guests." Matthew smirked. "Though it's never stopped Jordan."

Victoria noted that both Matthew and Alex had commented on Jordan's extracurricular activities. He either amused his coworkers or made them jealous.

She pulled up the security footage on her phone, turned it to face Matthew, and pressed play. "Do you remember this couple?"

Matthew frowned as he watched himself make drinks. "Kind of weird that there's a camera on me all night."

"You have great technique," Victoria said, trying to ease Matthew's worry and defensiveness. "Alex says you've been working here for a few seasons."

"Yeah. I have."

"Did you ever see this couple before last night?"

"No. Not that I remember," Matthew said, his voice flat. "Is she the one who died?"

"We're trying to determine that. Did you hear any of their conversation?"

Matthew looked away. "No. The bar was busy. I was swamped. Only noticed the guy seemed mad, and she looked upset. Figured she might want another drink."

When he turned back, Victoria nodded in encouragement. "Anything else you remember?"

"Not really." He shifted his weight. "That all happened before the avalanche. Haven't thought of much else since then."

"We need to identify the couple," Victoria said. "Was the cash the man put down a tip or payment?"

"A tip. Everyone gives me a credit card or their room number when they order a drink. If you tell me what time he ordered, I can get that information."

"I'll get you a time." Victoria rewound the footage.

"While I'm doing this, can you work with Josie?" Matthew asked Alex. "She doesn't know what she's doing. I'm afraid she'll walk out and hide in her room until the bar closes."

"Yeah, sure," Alex said. "I know how to make a few drinks."

"So do I," Ned added.

Victoria looked up from her phone and made a face. "Since when?" She'd never seen Ned drink anything except beer.

"Two summers bartending during vet school. Paid better than lab assistant jobs. There are still things you don't know about me, Victoria." He smiled. "Keeps things interesting."

Ten minutes later, Victoria had names for two male guests who had opened bar tabs around the same time. Jason Johnston, Room 420. Steve Foster, Room 309.

She thanked Matthew. "This is exactly what we needed. If you think of anything else, please let me know." She caught him staring at her hands.

"I forgot... You were on that flight," he said with awe in his voice.

"I was." She left it at that. He'd just reminded her she'd probably never work undercover again. "Thank you for the information."

Behind the bar, Ned had tied a towel around his waist and was explaining a recipe to Josie, who nodded and followed his example before looking up at him with a grateful smile.

"Where's Alex?" Victoria asked.

"The patrol team had to shut down all the lifts and trails," Ned answered, filling a beer mug. "Alex left to do a final sweep and make sure there's no one left on the slopes."

"Great," Victoria mumbled, not wanting to think about the escalating storm.

Ned untied the bar towel and addressed the waiting guests. "Hey folks, just a reminder that Josie's covering for the usual bartenders because of the avalanche. A little patience goes a long way."

A few people nodded, and one guest said, "No problem, we're not going anywhere."

Ned turned to Josie. "You've got this."

"Thanks so much," she said. "I wish you could stay."

"You'll be fine," Ned assured her before joining Victoria. "Did you get what you needed?"

"Maybe. I have two names with room numbers. Before we visit them, I need my laptop, my ID, and my weapon. If one of these guys is involved in a homicide, he won't be thrilled to see us asking questions."

Victoria cut off that line of thinking as two children licking candy canes approached the elevator bank. The same siblings she'd last seen messing around the coffee machines yesterday.

When the doors opened, Ned held them and gestured for the kids to enter first. "Which floor?" he asked.

"Same as you," said the boy.

As the elevator rose, the overhead lights buzzed and flickered.

"What the heck?" the boy exclaimed.

Ned's hand found Victoria's.

The lights went out, plunging them into darkness. The elevator jerked to a halt.

One child whimpered.

Ned activated his phone's flashlight, illuminating the small space.

"Is it going to fall?" the girl asked, her eyes wide.

Ned crouched to her level. "No chance. Modern elevators like this have safety systems. We're just taking a quick break until the power comes back. Where are you two from?"

"California," the girl said, her voice shaky.

"We live in Los Angeles," the boy added.

"That's a nice warm place," Victoria said. "We're from Virginia. Have you ever been to Virginia?"

The girl nodded with a rapid bob of her head. "We've seen the wild ponies there."

"Oh, the ponies. You know what? I'm a veterinarian. Every few years, we round the ponies up and give them shots to keep them healthy. They don't enjoy getting shots any more than we do, but we give them treats before we let them go. They do like those."

"What kind of treats?" the girl asked.

"Carrots. Apples. Delicious oats with vitamins."

Victoria watched Ned distract the children. Comforting them came so naturally to him.

The lights returned, and she exhaled as the elevator resumed climbing.

When they reached the fifth floor and the doors opened to reveal a mural of a red fox, the kids ran out and down the hall.

"That was excellent crisis management, Dr. Patterson."

Ned grinned. "Minor emergencies are my specialty."

"The whole 'modern elevators have safety systems' thing... what was that about?"

"I made that up." His expression turned more serious. "But for the rest of this trip, we're taking the stairs."

Down the carpeted hallway, Ned swiped his key card, and they entered their room. "A lot has changed since we left for breakfast this morning."

Victoria could hardly believe how much. They'd woken planning to ski and spend time with Alex and Minka, only to learn of an avalanche and then a dead body. The power fluctuations didn't help matters.

Victoria tapped the six-digit code on the safe to retrieve her service weapon—a Glock 19M, the FBI's standard issue. She checked the magazine and chamber, then secured her waistband holster. After sliding the weapon into place at her right hip, she concealed it with her sweater. Lastly, she pocketed her credential folio with the gold FBI badge and ID card.

"I'm starving," Ned said. "Do we have anything to eat in here? I burned through lunch a while ago."

"I wouldn't mind eating soon. For now, check the side pocket of my suitcase," she answered, distracted as she gathered her things.

Ned rummaged through her bag and pulled out a handful of protein bars and trail mix. "Should have known. You always pack snacks."

"I like to be prepared."

Ned tore open a bag and poured the contents into his mouth.

Victoria almost told him to slow down in case the resort's food supply ran short. She stopped herself. The kitchens and restaurants had tons of food. They couldn't possibly run out in two days.

"Ready." She checked her notes. "Jason Johnston, 420. Steve Foster, 309. Let's go see what they have to say."

TWENTY

The fourth-floor hallway mirrored the fifth floor's layout, featuring a bear mural instead of the fox, and a Christmas tree decorated with gold ornaments and plaid ribbons.

Victoria and Ned stopped outside Room 420. A woman's laughter reached them, followed by a man's deep chuckle, and some intimate sounds.

Ned raised his eyebrows. "Sounds like they're making the best of being snowed in," he whispered.

Victoria stifled her laughter. "May I remind you, you aren't very good at whispering."

He pressed his lips together, still grinning. "Should we come back later? We could try the other guy first."

"We're already here." Victoria tapped her fist three times. The sounds inside ceased.

"Who is it?" A male voice. He sounded annoyed.

"I'm looking for Jason Johnston. Is that you, sir?" Victoria asked.

"Yes, why?" More defensive than annoyed now.

"I'm with the FBI. I need to speak with you."

Hushed voices came from behind the door before it opened a crack, chain lock still in place. One brown eye peered out.

"What's this about?" Jason asked.

Victoria showed her identification. "We're investigating a recent incident. It would be helpful if we could speak with you briefly."

After a long pause, the chain rattled, and the door swung open.

Jason Johnston stood before them in sweatpants and an inside-out t-shirt. Behind him, a woman with tousled red hair and flushed cheeks adjusted her bathrobe. Victoria recognized them both.

"I thought it might be you!" Maura gushed. "How interesting!"

"Sorry to disturb you," Victoria replied. "You're not who I'm looking for."

Maura pulled her bathrobe tighter. "Is this about the woman who died? Was she murdered?"

"We don't know what happened yet," Victoria answered. "Might have been an accident."

"Accident? How could a person accidentally get strangled on the slopes?" Jason asked.

Victoria's blood went cold. "Who told you she was strangled?"

Jason frowned. "I thought that's what people were saying."

"What people?"

"I don't remember. A guy in the lobby, maybe?"

Victoria would have been more concerned about that person had the information been correct. She shook her head. "Please don't believe everything you hear."

"I don't." Jason narrowed his eyes. "Any idea when we can leave? My wife and I were supposed to check out tomorrow."

"Not soon. Road won't get cleared for a few more days," Ned replied.

"We've got another room to check," Victoria said as they walked away. "And stay alert. If Foster is our guy, he might not react well to being cornered."

They bypassed the elevator and took the stairs down to the third floor, where a rabbit mural shared wall space with another Christmas tree.

When they reached 309, Ned rapped his knuckles in quick succession and stepped aside.

No answer.

They waited, listening.

Nothing.

Victoria dialed the number Foster had given when booking his reservation. No ringing sound from inside 309, but her call connected and she left a voicemail. "Mr. Foster, this is Victoria Heslin with the FBI. Please call me back at this number. It's urgent." She hung up and turned to Ned. "Could have his ringer off and he's ignoring us."

Ned listened for a few more seconds, then made another attempt at whispering. "If he killed her before the avalanche, he probably left."

Victoria agreed.

They moved over to 311 and knocked.

"Who is it?" The voice sounded suspicious.

"Sorry to bother you. I'm with the FBI. We need to ask you a quick question."

A woman appeared in the doorway. She was in her fifties, with black glasses perched on her nose, and a drink of amber liquid in one hand. She looked Victoria up and down. "You don't look like a federal agent." Her gaze shifted to Ned. "You do. Did you two get your badges mixed up?" Her laugh was boisterous.

Victoria caught Ned's barely concealed smirk.

"What's this about?" the woman asked, opening the door wider.

Victoria held up her phone, displaying the shot from the bar footage. "This man, Steve Foster, was staying in Room 309. Have you seen him or this woman in the last twenty-four hours?"

The woman sipped her drink and pushed her glasses up. "Oh yeah, I saw them. Walking down the hall together yesterday evening. She was much younger than him. They were walking apart, not holding hands, but almost touching at the hip. The way they paid attention to each other, I knew they were a newish couple."

"Do you remember anything else about their interaction?"

"Not really." She lowered her voice. "Is she the one they found dead?"

Victoria deflected. "We're still investigating. Anything else you noticed?"

She took a gulp of her drink. "Like what?"

"Anything unusual."

"No, I wasn't really watching. I've been too worried about getting out of here. Wish we'd never come. Any word on when the road gets cleared?"

"Not yet," Ned said.

"Please take my number." Victoria handed the woman a business card. "If you see the man from 309, I'd appreciate a call."

Victoria and Ned worked their way down the hall. At Room 302, a man wearing a hotel bathrobe answered. "FBI? Jeez, what now?" He studied the photo and shrugged. "Sorry, I rarely notice people. My wife handles the social stuff. She's downstairs playing bridge."

No one else had seen Steve Foster or the woman. The few people who answered had been focused on their vacation activities, then on the weather, and hadn't paid attention to their neighbors.

Victoria felt the frustration of a cold trail getting colder. Jason's comment about strangulation nagged at her. How did the rumors get so specific so fast? And where was Steve Foster?

She had to keep digging.

TWENTY-ONE

At four p.m., they were back in Alex's office. He wasn't there. Neither was Elspeth.

Victoria sat behind her brother's desk and pulled her laptop from her bag. Ned settled into a chair across from her.

First, she called the manager to ask if Steve Foster's vehicle was still on the property. When Peter didn't answer, she left a message.

"While we wait to find out about Foster's car, I'm going to make sure he's the guy from the bar. Wouldn't have had to do this if we'd located him."

Ned leaned forward in his chair. "But that woman said she saw him yesterday."

"I know she did, but people make mistakes. You wouldn't believe how often. She was drinking when we talked to her. Maybe she'd already had a few before then."

When Victoria logged into her computer, the authentication process remained just as slow as it had been earlier. She and Ned watched snow fall in thick clumps outside the window until she could enter the FBI database again. She typed and clicked for several seconds. "Here we go. That's him. Steven James Foster. He's fifty-four and the CEO of a company he founded. Foster International in Denver. What they do is a little vague. Something with tech."

The photo on her screen matched the man from the security footage. Same eyes, same hairline, same confident posture.

"Clean record, no arrests." Victoria scrolled further, then stopped. "Hold on." Her frown deepened as she read. "Ned, look at this. Denver PD brought him in for questioning twice last year."

"For what?"

"Missing persons cases. Two women who worked for him vanished separately." She met his eyes. "Both young brunettes."

Ned let his mouth fall open as he listened.

"The first incident happened last year. A development manager never made it to her car after working late at the office. The second disappearance occurred a month later. A software engineer disappeared after a party. Steve worked closely with them. Both cases went cold."

"That's quite a pattern. Tracks with what we're seeing here. Another brunette. Dead after arguing with him. She might still be missing like those other women if Jordan hadn't spotted her before today's storm."

Victoria continued to search, pulling up more information. "Oh, he's married. His wife's name is Elaine Foster."

Ned scowled. "Our victim wasn't wearing a wedding band."

Victoria clicked on a link for Elaine Foster, then studied the polished headshot on her screen—platinum blonde hair, sharp blue eyes, mid-forties.

"What is it?" Ned asked.

She angled the display toward Ned. "This is his wife. Elaine Foster. Head of an interior design company. Former champion slalom skier."

"That's not the woman he was with in the bar."

"No. Definitely not."

"Which means he's a cheater."

"It's possible Steve and Elaine Foster separated or recently divorced. We don't know." Victoria continued to stare at the photo. Two brunettes had vanished. A third had died. What was going on with Steve Foster?

Ned exhaled through his nose. "Based on what you just found, Foster might be a serial killer who brought his latest victim here. Or... his wife might have something to do with this. Maybe she followed him here or had him followed. Perhaps he's another victim and his body is somewhere on this mountain."

"All possibilities... among others," Victoria said. "Until we find Foster, dead or alive, we don't know."

"What should we do next?"

"Search his room."

TWENTY-TWO

Yesterday

My chest is tight. Muscles constrict between my ribs, squeezing my torso, and it's hard to breathe. I used to think that meant I was having a heart attack until I learned it was panic clawing at my insides.

My key card is ready when I reach the door. I slap it against the card reader, pushing the handle down before the green light comes on. The light stays red, and the lock holds. "Come on, come on." My hands shake as I try again.

When the lock releases, I burst into the room. "Steve?"

His toiletry kit isn't on the bathroom counter next to mine. The closet door stands ajar, and the space beside my hanging clothes is now empty. His chargers no longer dangle from the base of the bedside lamp. His coat and boots are missing.

That was fast. Too fast. He's already packed up and left.

The drawers on the right side of the dresser are partly open. That's the side where I put my clothes and hid my small black purse.

"Oh, no. No. No. No," I moan, yanking the drawer out further and plunging my hands into my clothing. I toss aside underwear and bras, then fling jeans onto the floor. Maybe I'm wrong. Maybe I moved it. After yanking open the drawer above, I pull out sweaters and shake them, but nothing falls out. I claw through socks, scarves, belts, and fling everything behind me until all the drawers are empty.

Pacing the room, I tug at the roots of my hair. My purse is gone, and I must get it back, or else. That means going after Steve before he can leave Black Ridge. He doesn't have much of a head start on me.

I gather clothes off the bed and floor to stuff them into my suitcase, then give up. If I'm going to catch him, there isn't time. I have to go.

Outside, the storm means business. Snow hits my face with stinging force.

A plow with bright lights pushes snow around the parking lot, creating towering white walls along the perimeter. A thick, icy layer remains on the ground, crunching beneath my footsteps. I slip and almost hit the ground. I'm wearing cute suede boots, not my winter ones with good grips on the soles.

Besides the person driving the plow, there's no one else around. No one is foolish enough to be outside in these conditions unless they're desperate.

Steve dropped me off at the lodge when we arrived, so I don't know where he parked. The lot is a maze of snow-covered vehicles.

With gritted teeth, I weave between them, searching for the boxy shape of his SUV. The wind whips hair across my face and pushes me back. Steve has no idea what he's stolen from me, or the danger he's put me in by taking it.

Finally, the shape of a hulking vehicle right in front of a sign with a giant rabbit. I swipe snow from the front corner of the window, revealing the blue and green sticker for his country club. It's Steve's SUV. He hasn't left yet.

A ledge of snow has been disturbed on the driver's side. Someone opened that door recently. I peer through the window but don't see my bag. It's small and black, the same color as the vehicle's interior. It could be in there, and I just can't see it, or he could have it with him.

Waiting by the car, I shuffle my feet to keep them from freezing. I'm growing colder and more miserable by the second. This storm already seems worse than yesterday's. Driving snow slices into me from every angle.

I call Steve's burner phone, then his real phone, but he doesn't pick up. He's ignoring my calls.

Should I keep waiting? Maybe he's not leaving; it's late, and he's had a few drinks. The roads are dangerous. Steve wouldn't risk his life, no matter how angry he is with me. Maybe he just switched rooms and took my bag with him out of spite. I just hope he didn't open it.

Then I remember his skis. They're custom-made, high-tech, worth thousands. He'd never take off without that equipment. If he is leaving, he'd go back to the locker room to collect them.

I retrace my steps through the parking lot, back toward the buildings. Snow has already filled my tracks.

A flash of movement catches my eye. I spin around as a dark shape disappears behind the trees.

"Steve?" I call, but my voice gets drowned by the wind.

I pick up my pace, though I'm struggling to see what I'm following. This side of the resort is darker, more isolated. Snow has buried the pathway lights. Without goggles, the best I can do is shield my eyes by cupping my hands around them.

The locker rooms are ahead.

Another movement in the darkness. I'm not alone.

"Steve?" Desperation pitches my voice higher. I won't look good when he sees me. My nose will be red, my eyes puffy and teary, my hair a mess, but there's nothing I can do about that now. It's more important to get my purse back and get out of here. This place is no longer safe for me.

The wind dies for a moment, creating an eerie pocket of silence aside from the crunch of snow under my boots.

After walking a few more yards, I enter the dark locker room, grateful to escape the storm. A long table runs along one wall, cluttered with ski tuning equipment: metal scrapers, files, and a steel vise bolted to one corner. A low bench sits in the middle of the room, with a metal toolbox open on the floor beside it. Ski storage racks jut out from the wall at head height, skis and poles slotted between them like weapons in an armory.

"Steve?" I call, moving my hand over the wall in search of a light switch. "Please. Let's just talk about this."

A clicking noise makes me jump.

"Looking for someone, Anna?" The voice is calm and terrifying.

I whirl around, heart hammering against my ribs.

A dark figure emerges from the shadows, face obscured by ski goggles and the hood of a coat.

I can't tell if it's male or female, young or old. Just a voice and a presence that make my skin prickle.

The figure moves forward. "People get lost in storms like this. Sometimes they're never found. You shouldn't have come out here alone." A pause. "But it makes this easier."

I move backward, and my boot heel catches an object on the floor. I stumble against the bench and bump into the upright ski poles. My sweater snags on a sharp protrusion and tears. I look up a split second later, but I'm too late. There isn't time to duck or jump aside. Only a fraction of a second to see the metal toolbox arcing through the air, tools spilling out as it flies toward my skull.

The blow sends stars across my vision. I fall to my knees on the cold concrete, then continue to fall sideways.

Darkness overtakes me.

TWENTY-THREE

T hrough the large windows of the manager's office, nightfall had further darkened the cloudy sky.

Peter stood between his desk and the window, holding a tablet and a handheld radio like the ones ski patrol used. The creases lining his forehead were more pronounced than earlier.

Victoria got right to the point. "Have you heard anything from guests about our Jane Doe?"

Peter answered, "No one has reported a woman missing, and every registered female guest is now accounted for."

"So she wasn't an overnight guest?" Ned asked.

"Not officially registered. We ask for names at check-in, but we only know what people tell us. We charge per room, not per person, so we don't police occupancy. Some people want privacy." Peter rubbed his temples. "It's also possible she was here hanging out at the bar, but unlikely. Most of our bar patrons left early because of the storm, if they had any sense."

"What about male guests?" Ned asked. "Are they all accounted for?"

"Except for one. We haven't seen him, nor have we been able to reach him."

"What's his name?" Victoria already suspected the answer.

Peter opened his tablet and searched. "Steve Foster. He checked in three days ago for a four-night stay. He didn't check out, but he might have left without telling the front desk."

Victoria and Ned exchanged a look. "We were just trying to find him," Ned said. "We have him on security footage arguing with our Jane Doe at the bar last night."

Peter widened his eyes. "Arguing?"

Victoria nodded. "We need to locate and speak with him as soon as possible. I left you a message about his vehicle."

Peter looked apologetic. "Sorry. I haven't gotten to it yet."

"What other information do you have on him?" Ned asked. "His room charges might tell us if he was traveling alone."

Peter consulted his tablet again. "He provided one name but requested two key cards. He had charges from the restaurant and bar each night. Always two meals. Spa services yesterday: two ninety-minute massages, one right after the other."

Victoria made a note on her phone. "Is your masseuse here? I'd like to talk to him or her."

"No. I wish he were. We could offer free neck massages. Wait." Peter stared at his screen. "He bought a bottle of champagne yesterday afternoon. Dom Pérignon."

Everyone fell silent at the mention of the champagne purchase.

"No other charges since drinks at the bar last night. Nothing for today," Peter added.

Ned crossed his arms. "Do you have his vehicle information?"

"We require it if guests drive here." Peter scrolled through his tablet. "He registered a silver Lexus GX 550. Colorado plates." He read off the license number, and Victoria typed it into her phone.

Ned glanced at Peter, then back to Victoria. "We should check if his vehicle is still on the property."

She nodded. "But first, we search his room."

Peter was already moving. "I've got a manager's key. Let's go."

When they reached 309, Peter knocked on the door. "Mr. Foster? Resort management."

They waited. He knocked again. "I'm the general manager, and we need to conduct a wellness check. We're coming in."

Silence.

"Has the cleaning crew been on this floor today?" Victoria asked.

"No," Peter replied. "With the staff shortage, we haven't cleaned like usual."

"Good. Please wait out here and don't touch any door surfaces," Victoria instructed. "We have to minimize contamination in case this room becomes a crime scene."

Victoria's heartbeat quickened as she held out her left hand for the manager's keycard. Her right hand rested on her weapon, ready to draw if necessary. When the electronic lock disengaged, she nudged the door open with her elbow, preserving any potential fingerprints.

"FBI," she announced.

Scanning from left to right, she cleared the entry, then the main room, closets, and bathroom.

Clothes lay on the floor and across the bed. A few items hung out of the drawers on the right side. All women's clothes. Size small.

She used a pen to open the drawers on the left, one at a time. Empty.

A pair of shoes sat on the closet floor. Black heels, size seven and a half. Nothing belonging to a man.

The bed was made with housekeeping's precise corners.

She returned to the bathroom. The only toiletry items belonged to a woman. The medicine cabinet was empty. Towels hung on the racks. The hand towel by the sink was askew.

A sticky liquid had dried on the marble around the sink. It smelled of alcohol.

Crouching, Victoria examined the trash can contents: several tissues with makeup residue, a receipt from the resort's gift store, and the tag from a women's clothing item. No one had slept in the bed since the housekeeper's last visit, but someone had been inside the room.

Victoria checked under the bed and spotted a small hairbrush on the floor behind the nightstand. She had to stretch to retrieve it. The bristles held several strands of brown hair. Same color as their victim's. She bagged the brush, possibly the second solid link between Foster and the dead woman.

Examining the desk, she noted impression marks on the notepad. Someone had written on the previous page. She removed the pencil Peter had given her earlier. Using the side of the lead, she shaded across the paper, revealing the imprint of a phone number with a 303 area code. Denver. She took a photo of the paper and the number.

A keycard lay on the dresser with cash beneath it. Three twenty-dollar bills.

There were no signs of a man's belongings.

Victoria photographed the cash and key card arrangement. "We need security footage of the area outside his room."

"No hallway cameras," Peter said with obvious frustration. "Management's policy. Guests pay premium rates for discretion."

Perfect for people like Steve Foster, who vacation with women who aren't their wives, Victoria thought, though she kept the commentary to herself. Like she'd told Ned, they didn't have all the facts yet. Only fragments.

Peter cleared his throat. "However, I can access the security system and tell when someone entered his room last night."

"Good. Any information might be relevant," Victoria said.

"I'll send it to you once I have—"

A gruff voice came through the radio, cutting Peter off. "Boss? Can you come down to the main generator? What I have to show you isn't good."

The color drained from Peter's face. "Copy that, Bob. On my way." He clipped the radio back onto his belt. "Bob was trying to rig a temporary fix. I have to go."

As Peter hurried away, Victoria took one last look at the room, her eyes landing on the pile of cash.

Steve Foster's things were gone. A tip left behind. A woman's belongings remained, scattered around. It didn't make sense yet.

Time to search for his car and figure out where he was.

TWENTY-FOUR

Bundled in their coats and gloves, Victoria and Ned braced themselves for the frigid air outside. Clouds blocked the moonlight, but streetlamps illuminated the haze of thick snow falling over the parking lot.

Ned tugged his hood forward, then adjusted Victoria's scarf to cover more of her face. "There. You look like a beautiful bank robber." He slowed his usual stride to match hers as the wind blasted them.

"Let's go over what we know for certain." Ned's breath formed white puffs as he spoke. "It looks like Foster took off because his stuff is gone. Leaving a tip behind strikes me as odd. Would most people remember to do that if they were fleeing the scene?"

Victoria wrapped her arms around herself and shivered. "It is odd. Maybe just an ingrained habit."

"And we still have no information on the woman he was with, except that she appears to be our victim. There's also the champagne bottle, though he might not be the only person who ordered Dom Pérignon or brought a bottle from home."

"Appears is the key word," Victoria admitted, appreciating how Ned didn't jump to conclusions. "At this point, almost anything is possible."

"The champagne bothers me," Ned said, brushing snow off another car. "Maybe he bought a bottle to bring home to his wife to make up for cheating but forgot it."

"Does that mean if you bring expensive champagne home, I should be suspicious? Because if you ever vacation with another woman, it's going to take a lot more than a bottle of expensive champagne to get me back."

"I hope you're joking, because I would never do that." Ned turned to walk backwards so he could face her. "You know that, right?"

Victoria's expression softened. "I do."

She began scanning vehicles. They looked like hulking beasts hidden under the snow. "Let's find this car. The sooner we figure out what happened to our Jane Doe, the sooner we..." She ended her line of thought, pulling her scarf back from the wind. Things might seem worse once they solved this case and had nothing to do except wait for the road to reopen.

"The front desk assigns parking based on floors. Foster was supposed to park in the rabbit section." Ned pointed to a lamppost sign with a rabbit that matched the third-floor mural. "His SUV is new and hard to get. A friend waited months for one. Even at a place like this, there shouldn't be many."

They worked through the rows of cars, staying close together. Victoria tucked her chin against vicious gusts of wind, thinking of almost nothing except getting back inside.

Twenty minutes later, they'd uncovered luxury SUVs, high-end sedans, and sports cars, but not the silver Lexus they wanted to find.

"He must have left before the avalanche," Ned said. "He got lucky."

"Or he hid his car so we won't know he's here," Victoria replied. "Let's check the employee lot."

"Why would it be there?"

She shrugged. "I don't know. I'm just being thorough."

Further down the road, they found the employee parking area. It was smaller, with fewer vehicles and less expensive models.

"It's not here either," Ned shouted over a gust that nearly knocked Victoria sideways. "He's gone. Let's go back inside."

Victoria wasn't convinced. Maybe Steve or someone else wanted them to think he was gone. She looked back toward the lodge, its windows glowing like eyes. That person could be in there now, watching them.

Back in the heated entryway of the building, instrumental Christmas music played as they stamped snow from their boots and shed their winter gear. Victoria's cheeks burned from the warmth.

"We still have that phone number from the notepad," Ned said, rubbing his hands together. "Maybe that will tell us something."

They moved to a corner, found the number, and dialed.

After three rings, a recorded message played: "You've reached Jewel Security Service. Our office is currently closed. If you're a current client with an urgent matter, please press one to reach our 24-hour answering service. Otherwise, leave your name and contact information after the tone."

Victoria disconnected before the beep and opened her browser to search for the company. Their professional website displayed a dark blue background with gold accents that screamed law enforcement.

"Jewel Security & Investigation," Victoria read aloud. "Services include infidelity cases and background investigations."

"Infidelity cases," Ned said. "Interesting. Seems relevant."

Victoria had been thinking about the security services they offered. "Or maybe one of them needed protection."

She pulled up the photo of the notepad impression again, studying the pen strokes. Two people had shared that room. Either could have written the number. Now, one was dead.

TWENTY-FIVE

Back in Alex's office, Victoria hung up their coats, then took a seat. There was no sign of Alex or Elspeth.

Outside the window, the storm had devoured the slopes, the lifts, and the signs, replacing them with a writhing curtain of snow. Every familiar landmark had disappeared.

Ned took the chair across from her as Victoria returned to the security company's website, still open on her browser. She couldn't stop wondering why the number was on the notepad. Did it involve the need for investigative services or protection?

She called Jewel Security again. This time, she didn't hang up when the recording played.

"I'm with the FBI, working a homicide case and have some questions about a potential client contact."

Soon after leaving her number, a man with a gravelly voice returned her call. "This is Ricky Morales. You said you're with the FBI?"

"That's correct. I'm investigating a death at the Black Ridge Ski Resort in Colorado. I need to know if Steve Foster contacted your firm." She had no way to ask if the victim had called, since she didn't know the woman's name.

"If you're an agent, you know I can't discuss client information with you. I'd need to see credentials and a warrant."

"I understand," Victoria said. "But I'm not asking about existing clients or case details. I'm asking whether Foster contacted your firm at all. A simple yes or no."

A pause. "I'm sorry. I could lose my job." He hung up without saying goodbye.

Resting her chin on her hands for a second, Victoria sighed. "Before we theorize further, I want to verify the information Foster gave the resort. Fake addresses and burner phone numbers are common with people hiding things." She logged into the FBI database, summoning the patience it took to wait with the slow signal.

When she finished her search, the results surprised her. "Everything checks out. His Colorado address. The vehicle registration."

She scrolled to a new screen, found a number for the FBI's Denver office, and called.

"This is Special Agent Victoria Heslin from the Washington, D.C. Field Office. I need help with a potential homicide investigation."

"You're speaking with SSA Kerri Coleman. Go ahead, Agent Heslin."

After the Supervisory Agent verified Victoria's credentials, she outlined the situation. "I'm at Black Ridge Ski Resort, cut off by an avalanche. We discovered a deceased female earlier today, approximately twenty-five to thirty years old. No ID, no personal effects. No prints in our system."

"Jane Doe. Need identification," the agent repeated.

"I've identified a person of interest. Steve Foster. White male. Fifty-four. He left the resort last night. I need a welfare check at his residence and want to interview him as soon as he's located."

"How did you get there?" SSA Coleman asked. "My understanding was that no one was coming in or out."

"I was already here when the avalanche hit. They suspended the road clearing because of the approaching storm. We're looking at another forty-eight hours minimum." Mentally, she was preparing for longer.

"Got it." Keyboard clicks sounded in the background. "I'm pulling Foster's details now. Any reason to consider him dangerous?"

"Possibly. Security footage shows he was one of the last people seen with our victim. He has a history. Two people he worked with disappeared under suspicious circumstances. Those cases remain unsolved. I just want to talk to him."

"Understood. I can dispatch agents within thirty minutes and set up a video connection when we make contact."

Victoria opened her photo app. "I'm sending you an image of our Jane Doe. The sooner we know who she is, the better. Please check missing persons reports filed yesterday or today."

"We'll run everything through the databases. The field team will contact you once they're at his residence. Anything else?"

"I need a federal warrant for Jewel Security and Investigation Services in Denver. I found their phone number in the victim's room and need to access their client communications relevant to Steve Foster. This could be the key to identifying our victim or establishing motive."

"What's your probable cause?"

"Homicide victim found with evidence linking to this security firm. The suspect fled the scene and has prior connections to missing persons. Given our isolation and the time-sensitive nature of the situation, I need those records to prevent further harm."

"I can expedite that. I know the judge who's on call tonight. We should have the warrant within two hours, assuming your probable cause holds up."

"It will. Send it directly to Jewel Security. I'll follow up with them."

After the call ended, Victoria took a deep breath.

"What's bothering you?" Ned asked.

"Besides being stuck here... the fact that we still don't know who she is." Victoria got an idea. Their victim might have shared photos on a social media app and tagged the resort. Pulling out her phone and navigating to Instagram, she searched "Black Ridge Ski Resort."

What she found made her stomach turn.

Recent posts weren't the usual glamorous ski vacation pictures. Instead, clip after clip showed deteriorating conditions inside the resort. The mohawk guy and his friend had been busy, and the algorithm seemed to love their stories.

In one reel, Hawk grinned and sang off-key. "Oh, the weather outside is frightful..." He turned the camera around and panned the crowd of stranded guests, then added with dark amusement, "But the inside's so much worse." The video cut to shots of unemptied trash bins, dishes piled in hallways, and the women's restroom where he'd opened each stall to show unflushed, clogged toilets with no toilet paper. The reel concluded with a mess of water and paper towels on the ground.

The caption read: "Day two of vacation hell."

Victoria hadn't used the common bathrooms near the lobby recently. Had they really gotten that bad?

She returned to the task at hand and scrolled through every picture and video, searching for ones from before the woman died. Finding nothing with their victim or Steve Foster, she switched to a different platform.

The hashtags were brutal: #MurderMountain #CantCheckOut #BlackRidgeNightmare

One showed Alex and Jordan skiing with the stretcher between them. The caption read: DEAD BODY at Black Ridge Ski Resort! We're trapped with a killer!

Another reel showed ski patrol transferring the body from the sled onto a gurney, with the caption: Murder at Black Ridge! #MurderMountain #WhoDidIt?

Hundreds of comments followed the video. Most with questions or speculation about what happened. A chilling thought occurred to her.

The killer might be in the lodge now, watching these same videos, seeing how much attention the case was getting. They might have commented, blending in with hundreds of strangers, and influencing the narrative.

Victoria continued scrolling through the location tag, looking for content from earlier in the trip, before everything went wrong. Finally, she started seeing normal vacation photos from three days ago: shots on the slopes, cozy lodge pictures, happy couples holding wine glasses by the center fireplace. Hashtags like: First night at Black Ridge. #BlackRidgeResort #SkiVacation #Skilife.

Jane Doe wasn't in any of the posts. Neither was Steve Foster.

Victoria rubbed her eyes. "If they took photos or videos, they didn't share them."

"Makes sense if they're having an affair."

A new text came from the Denver field office: *Agents en route to Foster residence. Will contact you within the hour.*

Now she had to be patient until the field agents reached Foster's address. "I'm in the mood for a hot tea. Then I'd like to check our Jane Doe again and see if there's evidence we missed."

"Sounds like a plan." Ned stood and gathered their coats. "This is all interesting, though I'd prefer our vacations don't involve avalanches or dead bodies."

"That makes two of us. But at least we should have some answers soon." Victoria paused at the door. "I'm just not sure we'll like what we find."

TWENTY-SIX

N ed gestured to a sign on the door of the frozen storage room. DO NOT ENTER, handwritten in large capital letters. "Remember what Alex said about the danger signs acting like magnets for some people? Almost like they can't resist doing what they aren't supposed to do."

He held the insulated door open, and frigid air rushed out to meet them. The temperature inside was below freezing, but without the wind, more bearable than outside. Fluorescent lights hummed overhead, illuminating rows of metal shelving.

They'd positioned the body in the far corner, sectioned off with stacked boxes to shield it from view. Another sign clung to the side of the top box: DO NOT MOVE.

The body lay on a clean white tablecloth spread across a metal shelf. A white sheet outlined the unmistakable human form beneath. Victoria folded the sheet back to reveal the woman's face. She retrieved the hairbrush she'd found in Foster's room and compared the hair from the brush to the victim's head.

Ned moved in for a closer look. "They look similar to me."

"Similar. But not the same." Victoria frowned. "There's no way to know for sure without microscopic analysis, but it just doesn't look the same."

Ned huffed. "How many women were in that room?"

He pressed his hand against his abdomen as a growl erupted from his stomach.

"I'm hungry too." Victoria glanced at her watch. Two hours had passed since she'd promised they'd have a meal. "Let's grab dinner after—"

She stopped mid-sentence, her eyes fixed on the shelf where she'd placed the sealed evidence bags earlier. The champagne bottle sat where she'd left it, but the space beside it was empty.

"What the heck?" Victoria blinked hard, hoping her eyes were playing tricks on her. Both bags had been on that shelf when they'd stored the body. She was certain of it.

"What's wrong?" Ned followed her gaze.

"The evidence with the DNA samples is gone. I put it right there."

Ned moved closer to the shelf. "Could the manager have moved it?"

"Maybe." Victoria dropped to her hands and knees on the cold concrete floor and peered under the shelving units in case someone had accidentally knocked the kit over.

"I should have made sure everything was locked up," she said, checking behind boxes of frozen fish. "I can't believe I let this happen."

"Hey." Ned crouched beside her, his voice gentle but firm. "You specifically asked for a secure place. You asked for a lock. The manager said he'd provide one. It's not your fault."

Victoria sat back on her heels, staring at the empty spot, wiping grit from her hands and onto her jeans. "The person I asked is juggling too many issues. I should have taken care of it myself."

"You're not even supposed to be working, Victoria. We're on vacation, remember?"

Victoria stood and paced the storage area, checking the same spots again.

"Maybe there are cameras down here." Ned scanned the room, looking up at the ceiling corners.

"I don't see any."

The mechanical whirr and ticking of the freezer suddenly seemed louder, more ominous. She pulled out her phone and dialed Peter, pacing the small space out of frustration and to keep warm until he answered.

"This is Victoria Heslin. I'm in the frozen storage room. The DNA swabs are missing. The bag isn't where I left it. Did you move it?"

"What? No, I haven't been back there since we left together."

"Who else knew we performed the examination?"

"I mentioned it to Alex when we spoke earlier. That's it."

"That kit contained potential DNA evidence from the perpetrator. This isn't random. Someone might be covering their tracks. We need you to get a proper lock on that door."

"I'll see to it. Sorry that happened. I don't understand why it's missing, but I have to go." He clicked off.

Victoria turned to Ned. "I'm not letting any more evidence disappear. From now on, anything we find stays with us." She grabbed the remaining evidence bag with the champagne bottle.

Ned pulled the sheet back over their victim's face. "What about the body? We can't exactly carry it around."

Hands on her hips, Victoria stared down at the covered body. Their Jane Doe deserved better than this makeshift morgue with its hand-written signs.

She could think of only one reason for someone to have taken the biological evidence. That person knew what the DNA samples would reveal. Which meant whoever was responsible was still at Black Ridge. Either Steve Foster was still there even though his car wasn't... or someone else had done it.

As they headed for the exit, Victoria made a silent promise to find answers before anyone else got hurt.

TWENTY-SEVEN

Another handwritten sign sat on an easel at the entrance to the grill. It said: *Due to circumstances beyond our control, the menu is limited.* Below it was scrawled: *Patience Appreciated* in red ink.

A worker named Tyler took orders at the counter, sweat streaming down his face as he entered the information on a tablet.

As Victoria and Ned joined the back of the line, she hoped Alex had found a chance to eat a decent meal today. "Can you order for me?" she asked Ned. "Grilled cheese again?"

"Will do." He took her coat. "Where are you going?"

"I need to visit the kitchen."

Victoria slipped through the swinging doors into the industrial kitchen. A cook shouted, "I need more boxes in here now," while flipping burgers on a sizzling grill. A server weaved between prep stations saying, "Everyone's ordering multiple meals like they're stocking up for a war."

The kitchen staff worked as if the building were on fire and they had minutes left to finish and get out.

Victoria spotted her target: a young cook with earnest eyes and pants that were an inch too short. His face was scrunched in concentration as he monitored burgers sizzling on a huge grill.

She positioned herself directly in front of him, so he had no choice but to acknowledge her. "Hi. I'm Victoria Heslin. An FBI agent. I'm also Alex's sister."

He froze with the spatula mid-flip. "You're the one investigating the woman who died?"

"Yes. I need to dust a bottle for fingerprints, but I don't have the equipment. Can you spare a few minutes?"

He eyed the grill before setting down the spatula. "What do you need?"

"Plastic gloves, dark paper, fine powder, and a soft brush." She counted on her fingers, noting how his gaze caught on her missing fingertips before he looked away.

"A brush?"

She didn't know what to call it. Her skills were many but did not include cooking. "Whatever you would use to brush butter onto food."

"Pastry brush," he said, already heading toward the supply cabinets.

He gathered the supplies and led her to a small prep room off the main kitchen. Victoria helped herself to some nearby parchment paper, spreading it on a butcher-block table.

"One more thing. Scotch tape."

He disappeared and returned with a fresh roll. "We had it at the front counter."

Victoria pulled on gloves and set the bottle on the black paper he'd found. If this Dom Pérignon 2012 connected Foster to their victim, it could strengthen the case. Or it could introduce another suspect.

Ned arrived just as she was about to start. "Food's going to be awhile. People are ordering like it's the apocalypse. But your sandwich is in the queue."

"Great. You're just in time to see if I can make this work."

"Make what work?"

"Improvised evidence collection."

"You're looking for prints?" Ned asked. "Wouldn't the snow have ruined them?"

"It didn't help matters." She dipped the brush into cornstarch, tapping off the excess. Too much powder would obscure any prints; too little wouldn't reveal them.

As Ned and the cook watched, she applied the cornstarch in delicate strokes across the dark surface of the glass.

The white powder clung to the glass in random patterns, but nothing with distinctive whorls or ridges appeared. Victoria frowned. Many people would have touched this bottle. The bartender. Maybe room service staff. Even with professional wiping, there should be prints from whoever bought it.

"Nothing?" Ned asked.

"Not yet." Victoria continued dusting, working around the neck and base. The glass had been wiped clean.

Figures, she thought. Whoever took the DNA samples would have grabbed this too if they thought it held incriminating evidence.

But as she dusted the label, a pattern of faint ridges emerged against the burgundy and gold logo. "Got something."

She leaned closer, angling the bottle toward the light. Why the champagne bottle at all? The Dom Pérignon seemed like a prop designed to shape the narrative. To make people think: troubled woman, expensive alcohol, tragic accident in the snow. Or maybe that's exactly what it was.

Victoria pressed tape against the impression, then lifted it, transferring the impression to the black paper. She photographed it from multiple angles. The partial showed a thumb or index finger.

She made an impression of her fingerprint for comparison. The sizes were similar. The print belonged to a person with small hands.

Victoria sealed the bottle back in its evidence bag, adding tape and her initials.

"Cool," the cook said, already gathering supplies to return to his station.

Victoria tucked the evidence bag under her arm. Now she needed to find out whose print it was.

TWENTY-EIGHT

N ed and Victoria found a small table across from the gift shop where they could wait for their food. People had emptied the store of all snacks, like a grocery store before a hurricane.

Victoria opened the FBI's fingerprint database. It seemed like watching grass grow, but she managed to upload the photos of the partial print, adjusting the contrast and brightness to enhance the ridge details.

"We need at least eight to twelve matching points to make a solid identification, and this one's maybe seven points at best."

Her phone rang with an incoming call from the Denver area code.

"Victoria Heslin," she answered with a flutter of excitement. She couldn't wait to interview Foster.

"This is Agent Bruce Rork, Denver field office. I'm outside Steven Foster's residence. He's not here. Neither is Mrs. Foster, but we spoke with her."

"What did you find out?"

"She's currently out of town, driving back as we speak. Says she expected her husband home last night, but their security system shows he never arrived. She claims he was on a business trip, not a ski trip."

Victoria didn't want to imagine the awkwardness of that conversation. "Are the Fosters separated?"

"Not according to her. I asked. But..." Rork paused. "I sent her your photo of the victim over video chat. The photo from the bar. Mrs. Foster said she'd never seen the woman before, but what's strange is that she didn't seem all that shocked or surprised that her husband wasn't alone."

"She didn't seem upset?" Victoria asked.

"Not really. I'd say she was pretty composed considering."

Victoria made notes as she listened. "Where exactly was Mrs. Foster this weekend?"

"Aspen. A girls' weekend with a friend from college, she said. Left Friday morning."

"Did you verify that?"

"Working on it. I got the friend's name."

"When was Mrs. Foster's last contact with her husband?"

"He texted her at 9:12 p.m. on Saturday. She shared their text exchange with us. He said he was leaving early because another storm was coming. He had just left the hotel and started his drive home. What time did that avalanche hit exactly?"

"Around 10:30."

Victoria had seen Foster arguing with their victim at 8:30 p.m. His wife said he texted at 9:12 p.m. to say he was leaving. That wasn't enough time to take the victim up the mountain, get back down, pack his room, and get into his car. But the call was well timed if he was trying to establish an alibi.

"Elaine Foster is an interior designer, and she was a champion slalom skier in her twenties. Still skis regularly. I got that info from one of her platforms," the agent said.

"I saw it, too."

"I did a little research before I spoke with her. Police questioned her in connection with the death of her first husband in 2014."

Victoria straightened in her seat. "Death? What happened?"

"Her first husband was a real estate developer, a successful one by the looks of it, twenty years older than Elaine. He died at his home. Sudden heart attack, but his sister didn't think so. She opened a case against his wife, but it went nowhere. Lack of evidence."

"Interesting," Victoria said. Elaine Foster appeared to be an accomplished, competitive woman. The type of person who might not take news of her husband's affair lightly. Perhaps her first husband had also crossed her and paid the price.

"What else can we do while you're stuck there?" Rork asked.

"I need Foster's banking transactions for the past 24 hours. ATM withdrawals, credit card activity, and his cell tower pings. I need to know where he is now, and where he was when he made that call to his wife. Also, can you verify Mrs. Foster's whereabouts this weekend? Hotel records, credit card usage, anything that proves she was actually in Aspen."

"I'll get on it. Anything else?"

"Anyone in the missing person reports who might match our Jane Doe?"

"Nothing yet."

They said their goodbyes, and Victoria looked at Ned. "Foster told his spouse he was on his way home, but he never got there."

Across the lobby, Peter rushed between clusters of guests, a stack of papers clutched against his chest and his tablet tucked under one arm.

When he spotted Victoria and Ned at their table, he stopped mid-stride, his expression shifting from harried concentration to recognition. He hurried over, shuffling through the papers in his arms as he walked, nearly dropping his tablet.

"I have the information you requested. The key card data for 309." Peter sat on the edge of a chair, setting his papers and tablet on the table. He selected a document and smoothed it flat. "Here it is. This shows you the times someone entered Steve Foster's room last night. Three entries: 8:38 p.m., 8:55 p.m., and 11:02 p.m. Then not again until we went in today."

Ned picked up the paper. "Foster's wife said he left the resort at 9:12 p.m. So, who went into the room after he left?"

The overhead lights flickered ominously.

"Not again," Peter muttered.

A few seconds later, the entire lodge plunged into blackness.

TWENTY-NINE

The only illumination came from the dull red glow of battery-operated lights over the doorways. It wasn't enough.

Peter shot up from his chair. "I have to find maintenance." He pushed through the crowd of disoriented guests, his voice carrying across the lobby. "Everyone, stay calm! This is only temporary!"

But was it? Unlike most everyone else, Ned and Victoria knew there were issues with the generators.

They remained seated because it seemed like the sensible thing to do until they understood the situation. With her senses heightened, Victoria listened to a cascade of disbelief spreading through the darkness.

"How long is temporary?" "This is BS." "I can't see where I'm going." Anxious and angry murmurs mixed with the wind pressing against the windows as if it was desperate to get inside.

Shadows shifted near the restaurant's entrance as people funneled out, boots stomping across the floor, calling the names of their companions and family members.

The building began making strange noises, rattling and hissing inside the walls. She hoped it was the backup systems getting ready to come on. After what felt like minutes, dim light returned and grew a little stronger. Emergency power, not the full electrical system. Better than nothing, but the lodge remained cloaked in shadows.

The alarms stopped ringing. A man jogged past their table. "Elevators are stuck. We have guests locked inside."

By the fireplace, Hawk stared at his dead phone in horror. "What?" he exclaimed around the candy cane in his mouth. "No signal?"

Victoria checked her phone. Zero bars. No internet. The storm had finally cut their remaining connection to the outside world. Her heart sank as she realized what this meant for the investigation. No contact with the Denver FBI. No updates on Foster's whereabouts. No information from Jewel Security.

Several minutes passed before Peter spoke over the PA system, quieting everyone.

"Hello. This is Black Ridge Resort's general manager. Unfortunately, due to the storm, we've lost main power and internet services. Until power returns, the resort will rely on backup generators for essential systems only. You will notice some changes, so please bear with us. We'll keep you warm, fed, and safe, but please conserve energy where possible. Contact Guest Services with immediate concerns. We appreciate your understanding and patience."

Victoria thought of Rosalie and Thomas, already overwhelmed at the front desk. She heard Thomas raise his voice: "I wish I could tell you more, but we only have the same information you do."

At least the phones weren't ringing. They were dead.

"Attention, everyone waiting for food!" Tyler bellowed from the restaurant entrance. "If you just ordered in the last ten minutes, we're sorry, but your food isn't coming. Our ventilation system isn't running. We have to shut down the kitchen for safety reasons."

Groans and complaints erupted from the guests. Someone shouted, "What are we supposed to eat?"

Victoria felt a stab of sympathy for Tyler, who had to deliver bad news to a room full of already agitated people.

"The convenience store is still open," Tyler replied, perhaps forgetting guests had already cleaned out the shelves.

Ned gathered his coat. "We ordered a while ago. I'll go check on our food."

Victoria stood as well. "I'll meet you in our room. I want to try my satellite phone."

She'd brought the other phone out of habit but hadn't taken the backup battery. With the snowfall and cloud cover, the connection would be spotty at best. She'd need to conserve its power. The way things were going, the worst was yet to come.

"Take the stairs," Ned said.

"Absolutely."

The stairwell felt like a tomb. No heat, no light, just cold concrete and metal railings. Victoria hurried up the steps to reach her satellite phone. The Denver FBI would call about the warrant and Foster's whereabouts, and she couldn't afford to miss those updates.

She was halfway to the second floor when faint cries came from somewhere below.

Victoria stopped moving. The cries came again. Children's voices calling for help.

She followed the sounds to the pool area entrance and called through the door. "Hello?"

"Help! We're stuck!" A boy's voice, frightened.

Victoria tried the handle. Locked. "Are you alone in there?"

"I'm with my sister. The lights went off, and we can't get out!"

"My name is Victoria," she called through the door. "I'm going to help you. What are your names?"

"Max and Kayla."

"Are you the siblings from Los Angeles?"

"Yes!" Kayla shouted. "How did you know?"

"We met in the elevator."

Victoria spotted a maintenance panel. She used her credit card to pop it open. "I'm working on it. Won't be much longer. Are you both okay? Not hurt?"

"We're cold. Really cold," Kayla said. "We don't have our clothes."

Victoria didn't know what to make of that, but she focused on getting the door open. She found a manual override and pressed it. When the lock released, the door swung inward, revealing the two siblings in bathing suits, barefoot, shivering, and close to tears. Goosebumps covered their skin.

"We were swimming." Max's teeth chattered as he spoke. "Then the lights went out, and the door was stuck."

Victoria crouched to eye level with Kayla. "Where are your clothes?"

Max pointed behind him. "Our lockers won't open. And my phone is in my locker, so I couldn't call my parents."

Victoria stood. "Well, the phones aren't working right now, anyway."

"Huh?" Max said. "Not even to call people?"

Victoria turned on her phone flashlight, and they led her to the lockers. The electronic keypads were dead. She removed one of her earrings and used the post to manipulate the mechanism beneath the digital display.

The first locker clicked open.

"How did you do that?" Max asked, grabbing his towel.

"Something I learned at work. They've taught me a few tricks." Victoria moved to the second locker, repeating the process.

Kayla shivered as she wrapped her towel around her body. "What is your job?"

"I work for the FBI."

"Cool," Max said. "Like the TV show. Did you ever kill anyone?"

"My job is mostly about helping people. And your parents must be worried sick. Let's get you back to them. Fifth floor, right?"

As they climbed the dark stairwell, Kayla took Victoria's hand. "Thank you for saving us."

"Always call for help when you need it," Victoria said, as they pulled away from her and ran down the hall.

She wanted to accompany them to their mother or father, but they had slipped through their door before she got a chance.

At her own room, her keycard still worked, and her door opened with no trouble. Inside, she tried to adjust the heat, but it wasn't getting any warmer, so she gave up and got her satellite phone out. She hoped the signal could penetrate the thick walls, because she couldn't bear to go outside again.

After dialing the Denver field office, an automated message answered: "Because of widespread power outages and damage affecting the region, emergency services are prioritizing life-threatening situations, and our offices are assisting. Please remain on the line only if you have a life-threatening emergency."

She set her phone down. Asking for help was usually an option, but that didn't mean it was coming right away.

THIRTY

The door clicked, and Ned entered, carrying a paper bag and two bottles of beer. "Food," he announced, setting it on the console. "Glad we ordered when we did."

"Smells good." She inhaled the aroma coming from the bag. "So, it turns out the storm didn't just hit us. It's crippled communications across the entire area."

He opened the bags and began removing their dinner. "I figured."

"People are getting stuck. Our little friends from the elevator got locked in the pool area." She was about to go into details, but Ned had finished unpacking the food bag and was staring at the table. His mind was elsewhere.

He looked up at her. "Something strange happened after you left."

"What kind of strange?"

"I thought I saw the woman from the bar. I was almost certain it was her."

Victoria gave Ned her full attention.

"I didn't know how to straight out ask if it was her, so I asked if she owned a silver sweater with black around the neckline." He drew his finger from right to left to describe the design.

"What did she say?"

"She said no. Then she took off her hat. She had blonde hair. It was pulled back, that's why I didn't notice at first. Until then, I really thought it was her."

"Did she ask why you were asking?"

"No. She gave me a look like I was..." He paused, searching for the right word. "She probably thought I was hitting on her." He laughed. "I was wrong about who she was, but it made me realize something. We don't know for sure that our victim is the woman from the bar. All we have is the security footage we saw. She never even turned to the camera."

Taking her grilled sandwich, Victoria sank into the corner chair to think. He was absolutely right. She'd focused her investigation on the assumption that the victim knew Foster and they'd argued the night of her death. He was a suspect or a potential witness with information. But what if she was wrong and the deceased woman and Foster had never met? More than one brunette might own the same sweater.

A good agent verified facts before building theories. She'd built an investigation around circumstantial evidence and resemblance, letting the silver sweater cloud her judgment. A rookie mistake, if it turned out she'd made one.

Setting her food down, she wrapped her arms around her body to protect against the growing cold. "I can't believe we still don't have a name. There are hundreds of people here. One of them must have seen her around."

Victoria picked up her sandwich again, grateful for warm food while they still had it.

The television came on, displaying a bit of blue light around the black center. There was no internet or cable. With nothing to distract them, they ate at the small bistro table as the room grew chillier.

"At least we have food, a decent room, and each other." Ned raised his beer in a mock toast.

After clinking their glasses, he scooped up his phone and started typing, then stopped. He'd already forgotten about the lack of cell signal.

Victoria glanced at the satellite phone on the console. "I should call Minka. She might be worried about Alex."

"What are you going to tell her?" Ned asked. "We haven't seen him for hours. Won't that make her more worried?"

"Maybe she's heard from him."

"If she has, you'll feel better. If she hasn't…"

"I know, but I think she'll be grateful for the contact."

The satellite connection fizzled before Minka's voice came through. "Hello?"

"It's Victoria. I'm on a satellite phone."

"Victoria!" Relief flooded Minka's voice. "I've been trying to reach Alex for hours. The news says the entire region lost power and communications. Is Alex there? Please tell me he's with you."

"He's not here right now, but I'm sure he's fine." The lie felt hollow. She was just as worried as her sister-in-law. "But we were with him earlier."

"When were you with him? What were you doing?" Minka's voice sharpened. "Victoria, what's really happening there?"

"There's just a lot going on because of the storms. Things got a little strange earlier. Ski patrol found a body on the mountain." The silence stretched so long that Victoria thought the connection had failed.

"A body?" Minka sounded incredulous. "Someone died there? What happened?"

"We don't know yet. I'm investigating, and Alex was helping earlier until he had to head back outside. Everyone here depends on him. Especially now, with the weather."

"You're investigating? That means it's a murder investigation? On top of everything else?"

"We really don't know yet."

"I hope it isn't. Just please promise me you'll find Alex. Make sure he calls me as soon as you see him."

"I promise. The moment we find him, I'll put him on this satellite phone myself."

"I love you both. Tell Alex that when conditions are dangerous, like they are now, I need to hear his voice every so often."

"I will, Minka. Try not to worry."

The connection hissed with static, then went silent.

Minka's fear and her own growing anxiety about Alex's safety made Victoria's mouth dry.

Ned wrapped his arms around her, pulling her against his chest.

"Do you think everything will be okay?" she asked. He had no way of knowing, but she wanted to hear his reassurance.

"It's okay for now, and that's good enough. Let's try to get some sleep. Things might seem better in the morning. Maybe the power will come back by then."

Victoria's mind wouldn't quiet. She kept circling back to what Ned had said earlier. He thought he'd seen the woman from the bar. Except she had blonde hair. Victoria felt a spike of adrenaline as she connected some pieces. Elaine Foster. Platinum blonde, competitive skier. Had Ned recognized Elaine from the photos they'd seen earlier, and he just couldn't place her?

Elaine was supposedly in Aspen for a girls' weekend, but what if she'd never gone to Aspen at all? What if she'd followed Steve here, discovered his affair, and killed his mistress in a jealous rage? A former champion slalom skier would know how to move through snow and terrain that would challenge others.

Outside their window, the storm continued to shriek against the walls of the building. Somewhere in the darkness, a killer might be watching, waiting, staying several moves ahead, possibly using the chaos to their advantage.

THIRTY-ONE

An explosion shattered the predawn calm, the concussion wave vibrating through the walls. Victoria jolted upright in bed and turned to Ned.

A second blast followed, accompanied by a sustained rumble.

"Avalanche control," Ned said. "Must be Alex's team working nearby."

Victoria pictured Alex outside, calculating trigger points as the sun rose.

Electricity had not returned. That much was obvious. Even under the duvet with Ned's body beside hers, the cold chilled her bones. A phantom ache came from her missing fingertips, almost like a warning. She snuggled against Ned, not wanting to leave the pocket of warmth they'd created.

"I have to get up." He kissed her forehead before swinging his legs out of bed. The moment he left, cold air rushed in to claim his space. If it was this cold with the generators running, how cold would it get if they stopped?

Victoria pulled the covers to her chin. This weather was perfect for reading while wrapped in blankets with a cup of hot tea. But downstairs, a corpse waited in cold storage, and too many questions remained unanswered.

With a sigh, she pushed herself up as Ned opened the blinds. Weak morning light revealed a world washed in white. Snow had covered the lower pine branches, and fresh drifts reached nearly to the second-story windows. Worst of all, it was still snowing—not heavy flakes like yesterday, but a steady flurry.

Two ski patrol members stood together, staring off into the distance, one of them pointing. Neither was tall enough to be Alex.

Victoria had to look away. She didn't want to see how the snow had climbed higher overnight. She didn't need a reminder that they were slowly being entombed.

They did push-ups and core work, exercises they did every day, and it felt both necessary and normal.

Children hollered in the hallway. Footsteps pounded past their door. Victoria pictured Max and Kayla and wondered why they were up so early and unsupervised again.

"I'm going down to check on things," Ned said, pulling on his coat. "Want me to bring breakfast back?"

"No, I'm coming." She wasn't about to stay behind alone in the frozen room while there were still answers to find.

<hr>

On the main floor, the easel by the entrance bore a stark warning in large letters: STAY OFF ALL SLOPES. UNSTABLE SNOW CONDITIONS. AVALANCHE DANGER.

Another sign announced the cancellation of all outdoor activities.

In the lobby, guests crowded around the central fireplace, most wearing the hotel's white blankets over their winter coats. Some clutched paper cups. Victoria's gaze fixed on those cups. People had found coffee somewhere. She needed to do the same. But first, she scanned the crowd for Steve Foster. Though his vehicle was gone, she couldn't stop looking for him. She was also hoping to see the woman Ned saw, the one who might be Elaine Foster.

The yoga class had moved to a corner of the lobby since there was no heat in the studio building. Guests in leggings and sweatshirts held poses on their mats. Victoria took a good look at each of their faces before shifting her focus elsewhere. Still no blonde woman matching Elaine Foster's description.

A child wailed, "I'm cold. This isn't fun. When can we go home?" His mother shushed him, though he'd simply voiced what everyone else was thinking.

Victoria followed Ned toward the reception desk.

"My insulin is going bad in the dead refrigerator," a man shouted at Rosalie. "This is life or death!"

"How about putting it in the snow?" Rosalie suggested. "Maybe collect some snow and put it in your refrigerator, replacing it as it melts."

Behind him, other guests demanded toilet paper, internet access, updates on when they could leave.

"I don't know when the roads will open," Rosalie said with no trace of a smile, her composure finally cracking. "And no, we're being told we can't helicopter anyone out in this weather. It's not safe with these winds and the poor visibility."

Two men pushed to the front. One was the guy with the crewcut Victoria had seen around. The man with him had similar features. Crewcut's jaw was set, hands clenched into fists. His friend put a hand on his arm, but Crewcut said, "No, I'm done listening to this."

Victoria tensed, forgetting about the coffee. Acting on instinct, she headed toward them, Ned already beside her.

Rosalie looked up at Crewcut with wide, frightened eyes as he pushed through the crowd.

He placed both palms flat on the counter, his muscular frame towering over her.

"You need to hear this now," he began.

A shocked quiet followed.

Victoria was close enough to intervene, heart rate elevated, ready to spring into action.

"You're doing incredible work under impossible conditions," he said to Rosalie. "What can *we* do to help?"

Victoria let out a long breath. She'd been so certain he was about to explode that his kindness seemed almost surreal. Ned caught her eye and shook his head with a rueful smile. They'd both expected something terrible to happen.

If people were offering help instead of demanding answers from an intern at the front desk, maybe human decency would prevail over desperation, and no one would turn into their worst selves.

Shaking off the tension, they walked to the dining area, Victoria's thoughts returning to coffee. The buffet was reduced to fruit and cold cereal, with a sign reading: PLEASE TAKE ONE MEAL ONLY.

Unsmiling, Tyler stood guard, rationing supplies that had seemed unlimited days ago. The next guy who walked up took four boxes.

Tyler started to speak, then stopped. Frowning, he made a note on his clipboard as the man disappeared into the crowd.

Tyler shrugged. "At this rate, we'll be out of food soon. But Mr. Stanhook says not to argue with the guests."

Victoria had hoped the crewcut man's kindness was a sign that people would pull together, but watching a man blatantly ignore rationing rules while staff stood powerless to stop them suggested otherwise.

When she found the coffee station, she nearly groaned. The outlets behind the gourmet machines weren't working. Two simple single-carafe machines brewed coffee. A long line of guests waited, and Victoria joined them.

Later, tepid drinks in hand, she and Ned found seats with an older couple.

"If the heat doesn't come back, we're sleeping in our electric vehicle tonight," the man said. "The battery might keep us warm for days."

"I don't know if I want to do that," his wife answered. "What if we drain it while we're sleeping? If the road gets cleared before the power returns, we won't be able to leave. Then we're stuck here longer than necessary with no power *and* no car."

Victoria tuned them out, thinking about her investigation. The body in storage might be a low priority for everyone else, but she wasn't giving up.

The PA system emitted a screech of static, alerting them to a new message. "Any guests with medical training, please report to ski patrol headquarters as soon as you can. We have an emergency."

Ned was already standing, zipping his jacket.

Victoria grabbed his arm. "Ned."

"What?"

"There's probably a physician here, don't you think?"

"If there is, they won't need me. But in case there isn't... someone needs help. Maybe Alex." His eyes held that determined look she knew meant arguing was useless. But when he saw fear flash across her face, his expression softened.

"I know you want to keep everyone safe, but I can't just sit here." He gestured around the lodge. "You understand that. You're working the investigation because that's how you cope when everything's falling apart. This is how I cope—by helping where I can. I'm not trying to be a hero. But after what we went through, I know more about hypothermia than most doctors. If that's what this is about, I might help save a life."

Victoria wanted to protest, to keep him in the relative safety of the lodge, but he was right. Their plane crash experience had taught them excellent survival skills. Still, the thought of him venturing outside made her ill.

Alex knew what to look for, where to step, and what was safe and unsafe. Ned didn't.

"Promise me you won't do anything stupidly heroic," she whispered.

"Define stupidly heroic," he said with that half smile she loved.

"Anything likely to get you killed or maimed."

"I'll try to avoid both. Besides, I'm just going to the ski patrol station," he said, already heading to the door.

"Wait," she said. "You forgot something."

He returned and kissed her. "I love you."

"I love you, too. Be careful and come back soon."

He smiled. "I'm not going to war, Victoria. Just going outside."

Victoria watched him stride toward the exit until she could no longer see him.

THIRTY-TWO

With Ned gone, Victoria pursued the lead that had been nagging at her since last night. His comment replayed in her mind: *We don't know for sure that the victim is the woman from the bar.*

She pushed through the resort boutique's glass door and walked through the overpriced apparel. Long shadows fell over racks of ski wear and Black Ridge logo merchandise. The weak generator lighting made everything look gray and lifeless, like the inside of a cave. The shop was nearly empty anyway, except for a couple buying the last pair of earmuffs.

Victoria moved through the women's section, pushing hangers aside in search of the distinctive silver sweater with the black neckline. She examined soft cashmere, synthetic ski pullovers, and wool blends, checking stacks of folded sweaters on shelves. Nothing matched the sweater the victim had worn.

"Can I help you?" A woman with braided hair asked from behind a counter, wearing an Aztec print shawl and wool mittens. Her smile resembled the strained expression of a retail worker forced to be helpful.

"We don't sell food, if that's what you're looking for. We sold out of throw blankets, but we have bathrobes. Extra small. And a few cardigans, also in extra small. That size would work for you. They're going fast."

"I'm looking for a specific sweater," Victoria said. "A wool blend. Silvery gray with a black design around the neck."

When the employee tilted her head, the poor lighting made her eyes look sunken and haunted. "Is it one of ours? A sweater you saw here earlier?"

"I'm not sure if you sell it here."

"Do you know the brand?"

Victoria showed the photo she'd taken of their victim. She'd cropped it so only the sweater showed. "The label said Eakes and Rhyme."

"Never heard of that line."

Victoria caught a whiff of cigarettes as the woman leaned in and took the phone into her mittens, giving the photo a long look.

"Actually, hold on. I *have* seen that sweater. A woman came into the store with her husband. Or boyfriend. I don't think they bought anything."

"When did you see this woman? What day?"

The employee frowned, thinking. "Maybe two days ago? Hard to say with everything that's happened. I only remember because I liked the sweater. I'm great with fashion details, not so much with faces. So many people in and out, you know?" She handed the phone back.

"How was the couple acting? Did they seem happy?"

"Yeah. They were touchy. Holding hands. Whispering to each other." The employee's expression grew wistful. "Made me miss my boyfriend back home."

"Can you describe the man?"

"Older. Silver at his temples. Expensive coat."

Victoria showed the picture of Steve Foster and his companion from the security footage.

"Yes, that's them." The employee frowned. "You've got their photos? Did you ask her where she got it?"

"No. I wish I could ask her that, and a few other things," Victoria answered. "Thanks for your help."

The employee had confirmed what Victoria had already seen in the lodge—a woman wearing that distinctive sweater and a male companion acting like a couple. But was she the victim? Or someone else?

Without Steve Foster to question and with no word from the Denver office on his whereabouts, Victoria felt like she was fumbling with a puzzle in the dark. One small piece at a time, unsure if she was building the correct picture.

She still didn't even know the victim's name.

THIRTY-THREE

Peter leaned over his desk, hands planted flat on its surface. When he spotted Victoria, he winced as he straightened, pressing his hand against his lower back.

"Any progress identifying the deceased?" he asked straightaway.

"No hits on facial recognition or prints. So we're still working on it." Knowing the manager had a lot to deal with, Victoria was equally direct. "Have you confirmed whether all the cars in the parking lot belong to registered guests or staff? A vehicle that doesn't match your records might belong to the victim. I'll trace the registration and finally get an ID."

"Jordan took care of it. Not a simple task." Peter showed her pieces of paper with license plate numbers and checks next to all of them. "Finding that woman in the woods really hit him hard. He wants answers. He did a full sweep of both parking areas this morning. Every license plate matches our guest and employee records."

Victoria sighed. Another dead end. "I need to show her photo to your staff. All of them, if possible."

Peter rubbed his bloodshot eyes. "I need an all-hands meeting, but I'm unclear on how we can do it. We're falling apart out there. We never planned for a total communication breakdown while fully occupied. Our emergency protocols assumed we'd either get people out or keep the lights on. Not this."

"How bad is it, really?"

"The generator's my biggest concern. It wasn't built for extended use and needed repairs before this storm hit."

Victoria felt her stomach drop. "If it dies... is that it?"

"Backup units might give us another twelve hours. Maybe."

"There's nothing you can do?"

"Not until the road opens."

"Anything else of immediate concern?"

"My staff. Half of my team is on the other side of the avalanche. The ones here have been working overtime for two days straight. They're making mistakes, snapping at guests. And the guests are another matter." Peter's laugh held no humor. "This morning, I broke up a fistfight over the last of the blueberry muffins. A lawyer is threatening to sue me personally because he's not able to leave."

He didn't need to go on. Victoria had seen enough to understand. "How are you communicating with your employees now?"

"That's the problem. Ski patrol and security have radios, but housekeeping? Food service? They're scattered. Internal phones died with the power, and our usual group texts and emails require internet or cell service. We've got the PA system, but I can't say everything I need to say with guests listening."

"Like the medical issue earlier. I'm sure you didn't want to broadcast that."

"Exactly."

"What was it about?"

"One of our guests took a fall on the stairs and needed stitches. We gave him the care he needed, but I'm sure he'll sue us, as will everyone else."

Victoria pressed her hand to her heart. Not another death. Just an accident. Someone had simply fallen while navigating the unfamiliar stairwells in the dark.

Ned was an expert at closing wounds. He did it daily during pet surgeries, working with precision and care whether he was stitching up a dog that had tangled with barbed wire or a cat that had lost a fight with another animal. His hands were steady; his technique was excellent.

Maybe he'd be back any minute, walking through the door with that satisfied look he got when he provided help. She pictured him chatting with whoever he'd treated, making sure they were comfortable, giving them detailed aftercare instructions. If not, he was probably still in the medical room, monitoring that head injury. Concussions could turn deadly fast.

"I'm at a loss," Peter said, pulling Victoria from her worries.

"Call a meeting. Ask for one person from each department, or more if they can spare them. Once everyone gathers, you can address your issues and their questions. It's also an opportunity to boost morale, which has to be strained by now. And I can get the victim's photo in front of everyone."

"Good idea."

"Have you seen Alex today?" The question had been bothering her since she'd woken up to the explosive charges. Her little brother was out there somewhere in the avalanche zones, and she hadn't heard his voice since yesterday.

"I saw him briefly this morning before he left with the patrol team. That was..." Peter glanced at his watch. "Three hours ago?"

"Is that normal?"

"Oh, yeah. They contact me only when there's an issue. Though radio contact's been spotty with all this interference."

Victoria tried to push away the worry that was becoming a constant companion. Alex knew these mountains better than anyone, but avalanche control was dangerous work even in good conditions. And these weren't good conditions. She'd have to trust that no news was good news for now.

An hour later, the main conference room was packed with workers hunched against the building's pervasive chill, arms crossed, some shivering. Getting word to everyone without phones or radios meant sending runners to each department, but they'd managed decent representation.

The conference room displayed evergreen garland along the windows and a darkened Christmas tree in the corner.

Victoria didn't see Alex. Jordan was the only one there from ski patrol. His flushed cheeks made it look like he'd just come in from outside. When their eyes met, he looked away, fascinated with his radio controls.

Victoria's instincts prickled. Jordan's body language screamed guilt. He was acting nervous. But pushing Alex's patrol partner during a crisis seemed like a bad idea.

"Thanks for coming," Peter began. "I know you're all doing more than your share, and it's freezing in here."

"Are we getting overtime pay for this disaster?" Thomas asked. His attempt at humor fell flat. Everyone was waiting for an answer.

Peter nodded. "All staff and guests will be reimbursed for their inconvenience. Corporate is working on that."

"Yeah, waiting to see how bad it gets before they decide how little they can get away with paying us and reimbursing guests," Thomas mumbled from the back. A few people nodded in bitter agreement.

"Probably depends on how many lawsuits they're facing," Tyler said. "Corporate's probably sitting in their warm offices right now, figuring out how to spin this."

Thomas chuckled. "Good luck with that. Have you seen the videos going viral?"

Victoria stepped to the front of the room. "Before we get to logistics, I need your help with an urgent matter. I'm Special Agent Victoria Heslin, FBI. I'm also Alex Heslin's sister."

Some nodded; others moved to get a look at her.

"As I'm sure you're all aware, ski patrol found a deceased woman. We still haven't identified her or located the man she may have been traveling with."

Victoria selected a photo of the couple at the bar. After considerable internal debate, she'd chosen that image over an image of the corpse, whose frozen state made it look like a doll with waxy skin. Staff would be more likely to recognize a living person or the distinctive silver and black sweater.

Victoria held up her phone. "This is Steve Foster. He was a guest in 309, and we believe this woman was his companion. I need everyone to look at the two people in this image."

She handed the phone to Tyler, who stood to her right. "Pass it around. If you know the woman's name, or anything about her, please raise your hand."

As the phone began its circuit, Peter addressed the group. "Here's where we stand," he said, glancing at notes Victoria had helped him prioritize. "The access road remains blocked, and clearing can't begin until the storm settles. We're looking at forty-eight more hours minimum here. However, power could return at any time."

He turned to the man in a chef's hat. "I'm aware guests are panicking about meals. Do they have a reason to be?"

"We've inventoried everything," the chef answered. "We're making pre-portioned boxes, using perishables first. Smaller servings, limited choices. If we ration, we're limited but okay for three days. After that..."

"They're already hoarding," Tyler said. "Ordering multiple meals, stashing food in their rooms like squirrels."

"Starting now, one meal box per person per meal period," Peter said. "No room charges. Just track distribution. Most people will cooperate."

"What about the ones who won't?" Tyler asked. "Yesterday, some guy demanded five dinners for his 'family.' I've seen his family. It's him and his wife. Then this morning, I caught a guy filling a bag with granola bars. When I told him one meal per person, he said, 'What are you gonna do about it?'"

Rosalie spoke up from near the door. "The lobby's getting scary. People are going stir-crazy and taking it out on us. Someone screamed at me for five minutes because the Wi-Fi's down. He was acting as if I had destroyed the Internet myself. Can we open any activities? Anything to get them outside?"

Jordan answered. "The lifts don't have power. Even if they did, the snow isn't stable. We're triggering slides, but new snow is accumulating faster than we can clear it. No one should go out there now. If snow moves at the top, everything beneath it is at risk."

"Including us?" The question came from the back.

Jordan crossed his arms. "We're doing everything possible to keep everyone safe."

As her phone continued around the room, Victoria observed faces. Some took a quick glance and passed the phone along. Others studied the image longer. But no hands went up. No spark of recognition.

"I don't know when our main electric source will return. That's out of our hands. And the generators won't last indefinitely. So here's our new reality," Peter continued. "At six-thirty p.m., we're closing the restaurants and bars. Guests need to stay in their rooms after dark until sunrise. It's for their own safety and to conserve generator fuel."

Rosalie raised her hand. "Safety from what?" she asked, looking from the manager to Victoria. "Each other?"

Peter nodded.

"They're not gonna like that," Thomas said.

"We won't force anyone," Peter added. "We can only encourage them to do so. At six-thirty p.m., we'll shut off the heat to the main lodge and redirect it to guest rooms. At least they'll have a reason to want to stay put."

Thomas raised his hand. "What do we tell people? Hey, now you get to sit in your room with no lights, internet, or television?"

Peter moved from one side of the room to the other. "I know it sounds impossible. But we have to rise to the occasion. We want to get through this experience knowing we did our best as hospitality professionals."

Victoria cleared her throat. "When people feel powerless, those feelings can manifest as anger. Don't take it personally and don't argue with them about things you can't control. Acknowledge their frustration and give them what information you can."

"What if the generator dies next?" asked a woman in the back wearing a housekeeping uniform.

Peter's pause lasted too long. "We'll cross that bridge when we come to it."

Rosalie raised her hand again. "What was the medical issue today? I've gotten a lot of questions about it."

"A minor incident requiring stitches. It's nothing." Peter looked around the room. "However, everyone needs to be extra careful, particularly in the dark stairwells. Anything else?"

"Yeah," Thomas said. "Are we going to get through this?"

The room fell silent. Peter looked out at his tired staff.

"Of course we are," he said finally. "What you've all done these past two days is incredible. You're keeping hundreds of people relatively comfortable in an impossible situation. But pace yourselves. I won't lie to you. The next forty-eight hours, or longer, will not be fun."

The meeting broke up, and staff began filing out, faces grim with a fresh understanding of their predicament. Victoria's phone completed its circuit and returned to her hand without a single identification. Another dead end in a case full of them.

THIRTY-FOUR

Victoria remained in the conference room as the staff members filed out. A woman with jet-black hair in a severe bun approached. She was the person from housekeeping who had asked about the generator failing. Her name tag said Marjorie.

"Excuse me, please." Marjorie's accent made her speech sound formal. "I want to tell you that everyone loves your brother. He's a wonderful man. Very brave."

Victoria smiled. "Thank you. He's always been fearless." Too fearless, she thought.

"You wanted to know if any of us talked to the couple in the photo?" Marjorie's dark eyes were earnest.

"Yes, absolutely."

"I didn't speak with them, but I saw the man. Two days ago. Before the avalanche."

"Please tell me what you saw. Anything might help."

Marjorie pulled her cardigan tighter. "I was doing my evening checks. I saw him come out of his room on the third floor. He had a suitcase and a computer bag. He was in a hurry. Not smiling."

Victoria showed her the photo again. "This man?"

"Same one. Wearing that blue sweater, like in the picture."

"What time was this?"

"Late. Maybe nine o'clock?"

"How large was his suitcase?"

"Huge. I thought he was trying to leave before the storm got worse." She shrugged. "I didn't think it was smart. Not safe with the weather, but I kept quiet. Not my business what guests do as long as they don't destroy the rooms."

"Was he alone?"

"Yes, alone."

That timing matched what Elaine Foster had told the Denver agents.

"After he left, I cleaned two rooms whose occupants requested late service, and then I saw a woman with blonde hair go into his room."

"Did she knock or use a key card?"

"She went right in. She had a key card."

"How would you describe her?"

"Pretty. Hair to here." Marjorie touched her shoulders. "With a very sharp edge to the style. Taller than me. Thin."

"How would you compare the color of her blonde hair to mine?"

"Yours is pale blonde. Hers was bright."

"Did you see her leave the room?"

Marjorie shook her head.

"Please let me know if you see her again."

Another explosion echoed from somewhere beyond the building. The lights went out, and all sounds ceased.

Marjorie's sharp intake of breath matched Victoria's.

They waited. Ten long seconds.

Finally, the generator power kicked in with a reluctant hum.

Marjorie shivered. "I have to go back to work."

"Thank you for sharing what you saw."

After Marjorie left, Victoria opened her notepad, writing before the details faded:

Foster left with a suitcase around 9 p.m. A blonde woman went into his room after he left.

She stared at her notes. She was thinking about Elaine Foster when the PA system came on, the sound more strained than before.

"Attention, all guests and personnel." Alex's voice. Finally. Victoria was relieved to hear him.

"Because of ongoing avalanche mitigation, all exterior areas on the ski slope side of the resort are off-limits. For your safety, do not go out there. If you need to go outside, you may walk in the parking lot directly behind the building. Thank you for your cooperation."

Victoria let Alex's words sink in. If the parking lot was the only safe space outside, it was because the building would act as a massive barrier in the event of an avalanche.

Danger was imminent.

THIRTY-FIVE

Victoria pushed open the medical area's door, hoping to find Ned inside. Instead, a middle-aged man sat on the examination table where she'd recently examined Jane Doe. A bandage covered one side of his forehead. Small spots of dried blood stained his white shirt collar.

A woman of similar age held his hand. A younger woman stood opposite, shining a penlight into his eyes.

"Everything still looks good, Mr. and Mrs. Walsh," the younger woman said, her tone professional. "You got lucky."

"Thank you. What about sleeping?" Mrs. Walsh asked. "Is it safe for him?"

"Yes. He can sleep, but to be on the safe side, wake him every few hours to make sure he responds normally. Ask him questions like his name, where he is, and what day it is. If he can't answer clearly, then there's a problem. Also monitor for vomiting, extreme headache, and dizziness."

"And if those things happen?"

"Chances are good he's not concussed. So please don't worry too much."

Victoria waited for a pause in the conversation. "Excuse me, are you a doctor?" She asked without introducing herself.

"I'm a physician assistant," the woman answered.

"Was there anyone else here helping earlier? A veterinarian?"

Confusion crossed the PA's face. "I'm not sure."

Dread crept into Victoria's chest. Her relief about Ned had been premature. Where was he? "There was an announcement asking for anyone with medical training. My fiancé responded. He's a veterinarian."

The PA moved away from the exam table. "I think I saw him. Tall, fit guy?"

Victoria nodded.

"I don't know where he went. I got directed here to help Mr. Walsh after he fell on the stairs."

"Fell?" the man on the examination table repeated, his voice sharp with anger. "I didn't fall. I got pushed."

"The stairwell was so dark," Mrs. Walsh said. "It's possible you missed a step."

"It *was* dark, and that's another reason we're going to sue this place, but I didn't miss anything." His eyes got a wild look. "I felt hands right between my shoulder blades, then a big shove." He touched the bandage with his fingertips. "If I hadn't grabbed the railing halfway down, I might have broken my neck."

"Did you see anyone in the stairwell with you?" Victoria asked.

"No. It happened too fast. I was on the ground, shocked, and my head hurt. By the time I looked around, my wife was there. The person who pushed me took off."

"I was just a few seconds behind him. I didn't see anyone else," Mrs. Walsh said.

"Yeah, obviously, the guy didn't stick around. He exited on another floor. Look, I'm not paranoid. I know what I felt before I went flying. Someone here has serious problems. Maybe losing it already."

"Does anyone here have a reason to hurt you?" Victoria asked.

"Of course not," the man answered.

His wife let go of his hand and clasped her own. "You've been confrontational with half the staff here, and I'm sure you annoyed plenty of people, but that's not enough for anyone to want to hurt you."

The PA picked up the bandage wrappers and dropped them into a trash can. "Well, I need to get back to my family. Here's my room number if you have questions. I think you'll be fine."

"Thank you for all your help," Mrs. Walsh said.

Victoria watched the PA disappear down the corridor, her anxiety spiking. Ned had responded to a request for help hours ago, but he wasn't in the medical area. That meant there was another situation. One serious enough to keep him away this long. In a place where people were already on edge, that couldn't be good.

THIRTY-SIX

V ictoria studied the trail map on Alex's office wall, tracing the route to where Jordan had found the body. The pieces didn't fit.

At the scene, she'd considered a fall from the chairlift, but the lifts had closed early because of the storm. That night, she'd closed her curtains around 10 p.m. Thick flakes were still coming down then, but snow hadn't buried the corpse.

So, sometime after 10 p.m., when the snow was still falling, and before dawn, with the lifts closed, the victim had ended up near Red Fox Trail. A quarter-mile from the nearest access point, in darkness. In a storm. No one walks that far through deep snow wearing street clothes and suede boots. Not by choice.

Elspeth jumped up from her bed as footsteps approached. She trotted toward the door with her tail wagging. Victoria's heart leaped. Maybe Alex was finally back. But the dog's expectant gaze met only another resort worker walking down the hallway. She circled her bed before lying down with a disappointed groan.

"He's not back yet either. I wish he were," Victoria murmured, stroking the animal's head. Her brother and Ned had been gone for hours, somewhere in conditions Alex had called unsafe. The waiting was torture, but she couldn't help him by sitting here worrying. She could help by solving the case.

She forced herself to refocus on the investigation. Who had the means, motive, and opportunity to transport a body up a mountain after a blizzard?

A snowmobile. It was the only logical explanation. But only resort staff had access to the machines. If the killer used a snowmobile, then she was looking for a Black Ridge employee. A person who knew the mountain, had the right equipment, and moved around without raising suspicion.

Then she remembered Tom's radio call about the missing machine and keys. Someone had left a snowmobile outside the equipment shed. The keys were missing.

Victoria rested her head in her hands for a moment. She still had more questions than answers.

Elspeth let out a soft whimper. The dog probably needed to go out, and Victoria could use a break to clear her head.

She scrawled a message for Alex: *Taking Elspeth for a walk around the parking lot.* She added her satellite phone number in case he found a way to call her.

A winter coat hung behind the door, and Victoria grabbed it. The coat was huge on her frame and smelled like Alex, reminding her of the last time she'd borrowed his clothing. She wasn't sure when. Maybe his flannel shirt at their family's lake house? He'd worn the same cologne since he was in college. The scent hit her with unexpected emotion, making her throat tight.

"Come on, Elspeth." She grabbed the dog's leash. "Let's get you outside."

Victoria's dogs—greyhounds adopted from racetracks—would need sweaters and coats in weather like this. Their minimal body fat and thin skin made them vulnerable to extreme temperatures. But Elspeth was a different breed. Outside, she wore only her medic vest with its bright reflective stripes. Since they weren't venturing off the plowed roads and sidewalks, Victoria didn't bother with the dog's boots.

More guests had gathered in the common areas with warmth from the generator and the fireplaces. Crewcut and his brother had commandeered a corner and were encouraging people to join them.

"Glad you're here with us," he called in a cheerful voice that carried well across the large space. "Not that you have many options, but I won't take that personally. My brother and I come from Charlotte, North Carolina. We do trivia every Thursday at our favorite brewery, and we're bringing it to you right now. Get ready for five rounds. And without cell service, there's no way any of you can cheat."

Laughter followed.

Victoria admired the men's determination to keep spirits up. She smiled and gave Crewcut a thumbs up as she and Elspeth went out the door.

Wind-driven snow swirled in disorienting clouds. She couldn't tell what was coming down and what was getting redistributed. The parking lot still looked like a graveyard of white-shrouded cars.

"It's best if you make it quick," she told Elspeth.

But Elspeth took her time, following her nose with intense concentration, investigating scent trails invisible to Victoria.

Around the building's corner, trash surrounded the dumpsters. Bags toppled over each other, and their contents spilled out across the ground. The mess resulted from two missed pickups. What would day four or five look like? She didn't want to know.

Victoria jogged in place, stamping her feet against the numbing cold. From here, she saw only the mountain peaks and an endless expanse of white that could hide anything.

An explosion echoed across the mountain, farther away than the earlier controlled blasts. Outside, Alex was working in conditions capable of burying him in seconds if something went wrong.

When Elspeth finished, they returned to the building through a different service door, the closest entrance that would get Victoria into the building sooner rather than later. Inside, they turned left down a long hallway and faced an approaching figure. A woman with blonde hair tucked under a knit cap. She wore large aviator sunglasses, odd given the sunless day and poor lighting, and carried a white takeout box with a large blue X written on the side.

Victoria offered a polite smile. The woman nodded but leaned away, creating distance between them. A yellowish-purple bruise marred her cheek. The coloration indicated an injury two or three days old. She raised her hand to cover it, revealing a stainless-steel medical alert bracelet on her wrist.

Elspeth pulled toward the woman, nose working furiously. She barked with the insistent sound of a working animal who recognized a target scent.

Victoria shortened Elspeth's leash to keep the dog by her side.

The woman was already hurrying away. "Sorry. I'm afraid of dogs," she called back without turning around.

Something about her was familiar. Either she was a guest Victoria had seen earlier, or someone from her past. Victoria wanted to go after her, but not with the dog. Not only had the woman said she was afraid, but Victoria should return Elspeth in case Alex needed her.

The woman disappeared from view around a corner, but Elspeth remained fixated, straining against the leash with a low whine. Her behavior was unmistakable. It wasn't casual interest, but recognition.

Victoria couldn't shake the strange encounter. She had to know who that woman was. The takeout box might lead the way.

THIRTY-SEVEN

Tyler looked ready to collapse behind the grill's counter as he spoke with customers and scribbled on a clipboard. Josie appeared from behind him with a tower of white takeout boxes, moving with more confidence than she'd shown at the bar. She left the boxes on the counter, took the paper he handed her, and disappeared into the kitchen again.

Victoria waited in line, watching his system for order taking.

From the lobby, Crewcut called, "Round four has a common theme. Once you get it, the answers will click. Question one: What's a nickname for Seattle?"

When Victoria's turn arrived, she ordered three meals and watched Tyler write room numbers, adding "STAFF" next to Alex's name.

She leaned closer as he finished. "Quick question. What does a big blue X on a takeout box mean?"

He glanced up. "Special allergy meals. We prep them separately. No cross-contamination with nuts or seafood."

"Do you track who gets those orders?"

"Everything's manual now, but it's all here. Hold on." Tyler flipped through his clipboard pages. "Three blue X orders got prepared today." He showed her the list of room numbers, no names.

As Victoria jotted the numbers down, a loud, impatient huff came from behind her. Feet shuffled. She was holding up the line.

She moved to a corner table and placed the guest list on it to cross-reference the names with the room numbers Tyler had given her. The first two rooms were assigned to men with peanut allergies and the same last name. Probably family. But the third might be the name she was searching for.

Room 340: Lilly Childers. Severe shellfish allergy (anaphylactic).

That explained the silver medical bracelet.

After a few minutes, Tyler called her name. Victoria collected the three takeout boxes and thanked him as she mapped out her next steps. She needed more information about the woman in 340.

As she made her way through the lobby, heading for the guest wing, Crewcut's voice carried across the lobby: "What NFL team went winless for an entire season? The only time in history it's happened."

Carrying the three packaged meals in a bag, she headed straight to the third-floor guest wing and Room 340.

Victoria knocked.

When no one answered, she rapped again, then pressed her ear to the door. Nothing. Not even the sound of a person trying to be quiet. Strange. Where else would the woman have gone with her food?

A click came from behind her.

"I thought you were knocking on *my* door."

Victoria turned to see Mr. Walsh peering out from the room across the hall, head still bandaged.

"Hi, again. How are you, Mr. Walsh?"

"I've been better."

"I'm looking for the woman staying in this room. Have you seen her recently?"

His face twisted into a grimace. "Oh, her. No. Not today. She's been acting strange since she got here."

"Strange how?"

"She seems off." He stepped fully into the hallway, apparently eager to vent. "Eva got to talking with her a little on our first night here. I wasn't with them then. Neither skis, so they had that in common. Weird coming to a ski resort if you don't like to ski, right? Eva just likes getting away from home for a few days. She spends most of her time reading by the fireplace."

Victoria nodded, encouraging him to continue and get back to the topic at hand.

"Yesterday, me and that lady left our rooms at the same time. I tried to make conversation, just being friendly. I asked about her vacation. She said she had come all this way to ski, and then they closed the slopes. But just the day before, she'd told my wife, Eva, that she didn't ski at all. I didn't know what to make of that."

It seemed odd. "Are you sure you and your wife were talking to the same person?"

"Of course, I am. She had a sharp hairstyle. Eva said it was perfect. It looked pretty good. Maybe the lady does hair for a living."

"Anything else unusual?"

He smirked. "The sunglasses. Wearing them inside. She told me it was for migraines, but I didn't believe her." He lowered his voice. "Look, she had a bruise." He touched his cheek to show the location. "I used to work with a lady whose husband pushed her around." He shrugged. "I recognize the signs."

Victoria nodded. "When did you last see her?"

"Last night, maybe around seven? She was walking fast down the hall like she just wanted out of here. Maybe we're all freaking out now that we can't leave. It's making the weirdness in everyone come out."

"Did you see anyone following her?"

"No. Why are you looking for her? Is she missing?"

"I'm just checking on guests who might need assistance. She has severe allergies, and as far as I know, she's traveling alone. Or have you seen anyone else come in or out of her room?"

"Nah, haven't seen anyone else. But that bruise didn't get there on its own."

"Is your wife in your room? I'd like to ask her some questions."

"She's doing trivia in the lobby. Too noisy for me down there. She'll be back soon to check on me. I have to rest." He pulled his door closed a bit before stopping. "Hey, do you know anything about the heat situation? My room's like an icebox."

"I heard we'll have more heat in our rooms after 6:30 p.m. or sooner if the power returns."

Mr. Walsh went back into his room, and Victoria stood in the empty hallway. Partial clues floated in her mind. They weren't quite connecting. A woman who said she didn't ski. The sunglasses. The bruise. Elspeth's unmistakable alert.

Victoria still wasn't sure why she wanted to talk to Lilly Childers, but she trusted her gut. Whatever Lilly Childers was hiding or whomever she was hiding from, Victoria was going to find out.

THIRTY-EIGHT

Keeping my head down, I move through the lodge's main room. Everyone here has a reason for wanting to escape. Dare I say my reason is the most pressing? I wouldn't have left my room, but I'm hungry and going a little stir-crazy in there.

The resort offers single-serving cereal boxes. They're the sugary kind with cartoon mascots my mother used to buy when I was a kid. I liked them until I learned the truth. They aren't nutritious, just chemicals with vitamins sprayed on. Fake. Like most everything in my life lately.

The sign says we can only take one per person. I've watched others ignore this rule, as if five boxes of sugar cereal will be the difference between life and death, but I follow it. A worker stands guard, arms crossed, watching us. It's better for me to blend in rather than draw attention.

As I tear open my cereal box, I wonder where Steve is right now and how much he knows.

A familiar voice from a nearby table rises above the others. That copper-haired woman who's been holding court since yesterday, acting out every word that comes from her mouth. She says her name is Maura.

"I plan to hire an attorney and sue for the inconvenience," Maura announces. "We should band together. A class action suit."

Interesting, I think, but obviously, I can't be a part of that.

"Oh, look." Maura's voice rises a few octaves. "There she is. Victoria Heslin. The celebrity in our midst. You know, the FBI agent who was on Flight 745."

I turn to see a slim, athletic woman passing through the lobby, and I'm forced to swallow a lump in my throat that wasn't there seconds ago.

Victoria Heslin. I've heard of her, but I wouldn't have recognized her. She's a little taller than average, and more attractive than most, with no makeup and a simple shoulder-length hairstyle.

When she tucks a strand of hair behind her ear, her deformed hand confirms her identity. She lost fingertips on both hands after the most famous plane crash in recent history. Every post-rescue news article mentioned her frostbite. Victoria is a wealthy heiress; everyone knows that, too. She doesn't look the part. There's nothing ostentatious about her. No designer labels or jewelry. None of that polished glamour that sometimes comes with great wealth.

"I spoke to Victoria days ago." Maura's face is one big conspiratorial smile. "She's here on vacation with her fiancé because her brother works for Black Ridge. He's part of the ski patrol, the ones who found the body of that poor woman. The police asked Victoria to investigate. She's working the case now, interviewing people."

"Ooh, any of us might be next," a dirty blonde says, and I have no idea what she means. Next to be interviewed or next to die?

"I heard the dead woman was upset before she died. *Very* upset," the guest to Maura's right chimes in. "My husband got that information from the bartender."

Their conversation has shifted from their class action suit to a more interesting topic. I don't want to miss any of it. I drift closer and settle into an empty round-back chair, where I can easily overhear Maura entertaining her captive audience.

"Listen to this," Maura adds, not to be outdone by others' information. "They found a champagne bottle with the dead woman. One of the kitchen staff told me Victoria dusted the bottle for fingerprints. Apparently, the deceased had been drinking heavily before she died."

It's impossible not to smile. The story is already morphing the way rumors do when they go from person to person.

"One of the kitchen staff told me Victoria dusted the bottle for fingerprints and found one," Maura whispers.

I try not to look as surprised as I feel.

"Do you think she passed out and died from the cold?" I ask, angling myself into their circle with a concerned expression. "I can't imagine, especially in this weather."

The dirty blonde turns to include me, raising her brows at my suggestion. "But why was she drinking outside in a blizzard?"

I shake my head. "Who knows the things people end up doing when they're drunk?"

"Right." Maura lifts her hand to emphasize her point. "Terrible judgment. It happens. A few years ago, my cousin's best friend overdosed after her boyfriend broke up with her. So sad."

"Very tragic," I say. "Her poor family."

Everyone agrees.

"Speaking of family..." The dirty blonde drops her voice to a loud whisper and covers one side of her mouth with her hand. "Have any of you seen the dead woman's family or whoever she was with? Because I haven't."

Everyone's heads are shaking. No one has seen a grieving partner, friend, or family member. And they're not going to.

Maura frowns and tosses her red hair over one shoulder. "You don't think she was traveling alone, do you?"

Since I'm traveling alone, I don't want to stick around and hear them say how strange that is. Already, I've taken a risk by joining their conversation and giving people a chance to notice me. Getting up from my chair, I say, "I'm going back to my room. This whole situation is too much." I gesture around the lobby to encompass our entire predicament.

As I leave the gossip circle behind, I toss my cereal box atop a trash bin that's already too full. Instead of returning to my claustrophobic room, I brace myself for a walk through the storm to the spa's relaxation lounge. It's become my refuge at Black Ridge since the power died.

A sign on the locked door apologizes that it's closed because of staffing shortages. After picking the lock, I've got the place to myself. No one else has come out here. It's too cold and too far away from the main building.

I settle onto the leather couch facing the stone fireplace and light a fire using the supplies stacked nearby. The flames catch quickly, casting dancing shadows across the bookshelves lining the walls. Now I've got heat and light. I pull a throw around my shoulders, one over my legs, and select a book about mindfulness.

I can't stay cooped up in my room all day and night, replaying every mistake I made. Here, I can think and let my guard down.

Victoria Heslin just happened to be here on vacation, and now she's "investigating." I'm not worried. She might be an FBI agent with good survival skills, but she's surrounded by unreliable witnesses spreading distorted versions of events.

How can she possibly do her job well? How can she know what's really going on?

I don't think she can. In fact, I'm counting on that.

Besides, the FBI isn't who I fear the most.

THIRTY-NINE

Almost 4 p.m. The sun was still up somewhere beyond the wall of dark clouds, but the storm had turned the sky an endless gray. Still no Alex. No Ned. And no word from either of them. The lunches Victoria had gotten them sat untouched on Alex's desk.

Victoria took a deep breath. She had to focus on what she could control. She spread her notes out, creating three distinct piles. The evidence and timeline for Jane Doe's death on the left. Foster's information in the center. To the right, observations about the blonde woman with the bruise and medical bracelet.

She tore off a fresh sheet of paper and wrote out the questions she wanted to answer.

Who is the deceased woman? Where is Steve Foster? What is the deal with Lilly Childers?

One dead, one missing, one hiding. Three separate mysteries demanded answers, and she believed they were connected.

Elspeth got up from her bed, turned in a tight circle, then settled down with a soft groan.

"That blonde woman caught our attention, didn't she?" Victoria's tone caused the dog's ears to perk up. "But why?"

She returned her attention to the guest occupancy list and traced her finger down to the entry on Lilly Childers. There was a small 'W' beside her name.

"Let's find out what this means." She gathered her papers. "Come on, girl."

The trivia competition had ended in the lobby, replaced by a young man with dreadlocks playing a melancholy song on an acoustic guitar. The music amplified the lodge's unsettling mood, made worse by the unlit Christmas tree looming overhead.

She approached the guest services desk, where Rosalie and Thomas were leaning heavily on the counter. For once, no one was asking anything of them. Victoria hated to ruin that, but she needed help.

"Excuse me, Rosalie. I need information about a guest." She pointed to Lilly's name on the occupancy list. "What does the 'W' marking next to her name mean?"

Rosalie smoothed strands of hair over her ear. "The 'W' means walk-in. No reservation. She arrived and booked a room. We're usually booked solid during peak season, but with the storm warnings, we had several early departures and cancelations." She took a breath. "I'm sorry. You probably don't need all those details." Her eyes widened. "Is she the person who died on the slopes?"

"No. Lilly Childers is alive and well. I'm just trying to locate her. Is your computer still working?"

"Yes, it's one of the few systems on backup power."

"Please tell me what other information you have about her stay."

Rosalie's fingers flew across the keyboard. "Lilly Childers checked in for two nights. She has a local Colorado address. We scan driver's licenses. You want to see it?"

After walking behind the counter, Victoria studied the screen, then took a photo. "Do you have a Colorado driver's license?" she asked Rosalie.

"No, I'm from New York. But Thomas lives here."

Victoria turned to Thomas. "May I see your license?"

Thomas looked puzzled but lifted his wallet. "Sure, but why?"

"For comparison." Victoria held his license next to her phone screen, studying both documents. Thomas's license had a subtle holographic overlay, micro-printing along the edges, and a specific font for the state seal. Lilly's scanned license had all of those details, but the color saturation wasn't exactly the same.

"Thomas, where did you get your license renewed last?"

"The downtown DMV office in Denver."

Which meant Lilly's license was fake. Professional quality, but fake.

"Thank you," Victoria said, before walking away from the desk.

With Elspeth trotting beside her, Victoria climbed the stairs to the top floor of the guest wing.

The dog stopped to sniff the Christmas tree opposite the elevators as they passed it.

A harsh coughing fit came from behind one of the nearby doors, followed by a muffled voice complaining, "It's freezing in here. This is ridiculous."

The area beside the large window at the end of the hallway offered her best chance of satellite reception. With no heat in the guest wing corridors, ice coated the inside of the glass. The storm was slowly encroaching on the building, battling its way in.

She was relieved when her satellite phone connected to Agent Rork.

"Hi. This is Special Agent Victoria Heslin. Reception's terrible up here," she said without preamble. "The resort's completely cut off now. No internet or regular phone service. Wasn't sure if you'd tried to reach me."

"Not yet. We still haven't located Steve Foster or his vehicle. He has not used his phone or his known credit cards today. We'll keep looking for him. When he surfaces, I'll let you know."

"What about the warrant for Jewell investigations?"

"That's taking longer than I thought. Waiting for the judge to get back to me."

"Okay, thanks." Victoria sighed. Foster could be anywhere by now. "In the meantime, I need a background check on another person. Lilly Childers." Victoria read off the license information, squinting at her notes in the dim hallway light. "Fair warning, I suspect this might be a fake ID, but run it anyway, since fake identities often use real people's information."

"Any connection to your victim?"

"Possibly. Call me back at this number when you have information. I'll be waiting."

Victoria kept her satellite phone on, though conscious of its diminishing battery. She sat down on the carpeted floor and leaned back against the wall. It felt like a sheet of ice against her back, and she pulled her jacket tighter around herself. Behind her, snow whipped against the windows in violent gusts.

Elspeth curled up next to her thigh. Victoria stroked the dog's head. She hated just sitting there waiting, but this spot was the best place for satellite reception in the building.

More coughing, then an angry voice. "We need to find more blankets. I can't feel my toes."

Victoria's phone rang minutes later.

"Agent Rork here. Your Lilly Childers doesn't exist. The license number is fake, and the address is a mail forwarding service."

Victoria's stomach dropped. The questions were multiplying faster than she could solve them, almost as if the two women didn't want anyone to know who they were.

"Keep digging, please. Check missing persons and witness protection."

"Already on it. Sorry you're stuck there. How are people handling the situation?"

"They're not happy. Supplies are running low, and there's not much heat. We've had a few incidents. Arguments. One guest claims he got pushed down the stairs."

"What do you have there in terms of equipment?"

"Nothing, really," Victoria admitted. "I'm improvising. What about the rest of the area? How is it faring in the storm?"

"The entire region got hammered. Over four hundred thousand power outages. The National Guard is trying to reach stranded motorists. Just like your resort situation, it's all going to get worse before it gets better, even if everyone stays inside."

"I hope they do."

"Me too. Stay safe up there, Victoria. Talk to you later."

Victoria stared down the empty hallway. She rubbed her hands together, then up and down her thighs. The cold traveled through her clothes and made her joints ache. She pressed closer to Elspeth, thinking about Jane Doe and Lilly Childers again.

Elspeth lifted her head, listening.

An intermittent rattling sound carried from somewhere within the walls. An unsettling mechanical whine followed.

The generators shouldn't sound like that. No functioning machinery should.

The noise died away... then, nothing. An ominous quiet filled the hallway, interrupted only by the muffled sound of repeated sneezing.

Not good.

FORTY

O n their way from the top floor to the main floor, the stairwell was pitch black. Thinking about Mr. Walsh's "fall," Victoria kept a firm grip on the railing and Elspeth's leash. When she reached the bottom, weak light entered where an employee or guest had propped the door open.

Anxious voices grew louder as she approached the lobby.

The contemporary gas fireplace worked, though it generated little heat. Most of the warmth came from the central fireplace. Rosalie fed logs to the flames. The air carried a potent scent of marijuana as people dealt with their anxiety.

At least fifty guests had gathered in the space, with more streaming in.

She was just in time to see Peter step onto the stone hearth, his face pale and drawn. He cleared his throat twice before speaking. "Everyone, please remain calm. As you may have noticed, the generators have failed."

"How long until you fix them?" Maura asked.

Peter ran a hand through his now greasy hair. "We can't repair them until the access road opens." His voice wavered. "The main power might return before then. We're hoping it will." He forced what looked like a painful smile. "In the meantime, we're preparing a fabulous holiday barbecue for dinner. Our chefs are preparing the food now. A real feast."

"Before all the meat rots," Hawk shouted.

Peter ignored the comment. "I won't lie to you. It's going to get significantly colder in the building. Near our wood-burning fire is the place to be. We're also distributing thermal blankets." He turned to where Thomas was unpacking a box at the front desk. The crowd started funneling in that direction.

Maura's husband scoffed. "Those blankets look like the cheap things on airplanes."

Thomas held a stack of plastic-encased, folded fabric in his arms. "There's only this one box. Families with children and elderly guests get priority."

A man hollered, "I paid ten thousand for this week! I'm taking one."

Another man grabbed the same package. "I paid more than that. My wife is sick now, thanks to this place!"

The two men grappled over the blanket. One let go and pushed the other. Arms flailing, he stumbled backwards into the Christmas tree. It toppled in slow-motion, ornaments raining down and shattering. Screams erupted as people dove out of the way. The upper branches caught a woman who hadn't moved fast enough. She shrieked as the tree descended onto her. More glass broke.

"Tatum!" A man lunged forward. He tried to lift the massive decoration. "Somebody help me!"

Hawk filmed on his phone, circling the scene like a vulture. "Oh, man! More gold. Once I can post this, people are gonna lose their minds."

Guests rushed forward to help or to get a better look. Crewcut and his brother were the first to get to the fallen tree and reach into the branches. They hoisted the tree high enough for the woman to crawl out. The branches had pulled her hat off, leaving matted hair covering her face. She spat pine needles from her mouth.

Crewcut kneeled beside her. "Are you hurt?"

"I don't know," she gasped, wincing as her husband helped her to her feet. "My shoulder."

"Enough!" Thomas's face was a deep shade of red as he bellowed at the mohawk kid. "Put your damn phone down!"

Hawk grinned as he captured Thomas' angry expression and kept filming and narrating. "Guys, you're not gonna believe this. The power died, and people started brawling over airplane blankets. Then, the Christmas tree totally crushed a lady. It's insane here!"

"I'm okay, I'm okay," Tatum repeated with a dazed expression.

Her husband spun around and spotted one of the men who had been fighting over the blanket.

"You did this!" the husband shouted as he threw a powerful right hook.

Victoria moved quickly. "Gentlemen!" She jumped between them with her hands raised. "This is the last thing any of us need right now."

Both men stopped, blinking at her in surprise, as if shocked at what had transpired.

"Fire!" Tatum shouted. "The tree is on fire."

The dry evergreen branches crackled and popped as flames rose through the needles. Smoke billowed across the lobby.

Hawk held his phone higher, backing away but never stopping the recording. "Holy crap, the tree just went up in flames! This is next-level stuff, and it's real! I'm dying to upload this video."

Crewcut beat at the tree with his coat.

"Get back! Everyone, get back!" His brother shouted, stomping on burning embers. "We need more blankets!"

Several guests threw their blankets onto the fire. Thomas rushed over with a small fire extinguisher. "Out of the way!"

White foam sputtered weakly onto the flames. It was almost empty. Fortunately, the last of the flames had died out.

Smoke continued to rise from the charred remains of the tree and scattered debris.

The acrid smell of burning plastic and pine needles filled the air. People coughed and covered their faces. Terrified sobs came from a child.

Victoria stared in shock as things spiraled out of control. Disasters stripped away social conditioning faster than most people realized. Escalating misery would reveal the guests' true natures. Crewcut defaulted to protective leadership. Others revealed antisocial tendencies. If people were fighting over blankets now, Victoria's experience suggested they'd see hoarding, theft, and more violence when food supplies dwindled.

She couldn't bear to watch people morph into the worst versions of themselves. She had to leave or take charge of the situation.

Scanning the pandemonium again, taking in the anger and discomfort, her gaze stopped on a figure seated on the window ledge.

Lilly Childers.

She wore a red coat with a fur-lined hood and a blanket over her shoulders. A black knit cap with a pom-pom covered her platinum blonde hair. No sunglasses. She wasn't helping, nor was she reacting. Simply watching.

An odd feeling washed over Victoria. The same one she'd gotten when she first saw Lilly in the hallway. A sense of familiarity, like recognizing someone from a half-remembered dream. A person she'd seen recently.

Lilly held one arm up, rotating her wrist in a circular motion.

Something about that gesture...

FORTY-ONE

Despite the cold drafts coming through the glass, Lilly sat alone by the window. Her seat offered a perfect vantage point overlooking most of the lodge while positioned near a side exit. The kind of spot a person would intentionally choose if they needed to watch their back.

While everyone else gawked at the smoldering tree, Lilly's gaze moved across the crowd, never lingering too long on anyone. The movement might go unnoticed by the untrained eye, but it didn't fool Victoria. Lilly was reading the room in the same practiced way Victoria did.

Lilly rotated her wrist in a slow circle, sliding her medical bracelet up and down her arm. The gesture was unconscious, repetitive. Familiar. Victoria had seen it before. Two nights ago, the brunette who'd argued with Steve Foster had made that same movement. The same rhythm, only with black bracelets instead of the silver band.

The realization made Victoria's heart skip a beat.

This wasn't similar behavior. It was identical ingrained behavior.

The woman at the bar hadn't died. She was across the room, very much alive, wearing a blonde wig and a medical bracelet.

Victoria's entire investigation had just crumbled. Every assumption, timeline, and suspect. If the woman from the bar were alive and well... who was lying dead in the freezer?

As Victoria strode toward Lilly, two small figures jumped in front of her.

"It's the FBI lady!" Max called out, dropping to his knees to pet Elspeth.

Kayla plopped down too, reaching for Elspeth's ears. "She got us out of the pool and was nice to us in the elevator."

Their mother stood behind them, beaming. "Oh my goodness, you're the woman who rescued my children! I can't thank you enough. You have no idea how terrified I was. Max wasn't answering his phone. They never should have been in the pool area without us."

Victoria glanced over the woman's shoulder. Lilly was still there, but now partially hidden by the crowd.

"You're welcome." Victoria tried to move around them, but Max had his arms wrapped around Elspeth's neck, and Kayla had gripped Victoria's arm.

"Mom, can we get a dog like this when we get home?" Max asked.

"She's so soft!" Kayla squealed, burying her face in Elspeth's fur.

The mother continued her grateful monologue. "Again, I can't thank you enough. You must think I'm a terrible parent. They said you're with the FBI? That's so amazing. My husband's father was in the FBI. I'm sure he'd enjoy meeting you."

"Excuse me," Victoria interrupted as she scanned the crowd, seeing no sign of the black cap or blonde hair. Lilly had vanished into the sea of guests.

"Ladies and gentlemen." Peter's voice boomed across the lodge. "I'd like your attention once more for another important announcement. First, we need everyone to remain calm. Violent outbursts will not be tolerated."

"What are you going to do about it?" Hawk's friend asked with a taunting smile on his face.

"Enough!" Peter's voice cracked like a whip across the room. His face flushed as he slammed his palm against the wall, the sound echoing through the lobby. Guests jerked back, startled by the sudden violence of the gesture.

He stood there breathing hard, his shirt wrinkled and untucked, his hair sticking out at odd angles. For a moment, his eyes held the wild look of a man who'd reached his breaking point.

Just as quickly, he caught himself, smoothed his hair, and tucked his shirt back into place. When he spoke again, his voice had calmed, though his hands still trembled. "I've just learned that the electronic key card system is down. Guest doors are now unlocked."

"Wait, our doors don't lock?" Maura asked, her mouth hanging open.

Peter held up a hand to regain attention. "You can still lock your rooms from inside using manual deadbolts, but we cannot guarantee security for unattended spaces. If you're concerned about valuables, take them with you when you leave your room. Retrieve any items you need, but I recommend you come back to the lobby, where it's warmest." He had to raise his voice to be heard over the buzz of people speaking. "One more thing. Please listen. It's important. When you return to your room, turn the faucets on and let them drip so the pipes won't freeze."

People got up in droves, rushing to the stairwells that would take them to the guest wings, driven by an urgent need to secure their belongings.

The narrow opening to the stairs created a bottleneck of bodies jamming together to get through. A woman screamed and fell, disappearing beneath the surge of people.

"Stop pushing!" Peter shouted.

When the woman was on her feet and appeared to be okay, Victoria headed up the stairs with the others, three flights in near darkness. On the third floor, she walked straight to 340 and knocked hard.

No answer.

"Lilly? FBI. I need to talk to you." Victoria leaned against the door. Heard nothing.

The electronic locks were no longer working. If this door didn't open, that meant Lilly had engaged the manual deadbolt from inside.

Victoria grasped the handle and pushed it down. The door swung open.

Pausing at the threshold, she realized she was about to cross a line by entering a guest's space without permission, exactly what people feared might happen now that the electronic locks weren't working. But with a woman dead, possibly murdered, Victoria couldn't ignore Lilly's suspicious behavior. Lilly was the woman with Steve Foster in the bar. She had worn a sweater and bracelets identical to the victim's. Coincidence? Possibly. But taking that chance wasn't an option.

Warrantless searches were justified and admissible in court when there was a risk of evidence destruction. If Lilly was involved with the victim's death, or in danger herself, every second counted.

Leaving Elspeth in the corridor, Victoria drew her weapon and entered. "FBI. Is anyone in here?"

She cleared the bathroom first, then the closets. Empty.

Certain the space was secure, she holstered her gun and brought Elspeth into the room with her.

Blankets lay twisted and bunched on the right side of the bed, farthest from the door. The sheets and blankets on the left side remained tucked beneath the mattress.

Moving closer, she activated her phone's flashlight, wincing at the low battery warning. On the pillowcase, the beam caught a long strand of dark hair. Not blonde like Lilly's, but dark brown.

Victoria collected the strand and sealed it in a tissue from her pocket.

Moving to the dresser, she searched each drawer for the distinctive black and silver sweater. The drawers were empty aside from a few pairs of women's underwear and a top. No sweater.

A carry-on suitcase sat on the floor beneath the hanging clothes. Next to the suitcase, a white plastic bag held bunched-up used clothing. Size 6 black jeans. Long-sleeved T-shirts. Cotton underwear and a sports bra.

Why hadn't Lilly unpacked for a multi-day stay? Why was she living out of her suitcases when they had at least two more nights here?

Opening the suitcase, Victoria found more clothing in small and medium sizes.

The silver sweater wasn't there.

Was Lilly wearing it right now, beneath her coat? Or was there only one sweater like it at the resort—the one on Jane Doe?

Keeping one ear tuned for sounds from the hallway, Victoria shone her light inside the small trash can. Travel-sized bottles of face wash and shampoo. A toothbrush. Stuck to the bottom, beneath crumpled tissues, were two small particles of stiff brown plastic. Used contact lenses. Brown-tinted.

In the bathroom drawer, she found a toiletry kit with prescription bottles, all labeled for Lilly Childers. Lorazepam. Rohypnol. Muscle relaxants. Sedatives.

The pieces were forming a picture she didn't like.

FORTY-TWO

Victoria had just stepped out of Lilly's room and closed the door when Mr. Walsh exited the room across from her. A winter hat covered most of the bandage on his forehead. His wife, Eva, stood beside him. They each carried a large travel bag.

"That's her," he said to his wife. "The lady we saw in the medical area, the same one who was asking about the blonde."

Eva stepped forward. "My husband mentioned you were looking for the woman across the hall. Did you find her? I've been a little worried."

"I'm still looking for her," Victoria admitted.

Mr. Walsh glanced down at Elspeth, who was sitting at Victoria's feet. "They allow dogs at Black Ridge now? Or are all the rules out the window?"

"She's a ski patrol dog," Victoria explained. "Search and rescue."

Walsh nodded, seeming satisfied with that explanation.

"When did you last see the woman from this room?" Victoria asked.

Eva shifted her bag to the opposite shoulder. "I haven't seen her since before the avalanche."

"Can you describe her? I just want to make sure we're talking about the same person."

"She had shoulder-length blonde hair. An excellent cut, and she knows how to blow it out perfectly. Attractive, but not social. Although, she was friendly with one of your colleagues." Eva's eyes lit up as she emphasized 'friendly.'

Victoria wondered if Eva was talking about Steve Foster. He wasn't a staff member, but neither was Victoria, and the Walshs believed she was. People made assumptions, sometimes with the utmost confidence. Though Elspeth's presence and Victoria's visit to the medical area had certainly given them good reason to assume. "Which one of my colleagues?" she asked.

"The one my husband had an issue with."

Mr. Walsh crossed his arms over his chest. "I wasn't being difficult. All I did was ask legitimate questions about why they closed the upper trails so early. I've been skiing for thirty years. I know when conditions are safe."

"What exactly happened?" Victoria glanced between the couple.

"This big guy got aggressive, told me to follow the rules or leave the resort. Very rude. So, I complained to the manager about his attitude. A day later, as you know, I'm flying down the stairs."

"You think he pushed you because you complained to the manager?"

"I don't know why he pushed me. Does it matter? There's no acceptable reason."

The tension in his voice made Elspeth stand and stare up at him.

"I didn't see the actual disagreement or the fall," Eva said, "but I saw the woman across the hall go off with that same worker."

Mr. Walsh narrowed his eyes. "Maybe that bruise didn't come from an abusive husband after all."

"What was the employee's name?" Victoria asked.

Mr. Walsh shook his head, halting the movement with a frown as if it bothered him. "Uh… it might come to me, but I don't remember. Maybe I am concussed. Great, just great."

"Can you describe him?"

Eva answered for her husband. "Good-looking. Tall. Wore one of those ski patrol jackets."

A surge of nervous energy made Victoria a little shaky. "When did you see them together?"

Eva tilted her head and placed a finger on her lips before answering. "Two nights ago. I recognized her red parka with fur around the collar. Cute. Later, I saw them outside together. He had his hand on her behind. They went into the equipment building near the ski rental shop. It has a Staff Only sign on the door."

Victoria's mouth was dry. *Please don't let it be Alex.* The thought flashed into her mind before she could stop it. "I need you to identify the man you saw her with. There's a photo of the ski patrol downstairs. Would you come with me?"

"As long as it's quick," Mr. Walsh said. "They're having a barbecue downstairs. It's about time we got some decent warm food here."

They walked down the stairs to the main floor, all of them moving slowly with their hands on the railing, along with other guests headed back down to the lobby carrying purses, duffel bags, and even suitcases.

In the administrative corridor, Victoria's steps slowed as they approached Alex's office, where the patrol team photo hung on the wall outside his door.

"Was it one of these men?" she asked, holding her breath.

Eva studied the photo, hovering her finger over the faces as she moved it from left to right. She slowed at the center where Alex stood.

Victoria's throat constricted. She squeezed her hand tighter around Elspeth's leash.

Then Eva's finger moved to the right.

"This one." She tapped a fingernail against the glass. "Him."

"Yes, that's the guy with the attitude problem," Mr. Walsh added.

Eva had pointed at Jordan.

Lips pursed, Victoria blew out a quiet, deliberate breath. Not Alex, thank goodness. Guilt hit next, for suspecting her brother, even for a second.

Jordan was the one who had gone into the equipment shed with Lilly. A memory returned from when Victoria first met him. Alex had mentioned Jordan hooking up with a blonde.

Victoria stared at Jordan's photograph. The bruise on Lilly's face took on new meaning. Was he responsible for that injury and Lilly's reclusive behavior?

If Walsh was right about being pushed, Jordan resorted to violence when he was upset. If he'd shoved a guest to avenge a complaint, what else might he have done?

FORTY-THREE

After what Mr. and Mrs. Walsh told her, Victoria had to find Jordan, but the growing knot in her stomach wasn't just about him. She still hadn't heard from Ned and Alex. They'd been gone for hours, and Ned had to know she'd be worried. Where were they? Should people be out looking for them in case they needed help?

The smell of grilled meat hit her before she reached the lobby. Elspeth was interested. With her ears up, she stared intently at the buffet.

Outside, a few kitchen workers manned grills positioned just outside the back doors. With the power issues and refrigeration down, they were clearly rushing to cook everything before it spoiled.

"Fresh batch coming up." The chef carried a giant silver platter toward the long buffet tables. "Get it while it's hot!"

The Walshs were already in line, with Maura in front of them. "I haven't had a proper meal since we got here," she said. "It looks like there's plenty."

"More than enough," the chef answered, "but it's going fast. Grab a plate."

Rosalie and Thomas stood together in one corner, eating in silence. They needed the break.

Peter moved between tables, managing a strained smile as he checked on guests. "Chef figured we should cook it all at once rather than let it go to waste," he explained.

Hawk sneered. "So we should dig in today because there'll be nothing left tomorrow? This is our last supper before we have to eat each other?"

"Just... eat the food," Peter said, teeth clenched behind his tight smile.

"Agent Heslin?"

Victoria turned to see Tyler. "Can I get you a plate? We've got barbecued chicken, beef brisket, and some pork ribs that are falling off the bone."

"Thank you, but I'm okay."

Tyler looked puzzled.

"I'm a vegetarian."

"Oh. Well, there's some ... I think we have more granola bars somewhere."

"I'm fine, really." Victoria smiled at him. "But thank you."

"This is the best meal we've had since we got here." Maura's husband said, carrying a heaping plate on his way to a table.

For the moment, at least for those who ate meat, it seemed like their luck was finally turning around.

Victoria stood by the remains of the burned tree that lay pushed against the wall. No one had removed it.

Scanning every face, she didn't see any of the people she wanted to find, but she spotted another ski patrol member she recognized from the hallway photo. He was near the fire, still in his ski patrol jacket and ski boots, balancing a plate heaped with meat.

He eyed her as she walked toward him with Elspeth.

"Excuse me." She tried to keep her anxiety out of her voice. "I'm Alex Heslin's sister. Have you seen him recently?"

"Oh, hey. I heard you were here. I'm Corey. I was wondering why you had Alex's dog." His casual tone did nothing to ease Victoria's worry. His eyes looked glassy. "Alex is probably still out there doing his thing. He's always the last one in. You know how he is, right? He has to come back soon. Can't do much more work in the dark."

She wanted to press for more information but knew Alex wouldn't want her making a fuss. Her brother was outside doing his job. He's fine, she told herself. And Ned just better be with him.

"How about Jordan Deery? Do you know where he is?"

Corey dug into a slab of beef with his fork, then held it in the air while he spoke. "Jordan? He's probably somewhere inside. I heard he wasn't feeling well and backed out of our final rounds."

The timing felt convenient. Was he actually sick or was he hiding? "Any idea where he is now?"

"Nah, sorry. Haven't seen him since this morning." Corey pulled a piece of meat from his fork and fed it to Elspeth, who gobbled it down with enthusiasm.

Everyone seemed to enjoy the barbecue, but somewhere out in the dangerous storm were two men she loved. Why hadn't anyone seen them recently?

Stop. Focus. Maybe she was overthinking this. Or maybe she wasn't thinking dire enough.

Find Jordan first. Get answers. That she could do.

FORTY-FOUR

When Victoria moved away from the fireplace, the temperature dropped twenty degrees within yards. The hallways beyond the lobby were freezing. The building groaned around her, wood and metal contracting in the cold.

Maybe Jordan had slipped out of the lodge, feigning sickness, and disappeared into the storm where even ski patrol couldn't track him. But that seemed unlikely. No one was that desperate.

Wrapping her arms around her chest, she headed back to Alex's office with Elspeth. She rounded the corner and froze.

A tall figure crouched on the floor halfway down the corridor. A black backpack lay open on the floor beside him.

Victoria moved toward him. "I was looking for you."

Jordan zipped up his bag and shot to his feet. "Why?"

She started with Walsh's accusation. "A guest named Michael Walsh thinks you pushed him down the stairs."

Jordan's eyes went wide. "What?"

"He complained to management about your attitude when he questioned trail closures."

Jordan wiped his face with the back of his hand. "People give us grief over closures all the time.

"He believes you pushed him as retribution."

"I've never pushed anyone. Why would I do that?" His confusion seemed genuine.

"He said you were rude and told him to follow the rules or get out."

"I get tired of people thinking they know the mountain better than ski patrol does. But pushing someone? That's insane. I'd never risk my job." He clasped his hands together. They were shaking. "Is that what you wanted to ask me?"

"No, there's more. I have a question about the woman you were with the night of the avalanche. In the equipment shed."

His face turned pale. He looked younger, more vulnerable.

"What do you want to know?"

"She has bruises on her face. Are those from you?"

"What bruises? I didn't see any bruises." Jordan's back hit the wall, shoulders slumping. "Oh, God. It was just a hookup. I don't know who she is."

"Tell me what you know."

"Nothing. I know nothing." Jordan stared at his trembling hands. "We didn't even exchange names. I didn't know what room she was in or whether she was here with anyone. It happens sometimes with guests. They're here for a few days, looking for a good time. I must give off a vibe that I'm into that sort of thing. One thing leads to another. No one has ever complained. It's never been a problem before."

Jordan's emotional reaction surprised Victoria. She didn't understand why he was so defensive, unless he was guilty of giving Lilly those bruises.

"Do you always take your hookups into the equipment shed?"

"No, usually their rooms, or mine, but she wanted to go to the shed. I don't know why. But no one can get in except staff, so I figured it was a private enough location." Jordan's voice cracked. "After we... you know... she left first. Said she had to get back."

"Did she say who she was with?"

"No. Like I said, there wasn't much talking. But she checked her phone right before we, you know, started and right when we finished."

"Did you see her after that night?"

Jordan's face crumpled. "No. Not until..." His words tumbled out in a rush. "I swear I didn't hurt her." He choked back a sob. "I didn't see her again until I found her body in the snow."

Victoria's breath caught. Her voice came out just above a whisper. "What did you just say?"

"When I saw her again, she was already dead."

Victoria didn't understand at first, and then the horrifying truth hit her. Jordan hadn't been with Lilly Childers. He'd been with the victim.

FORTY-FIVE

Victoria tried to mask her surprise. "Jordan, I need you to be very clear with me. Is the woman you were intimate with in the equipment shed the same person you found dead in the snow?"

Jordan looked confused again. "Yes. I thought that's why you were asking about her."

Victoria processed the shocking information and regained her composure. "Why didn't you tell anyone you knew her?"

"At first, I wasn't sure it was her. The night we were together, she had blonde hair, not brown. But I recognized her face or thought I did. She looked different dead and frozen like that. I was freaking out, not sure what to think."

"That's why you vomited at the scene," Victoria said, clues falling into place.

"I panicked. I knew how it would look. Me finding her body after we'd been together. I was scared."

"Scared enough to steal evidence?" Victoria's voice hardened. "I took samples from the victim's body, and now they're missing."

Under Victoria's unwavering gaze, his shoulders slumped again.

"I heard Peter tell Alex about the evidence you collected," he admitted. "I figured my DNA would be there." He covered his mouth with his hand, apparently realizing how damning his actions were.

"You stole evidence from a federal investigation. That's obstruction of justice, tampering with evidence, and interfering with a homicide case.

Any of those charges can put you in federal prison for years." Victoria clenched her jaw. In normal circumstances, she'd have him arrested. But their situation was far from normal.

"I didn't do it." His words resonated in the empty corridor. "I just didn't want to be blamed for something I had no part in. I mean, if I were going to kill somebody, why would I leave the body on the slopes?"

"She was off the trail in the woods. Maybe you thought she'd get buried by snow until spring."

"But I'm the one who found her."

"Makes you look less guilty if you're the one to discover the body."

He winced. "This is exactly why I avoided telling you. No matter what, I'd get blamed. I didn't hurt her. I swear it."

"Where are the samples you stole?"

Jordan swung his backpack around to the front.

"Keep your hands where I can see them," Victoria shouted.

Jordan dropped his bag and raised his hands. "Whoa. I'm just getting it out of my bag. I was going to put it back once things calmed down. Once you figured out what happened."

Victoria retrieved the bag. Her initials were still on the seal. "I can only find the truth when I have the right evidence. This doesn't look good for you, Jordan."

"I know." He rocked back on his heels, wringing his hands. "But you have to believe me. I didn't kill her. We had sex, yes, but it was consensual. She initiated everything. The equipment shed... what we did there. I just went along with it. And when we finished, she was fine. Alive and talking about needing to get back to the main lodge."

Victoria studied him. "Is there anything else you want to tell me?"

"The woman I was with wore a medical bracelet. That's another reason I wasn't sure. The dead person didn't have a medical bracelet. And people don't take those off."

The corridor suddenly felt colder. Victoria leaned against the wall, processing the implications. Blonde hair. Medical bracelet. The conversation discrepancies that Michael Walsh had mentioned: Lilly Childers said she didn't ski, and then she said she did.

Someone had stolen the victim's identity.

That didn't clear Jordan entirely, but it meant another person was involved.

She told Jordan what she knew to gauge his reaction. "I think the woman you slept with wore a blonde wig. A different person is now wearing the same wig and medical bracelet."

Jordan's face lit up. "Who?"

"That's the question. Have you noticed anyone disguised as the woman you slept with?"

"No. But I've been outside working most of the time."

"Your DNA will be on the victim, and I'll need your fingerprints for elimination."

"I was in the military. My prints are in the system."

Victoria wasn't sure she believed him. "I'd rather not wait to access the system."

Jordan nodded. "Okay. Fine. I want to cooperate. What do I need to do?"

"After I get your prints, stay away from the other guests until the police arrive."

"Oh, believe me, I will."

"I'm trusting you to stay put, Jordan. Don't make me regret that decision. And if you're lying to me, I will find out."

In a normal investigation, she'd bring him in for formal questioning, maybe even arrest him. But here, with no backup, no holding cells, and everyone trapped together, keeping Jordan cooperative was more valuable than trying to restrain him. Besides, if he was telling the truth, there was someone far more dangerous walking free among the guests.

The pieces were reshuffling, a few clicking into place with alarming clarity. Jordan had slept with their victim the day she died. But someone else had stolen her identity—her blonde wig, her medical bracelet. They'd dressed the corpse in the silver sweater and black bracelets to complete the switch. It was an elaborate deception. But why?

Victoria had maybe 36 to 48 hours left before the access road cleared. After that, the impostor could vanish with her fake name and disguise, disappearing forever.

FORTY-SIX

Victoria hid the DNA swabs in her room, then retrieved the partial print she'd taken from the Dom Pérignon label

With the print cards on the desk, the difference was obvious. Jordan's fingerprints were large, consistent with his broad hands and tall frame. The partial print on the champagne bottle was smaller.

She'd already let Jordan go, and now she had to find the woman calling herself Lilly Childers.

From across her room, her satellite phone rang, and she answered, grateful for the contact.

"Agent Heslin, this is SSA Coleman, from the FBI's Denver field office. We have two updates on the Steve Foster situation."

"Excellent. Have you located him?"

"We have not. Still no phone activity or credit card activity. According to the phone company, his phone is still at Black Ridge. His wife hasn't heard from him, and she's concerned."

"You spoke with her again?"

"Elaine Foster showed up at our office an hour ago. She's still here, demanding we launch a full investigation into her husband's disappearance. She's convinced something happened to him."

"She's there right now?"

"Sitting in my office as we speak."

Coleman had just eliminated one of Victoria's theories. Elaine couldn't be at Black Ridge if she were in the FBI's office.

"Did you verify she was in Aspen before the avalanche?"

"Yes. Security footage and credit card records confirm she was there through the weekend. Her timeline checks out. About his being in danger... she's provided disturbing context we didn't have before."

"What disturbing context?"

"Steve Foster developed an algorithm for predictive market analysis worth hundreds of millions to the right buyer. Now that Foster is also missing, his wife believes someone is trying to steal the algorithm. She brought us documentation from the project team. Emails and financial projections for the eventual sale."

"Wait. Two women from Foster's company disappeared. Were they working on this algorithm project?"

"Let me check... yes, according to his wife's documentation, both missing employees were part of the development team. If there's a connection, this could be industrial espionage and theft. Professionals who specialize in becoming invisible."

Victoria stayed quiet for a moment, absorbing what this meant. It would explain why the woman she was trying to identify didn't exist in any of the FBI's databases. No records, no history, completely off the grid. She was dealing with thieves who were experts at deception and disappearing. Except the avalanche must have changed their plans. There was no disappearing from Black Ridge now.

Coleman continued. "Along those lines, we got the warrant from Jewell Security. Steve Foster called them at 9:08 p.m. on Saturday night."

"Just before he called his wife to say he was in his car and leaving Black Ridge," Victoria said, thinking aloud.

"He hired them to do an immediate background check on a woman named Anna Winters."

"Anna Winters? Do you know why?"

"He didn't tell them why."

"What did they find on her?"

"Nothing. And I can't find anything either. She doesn't exist. Just like Lilly Childers."

Victoria closed her eyes to think. It seemed like Foster had hired investigators because he suspected his mistress wasn't who she claimed to be. He'd been right. Too bad discovering the truth had probably gotten him killed.

Victoria ended the call with SSA Coleman feeling like she might be in over her head. Two fake identities. Possible corporate espionage and an algorithm worth killing for. The case was more complicated than murder. It had shifted into a different category of danger.

For the next hour, she checked every accessible, unlocked area of the lodge with Elspeth by her side. They swept through the dining areas where guests gathered around the last scraps of barbecue, searched the medical bay and the gym on the frigid lower level, and Room 340 in case the woman had returned there. Victoria checked behind the bar, in the gift shop, and anywhere else a person might hide or slip away unnoticed. The suspect had vanished.

Two days of investigation, and Victoria still hadn't identified the victim or the killer, but at least now, she understood why. She wasn't dealing with ordinary people caught up in a crime of passion or a random act of violence. This wasn't some jealous lover's revenge. These were professionals, trained to blend in, disappear or become anyone they needed to be. Criminal organizations often recruited people like that from prison, hence the tattoo.

But that still didn't explain why one of them had died or what had happened to Foster.

Elspeth whined softly at her feet, pressing against Victoria's leg.

"I hear you." She stroked the dog's back, letting the animal's solid warmth soothe her. "I'll take you outside soon."

Later, when she pulled her hood up, bracing herself to venture into the cold again, she wondered if the woman calling herself Anna Winters was hiding somewhere outside. The brutal storm made that unlikely. The wind was blowing with enough force to knock someone down, and the temperature had dropped so far below zero that exposed skin would suffer frostbite within minutes. Even someone trained for survival wouldn't last long in these conditions without proper shelter. Victoria's brief trip outside with Elspeth was pushing the limits of safety. No one, no matter how desperate, would try to survive out there for long.

So where were Alex and Ned?

Victoria kept Elspeth on a short leash. As the dog sniffed the snow, Victoria followed, her face scrunched up against the cold.

Elspeth stiffened and let out a low whine, tugging toward the line of trees.

"Nope. Sorry. This is as far as we're going."

Elspeth's tail wagged, her body vibrating with anticipation.

Victoria squinted through the swirling snow. A dark shape trudged toward them with a pronounced limp.

Elspeth barked and bolted forward, her leash slipping through Victoria's thick gloves. She ran straight to the approaching figure.

"Elspeth!" It was Alex, his voice hoarse but unmistakable.

Speechless, Victoria rushed through the snow and threw her arms around her brother. "Oh, you're back. But where's Ned? Wasn't he with you?" She scanned the trees behind him.

"He's coming."

A second figure appeared, his steps slow and deliberate.

"Oh, my God. I was so worried." She reached Ned and pulled him into a fierce embrace. For a moment, they stood in the howling wind, Victoria's eyes squeezed shut against unexpected tears.

"I'm sorry I couldn't contact you." Ned's voice was rough. "Long story."

"I want to hear every bit after you get inside."

In the lodge, the men peeled off their ice-crusted facemasks and goggles.

"Keep your coats on," Victoria warned. "The generators failed."

"When did that happen?" Alex asked.

"This afternoon. Things have been pretty tense since then."

Alex limped, favoring his right leg. Behind him, Ned moved as if he'd pushed his body past its limit. For a triathlete, a man who rarely showed weakness, that was saying a lot.

Questions came from all directions. "Have there been more avalanches?" "Are we in danger?" "Do you know when the power will come back?"

"What about the road?" Maura asked. "Are they clearing it?"

"What about the internet?" Hawk asked.

Victoria watched Alex force his shoulders straight despite his obvious pain.

"Alex!" Peter pushed through the crowd. He stopped, glancing at the guests surrounding them.

For an instant, Alex locked eyes with Ned. Victoria couldn't interpret its meaning, but she felt the skin prickle on the back of her neck.

"Everyone, please," Peter raised his hands. "Let these men sit down and rest. We'll update you as soon as we have information."

Victoria wanted to get them something to eat, but the buffet tables were now empty. People had devoured every piece of chicken, beef, and pork. Not even scraps remained on the serving trays.

Despite Peter's request, a man shouted, "We have a right to know what's happening."

"And you will know," Alex said with a tone that ended the conversation. "But not yet. Incomplete or incorrect information won't help anyone."

Victoria watched in admiration as her brother defused the tension, even while swaying on his feet.

"What happened out there?" She studied Ned's face for clues. "You were gone for so long. I thought..." She couldn't say the words aloud.

Ned's lack of energy was clear in every line of his body. "I need to lie down."

Whatever Ned and Alex had encountered in the storm, Victoria suspected it wouldn't bring comfort, only more questions, and perhaps confirmation that their situation was worse than anyone realized.

FORTY-SEVEN

L eading Ned down the pitch-black fifth-floor hallway toward their room, Victoria's hand trailed the wall for guidance. She walked into dishes and a metal plate cover, sending them clattering across the floor.

Ned grabbed her before she fell.

Her phone's flashlight revealed abandoned room service trays and broken dishes littering the hallway.

She read their room number on the door, then quickly shut off the light. The battery icon showed a sliver of red. "This is us," she said as Ned's foot sent more plates crashing together.

Inside their dark room, Ned sank onto the edge of the bed.

"You need to get your wet clothes off." She fumbled through his dresser drawers in the darkness. By touch alone, she pulled out thermal underwear and dry socks and created a pile on the bed. She added the resort's thick bathrobe and a large towel.

Ned didn't move. As her eyes adjusted to the darkness, Victoria recognized the thousand-yard stare she'd seen in colleagues after horrific operations, and in survivors after traumatic rescues. She kneeled on the carpet and began unlacing his boots.

"I can do it," he protested.

"I know you can." She continued anyway. When she peeled his socks off, his feet were like ice cubes. After covering them with dry socks, she massaged from his toes to his ankles. "Any numbness?"

Ned wiggled his toes within her grasp. "I'm good. We kept moving, and my gear held up. We weren't outside all day. Alex took us to a hut to get out of the wind."

Despite his assurances, when he stripped off his shirt, she turned on her flashlight again to examine him. A massive purple bruise had formed along his ribcage.

"What happened here?" She pressed lightly against the discolored area.

"It's okay. I fell. There's no serious damage. Nothing broken. Just bruised." His voice was matter-of-fact, downplaying the injury.

Once she'd bundled him in dry layers and he'd eaten their remaining snacks, they huddled together under all the bedding. Cold seeped through the walls, floor, and windows, claiming every inch of the room.

"It's freezing, but here's one way to look at it. If we'd had this setup when we were stranded in Greenland, we would have thought we'd died and gone to heaven," Ned murmured against her hair.

"That's very true. Can you imagine if we'd had a bed and all these blankets? The bathroom?" All it took was a few seconds of reminiscing to feel better about their current situation, yet she still couldn't relax, couldn't stop thinking about what Ned had experienced. "Please tell me what you were doing out there."

"I need sleep, Victoria. We both do."

"I can't until I know."

He sighed. "There's nothing we can do now, and I don't want you to say otherwise."

Victoria sat up straighter. "You're trying to protect me?"

"I just don't want you running out into the storm. We did everything we could. Alex will brief Peter, and they've probably called the sheriff."

The dread that had been building in Victoria's stomach all day crystallized into certainty. "What happened?"

Ned was quiet for so long that she thought he might have fallen asleep. Then he turned to face her, and even in the darkness, she could tell terrible news was coming.

"There was another slide on the access road," he said finally. "Smaller than the first, but enough to shift the avalanche debris." His voice broke. "There was a car buried under all that snow. At least one."

Her hand flew to her mouth as the full horror sank in. People had tried to escape the storm but got caught in the avalanche.

Ned grasped her other hand under the blankets. "We tried to get closer, but it wasn't safe. Alex fell into a crevasse when a section collapsed under him. That's how he hurt his leg."

"Were there any signs of life?" Victoria asked, though she already knew the answer.

"It's been three days. Even if someone survived the initial impact, in these temperatures..." He didn't need to finish.

Victoria closed her eyes, calculating the mathematics of frigid-weather survival. Hypothermia would have set in within hours.

"There's no way to reach them until the right equipment arrives. Especially not in a blizzard." Ned turned his head and coughed.

When his coughing subsided, Victoria leaned her head against his shoulder, feeling the weight of every worry about Alex and Ned, every crisis and complication in what had started as a simple vacation and turned into a nightmare.

"Wait, those barricades we saw. I thought they were in place before the slide."

"They were. Your brother and Jordan set them up on both sides of the avalanche zone. Someone must have moved them."

Victoria wasn't sure what to say.

"Your brother was incredible out there. I figured he was good at his job, but seeing him in action was eye-opening. He knew where it was safe to step and when we needed ropes. He risked his life trying to get to the vehicle we saw. His endurance is unreal."

"He's always been like that. It's why he was captain of every sport he played in high school and college."

"After today, we know each other so much better, and I'd trust him with my life. Because I literally did."

"I bet he feels the same about you." Victoria smiled. At least one good thing had come from their time at Black Ridge.

"Alex wants to try a different approach tomorrow at first light," Ned continued. "But tonight, there's nothing anyone can do. I need you to be okay with that."

Her professional instincts screamed against waiting and leaving people in their cars, but Ned was right. They had no safe way to access the unstable barricade of snow. Attempting a rescue in these conditions, in the dark, would only lead to more casualties. The rational agent in her understood this, but she hated it.

"I was so terrified something had happened to you," she whispered.

"Now you know what it's like for me when you're on a case and you can't call." He pulled her closer. "The waiting. Not knowing. Imagining worst-case scenarios. But I trust you."

She pressed her face against his shoulder. "It's not you I don't trust. It's everyone and everything else."

"We're going to be fine. We've been through worse."

They'd survived the plane crash that had nearly killed them both, dangerous assignments that had tested every limit and their relationship, and cases that had left physical and emotional scars. But as Victoria lay in bed listening to the wind lashing against the roof, she wondered if their luck would hold.

Would there be more victims before this nightmare ended?

FORTY-EIGHT

They lay quietly for several minutes, Victoria listening to Ned's steady heartbeat. The immediate crisis of getting him warm and safe was over, but her mind wouldn't settle.

"I keep thinking about the avalanche... the cars," she whispered.

His response was so quiet, she almost missed it. "I know. Me too."

She thought he was drifting off, but then he shifted and drew her closer.

"I'm sorry. I never asked about *your* day. Did you figure everything out while I was gone?"

"Not exactly. No. It's more complicated than I imagined." She hesitated. "Do you want to hear about it, or try to sleep?"

"Tell me what happened."

"The biggest discovery is that the woman who argued with Foster at the bar—she's alive. She isn't the victim."

Ned turned on his side. "So, I *did* see her yesterday."

"I think her name is Lilly Childers, but that's a fake name. She's wearing a blonde wig and a medical bracelet that used to belong to the victim."

"Wait, how do you know the wig and bracelet belonged to the victim?"

"Jordan told me. He was with her the night she died."

"Wait, what? Jordan knew the victim?"

"They had sex in the equipment shed."

Ned pushed himself upright. The bombshell she'd delivered had given him a second wind. "He had sex with her and then found her body? That's... that makes him a suspect, doesn't it?"

"Yes, but I don't think he's responsible for her death. There's more. The Denver office got a warrant for Jewell Security and Investigations. Foster hired them to look into someone named Anna Winters. Not her real name, we're sure, but I think she's the person we saw at the bar. She's a professional who targeted Steve to steal from his company. Now she's pretending to be the dead woman."

"So, did she kill her?"

"I don't know yet. Whoever she is, she's dangerous. Foster was on to her, then he disappeared. It's looking like he's the one in trouble, if he's not already dead."

"We're stranded with a trained killer who could be anywhere in the lodge right now. You need to be careful."

Victoria agreed. "We both do."

Ned lay down again, and Victoria nestled closer to him, wanting to dispel the coldness inside her that had nothing to do with the temperature. She'd locked and chained the door and placed her weapon within arm's reach.

"I was worried about you when you were gone."

"Me, too," he mumbled, already drifting off again.

The hallway outside their room was silent. Guests had either retreated to their beds to stay warm until sunrise or had remained in the lodge near the fireplace.

Ned's breathing gradually deepened as sleep claimed him, but Victoria remained wide awake. Somewhere inside Black Ridge, Lilly Childers was probably awake too, wondering how much Victoria had figured out, and whether her secrets were about to be exposed.

FORTY-NINE

Victoria stirred from a restless sleep. Bitter cold sliced through every layer of clothing and each blanket, an instant reminder of their predicament. The room felt like a walk-in freezer, and Victoria could see her breath in the pale morning light.

A distant boom reached them from somewhere outside. The ski patrol was already risking their lives to keep everyone safe. The thought filled her with a complicated mix of pride in her brother's dedication and concern for the dangers he faced, considering how much snow had fallen.

Beyond the frost-covered window, clear skies stretched endlessly. The snow had stopped, and the storm had finally moved on, offering their first real break since arriving at Black Ridge.

She turned back to watch Ned sleep, taking in every detail of the face she'd been afraid she might never see again. She loved everything about him: his steady, quiet strength, his courage and helpfulness, the way he never complained even when pushed beyond normal limits. Just by being himself, he grounded her in a way nothing else could.

He scrunched his face, then turned on his side, coughing. She hoped he wasn't sick.

Moving carefully to avoid waking him, Victoria peeled off a few layers of clothing and laid out her exercise mat on the floor. Three sets of twenty-five push-ups. Fifteen minutes of core work. Next, she endured a quick but brutal sponge bath with ice-cold water from the tap, gritting her teeth against the shock on her skin. By the time she was checking her weapon's position at her hip, Ned was dressed and ready to go.

"How are you doing?" she asked.

"Hungry." He covered his mouth, turned his head to the side, and coughed.

"You missed a big barbecue last night. They cooked all the meat from the refrigerators and freezers before it went bad."

"I missed a barbecue? Why are you even telling me? That's just cruel."

"Sorry. I should have made you a plate. Let's see what awaits us in the lodge."

Heading down the stairs, she hoped everyone would be more comfortable now that they'd had a big meal, the sun had risen, and the storm had passed.

As they reached the first-floor landing, a wet, retching sound echoed from somewhere ahead. The noise made Victoria's stomach clench. Someone was having a terrible morning.

Ned's jaw dropped when they entered the lobby. Light poured through the tall windows, revealing what looked like a disaster relief center for sick people. Guests clustered near the fireplace, some curled in fetal positions with the resort's white sheets and duvets pulled over their heads.

The acrid smell of vomit hung in the air. A woman stumbled past them toward the restrooms, one hand pressed to her mouth, the other clutching her stomach. A man sat doubled over in a chair, dry-heaving into a bucket while his wife rubbed his back with a helpless expression.

Thomas and Rosalie were nowhere to be seen. The guest services desk was vacant for the first time that Victoria could remember.

Peter entered the lobby with a wrinkled brow, one hand pressed against his lower back.

"What happened here?" Ned asked.

"Food poisoning. Most everyone who ate last night's barbecue is sick." Peter turned away. "Obviously, something went wrong."

Victoria's mind flashed back to the barbecue—the power issues affecting refrigeration, the rushed preparation, all the guests and staff devouring the meat.

"But you're okay?" Victoria asked.

"I was too busy and too stressed to eat. But my entire kitchen crew is sick. All of housekeeping. Some of ski patrol. You two are fine?"

"The food was gone when Alex and I got back last night," Ned said. "Victoria's a vegetarian."

"You got lucky." Peter let out a defeated sigh. He tried to move to the center of the room and the fireplace, but he couldn't get through without stepping on people. "Everyone!" he called from the front desk. "I have updates about our situation."

Most of the guests looked too weak and sick to care.

"First, we're doing everything we can for those who are ill. We have water bottles and Gatorade bottles available." Peter gestured to the drinks tucked into coolers packed with snow.

"The snow has finally stopped, and crews will resume clearing the access road today. The current estimate is still forty-eight hours until we can leave."

Angry grumbling mixed with moans.

"I know many of you would like some fresh air, but conditions outside remain extremely hazardous. Our reduced ski patrol team is conducting avalanche control operations. Some of them are just as sick as you. Please stay inside for your safety and theirs. We've cleared a walking path around the parking lot. Do not venture beyond the marked boundaries. The avalanche zones extend closer than you might think. Anyone who ignores these restrictions puts themselves and our patrol team at risk."

He paused, letting that sink in.

"If anyone has a genuine medical emergency beyond food poisoning, helicopter evacuation is now possible."

Tyler appeared, his skin pale and sickly, carrying a box. He unpacked it at the guest services counter and unloaded granola bars. Guests swarmed him, though with much less energy than before.

Victoria scanned the crowd, looking for the woman calling herself Lilly Childers. She wasn't among the sick guests huddled near the fireplace. Where would she hide at a resort where the only remaining heat was in the lobby?

"I need to check something," Victoria told Ned. "I'll be back."

"Be careful," he called after her.

FIFTY

Victoria checked Room 340 again, knocking first, then entering. Empty, as she'd expected.

She zipped her coat to her chin, pulled her hood up, and walked outside into the bitter morning air. Through the breaks in the clouds, sunlight reflected off the endless white landscape. The nearest lift house seemed half its original size, with the bottom portion, including the windows, buried in powder. The lower chairs sat motionless on their cables, each one covered by large mounds of snow.

Following the resort map signs, she made her way along a newly cleared path, then veered off toward the spa building. The structure looked dark and abandoned. A sign on the door read: Closed due to staff shortages. We apologize for any inconvenience.

Victoria tried the handle and found it locked. But knowing what she now suspected about Fake Lilly's skill set, a locked door wouldn't pose a barrier. Scratches around the keyhole confirmed her theory.

Fake Lilly wasn't the only one who could break in. Victoria got the lock open in seconds.

She pushed the door open, listening for any sound from within. She crept forward.

In the second room, not visible from outdoors, weak flames rose inside a small gas fireplace, more for décor than function. In the chair facing the fire sat her target. She appeared unaffected by the illness ravaging most everyone else.

Victoria edged toward her, reading the woman's practiced stillness, tense shoulders, and tight grip on her bag.

"Don't move," Victoria said, her hand on her weapon at her hip. "FBI."

The woman's expression held no surprise as she met Victoria's gaze.

"You need to answer some questions."

"About what?"

"About Steve Foster, Anna Winters, and Lilly Childers—the woman whose identity you stole."

"I'm Lilly Childers. Would you like to see my identification?"

"It's fake. Just like Anna Winters was fake."

The woman's expression didn't change, but she glanced past Victoria.

Victoria followed her gaze for an instant, but there was no one else in the dark spa. They were alone.

"Steve Foster hired investigators to look into Anna Winters. That's you, isn't it?"

No answer, just a blank stare.

"Where is Foster now?" Victoria asked.

"I swear, I don't know where he is or what happened to him."

Victoria wasn't sure if she believed her. "If you're in danger, I can protect you. But I need to know what's going on."

"You don't understand." Her voice trembled. "They'll kill me if they think I talked to you."

"Who will?"

"The people who... who made me do things. Terrible things." Her hand went to her bruised cheek. "They said if I didn't cooperate, they'd hurt my family."

"What did they make you do?"

She looked away. "I can't tell you. I shouldn't even be talking to you. They have people everywhere. Even here."

As the woman's hand moved protectively over the medical bracelet, Victoria glimpsed something beneath it. A small, crude marking on the inside of her wrist.

"Show me your wrist," Victoria commanded. "Pull up that bracelet. Now."

The woman slid the medical bracelet up her arm, revealing the same rudimentary star tattoo Victoria had seen on the victim's wrist. Same placement, uneven lines, and amateur quality.

"The woman who died here had the same tattoo. Were you in prison together?"

The suspect let out a haughty laugh. "I've never been in prison."

"That's prison ink. I've seen enough of it to know. You and the victim were working together, weren't you? Same employer. And your target was Steve Foster and his algorithm. But something went wrong. Or maybe one of you was always supposed to eliminate the other once you completed the job."

"None of that is true," the woman whispered, but her voice lacked conviction. She looked past Victoria once more, then met her gaze with desperation in her eyes. "Meet me in my room in ten minutes. Please. Room 340. I have to show you something."

"Okay," Victoria said, though she had no intention of letting the woman out of her sight.

Whatever game she was playing, whatever she was hiding behind that bruised face, Victoria needed to uncover the truth.

Following her into her hotel room might mean walking into a trap.

But it might be the only way to get answers.

FIFTY-ONE

Ten minutes. That's how much time I have to decide on my next move.

Victoria Heslin doesn't have the entire story right, but she knows more than I realized. Much more. How did she find out Steve Foster was investigating me when I didn't even know it?

She's better than I thought. I'm not sure how much longer I can get away with playing the victim. Is she even buying it?

As I leave my little spa sanctuary with her right behind me, I can't believe it's come to this. Two days ago seems like a lifetime now. Everything fell apart so fast. I keep replaying the events to piece together how it imploded, the exact moment my simple assignment became a death sentence. I had what I needed, but I was dragging the assignment out. Enjoying myself for once... right until I wasn't.

After Steve got those photos and stormed out of the bar, I'd gone to the locker room looking for him, hoping that he hadn't left, that he'd be there picking up his skis. I wanted to explain. I needed an explanation that wouldn't expose everything, a version of the truth mixed with careful lies. Even more pressing, I had to get my purse back. That's when a figure stepped out of the shadows and hit me on the head. In that split second, I thought my life was over. But that's not what happened.

I come to lying on the floor with my ears ringing as if there's an alarm going off next to my head, surprised I'm still alive. The left side of my face pulses with pain.

As my vision clears, I glare at the woman who just assaulted me. Even in her excellent disguise—a blonde wig that suits her coloring—I recognize my colleague. Lilly. I should have guessed. That explains the photos Steve received. Her style is to toy with people, torture them just a little for no other reason other than to watch them squirm. She enjoys inflicting pain.

Lilly glares back. "That was personal. I hate the cold, and I detest the snow. Yet here I am in the middle of an epic blizzard because you failed to get the job done."

I push myself up from the floor. The room spins. Lilly goes from single to double and back again as nausea settles inside me. Still off balance, I lean against the wall for support. "I had everything under control."

"Greytech doesn't think so. Foster's company was getting ready to sell those algorithms. You've had more than enough time to get them. You know what I think?"

Instead of answering, I touch the painful skin beneath my eye. There's going to be a large bruise, but there's no blood.

"I think you had other plans, Anna." Her voice turns sickly sweet and suggestive.

"This trip is the first time we've been together where he's had his computer with him. I have the intel. It's on a thumb drive in my purse. I have it," I repeat, hoping she believes me.

Blood pounds against my temples as I try to figure out how to get the thumb drive back. How much time has passed? Has Steve already gathered his skis and left Black Ridge?

"You had no right to interfere," I say, needing to first deal with the threat in front of me.

"Not my choice. They sent me to evaluate the situation, and after watching you and the target together, it's clear what's going on. You weren't acting, Anna. You've gone soft. As of today, I'm the primary on this operation."

"You're supposed to finish the job?" I ask, though I know that's exactly what she means.

"That's the plan." Lilly moves to block my path to the door. "Though now there's the added complication of you."

"I'm the one with the intel," I repeat.

Lilly laughs. "And that's why you're still alive. For now. But you've been recalled."

Recalled. Everyone at Greytech knows that term. Recalled means eliminated.

"I have to report that you were emotionally compromised, but I'll try to minimize that part. Save you some embarrassment."

"How generous," I say, my jaw clenched, though I really want to scream.

"It's more than you deserve. Foster was a simple job. Get close, get the data, get out. Instead, you're making plans like a happy couple." She cackles. "Did you really think you had a future with him? He has a wife, Anna. Why would he want more than a fling with you?"

The truth stings because my feelings for Steve weren't pretend. I think... or thought... they were real. But I've been lying to myself, pretending I could have a normal life with other ski vacations and so much more in our future.

"What about Steve?" I ask, though I already know the answer. He wasn't Greytech's first target. They had already "disappeared" two female employees at his company before realizing Steve was the only one in possession of all the data.

Lilly shrugs. "Collateral damage, and it's above our pay grade. Another asset is waiting to intercept him once he gets on the road. I might try to frame him for your death. Haven't decided yet."

Though my life is just as doomed, my heart goes out to Steve. It's partially my fault that an unfortunate "accident" will lead to his demise. And now, Lilly might make him look like a killer. I've understood the risks all along, but he didn't know we were playing a deadly game.

"Let's go, Anna." Lilly pushes me. "Enjoy your last few minutes on earth. Sorry, you don't get a last phone call. You know how it works. But I promise I'll make it fast and painless. You can even choose how I do it. Has to be quiet. Otherwise, it's your preference."

"Right." I swallow the lump that's formed in my throat. I understand Lilly has to carry out commands. She has no choice. That's how our company works. And if Lilly doesn't kill me, someone else will. Maybe today, before I leave the resort. Or tomorrow, when I enter my apartment. I'll always be looking over my shoulder until the day I die. The only guarantee will be that day coming much sooner rather than later.

"Move along," Lilly says. "We're going to grab that thumb drive now. I want to get the hell out of here before the next storm comes."

It sinks in that I'm going to die today. This is really it. My last everythings. Last thoughts, last breaths, last walk through the snow. So many things I'll never get to do rush through my head. Random things. Visit Thailand. Settle down in a fixer-upper bungalow house. Adopt a cat. It isn't fair. They've controlled and watched me for years. Finally, a taste of happiness, and everything gets ripped away. Greytech's reach is global. There's nowhere to run.

But as we walk toward the door, defiance flares inside me. I've spent years following orders, doing exactly what they told me to do. And for what? So they can discard me the moment I show a shred of humanity?

No. Not today.

Lilly's attention is on the door ahead.

My hand goes to the steel scraper on the workbench. I don't consciously decide to use it. My body operates on pure survival instinct. I can't flee. I have to fight. It's now or never.

I swing the metal tool.

Lilly is quick. Jumping back before the tool makes contact, she reaches for her ankle and the switchblade she probably has strapped there.

I don't have another instant to waste. With a leap, I deliver a powerful kick to Lilly's chest.

She falls, tumbling backward over the bench. Her head strikes the jutting corner of a ski rack.

Eyes filled with shock, she falls in slow motion. A knife slips from her grasp and clatters against the hard floor.

I wait, adrenaline making my heart race as if it wants out of my ribcage. She remains still.

"Lilly? Lilly, get up." My voice sounds strange and unhinged in my own ears.

No movement.

I snatch up Lilly's knife, then take a few steps back, expecting a trick. Sweat trickles down my brow. My hands shake. When she remains lifeless, I drop to my knees and press trembling fingers to her neck. Nothing. No pulse. Also, no blood. No gash where she hit her head. Lilly appears to be fine. But she isn't. The vacant stare, the unnatural angle of her neck. She's dead. She must have a closed head injury.

For a long moment, I can't breathe. When Greytech learns I've killed one of their assets, my death won't be quick or painless.

My gaze flies around the locker room, assessing options. I can hide the body outside in the snow. That will give me a day or two. But not much more than that. I'm a target now. At every border, every airport, every train station, Greytech will watch for my face.

Unless... unless they aren't looking for me at all.

FIFTY-TWO

Two days ago

An idea flickers, just a crazy thought at first... or maybe not. In a few heartbeats, it becomes a desperate plan. What if I can make Greytech believe Lilly isn't the asset who died in this locker room? What if they think things went according to their plan, and I'm the one who got eliminated?

Lilly and I are the same size. Neither of us has any information in any identification systems. Same tattoo. The wig is easily moved from her head to mine.

I'll pretend to be her. Report back to Greytech on "Anna's" demise. That will buy me time to warn Steve, to get us both away from Greytech's reach. Except... no, I can't trust him with a secret like this. I can't tell him who I am, what I do, or who I work for. Or can I? How am I supposed to know how much I can trust him?

First things first. I have to act fast before someone finds me here. Self-preservation is the strongest motive, and I dive into action, needing my plan to work. I search her pockets and find a second tactical knife, smaller than the one she tried to kill me with.

Next, her phone. It's locked, and I need access to it. Greytech will expect communication from her, and I can't afford to go silent.

Kneeling beside her body, I press her thumb to the phone's home button. The screen unlocks, and I disable the auto-lock feature. Turn off Face ID and fingerprint security. Set a simple four-digit passcode.

I scroll through her messages. There's only one, from "Grandma Gigi."

"Hope you're having fun on your trip, sweetheart. Remember to clean up after yourself while you're visiting Anna. Don't leave a mess. If things aren't flowing naturally, it might be best for your relationship to disappear. Love, Gigi XOXO."

This isn't from Lilly's grandmother. It's Greytech telling her to make sure there isn't a body to find. Make my death look like an accident or make me disappear entirely.

Lilly didn't respond. She was probably planning to text back after she killed me.

I double-check my new password on her phone, then continue searching.

There's a key card with the resort logo in Lilly's back pants pocket, still in a paper jacket with 340 written on the bottom.

Her front pocket contains two metal keys attached to a Black Ridge resort tag labeled *Snowmobile #5*. Random joyride? Or something more sinister? Was my "accident" supposed to involve a snowmobile crash? Send my body over a cliff to make it look like I'd stolen the machine and lost control?

I finish checking her jacket, pants, and even her boots. But no car keys. Did she drive here? She must have. Where are those keys?

Calling an Uber is not ideal, even if one can come for me in this storm. Maybe I can find that snowmobile and drive it to the next town if Lilly doesn't have a car. I'm thinking about how much I really need a vehicle as I unclasp Lilly's medical bracelet and replace it with my own black jewelry.

I strip off her jacket, sweater, and pants, leaving her in underwear and socks. Lilly's skin is still warm and pliable, which makes the task easier but also more disturbing. I half expect her to wake up, wrap her hands around my neck, and start squeezing. Another pulse check is necessary to convince me she's truly gone.

Quick as I can, I pull off *my* jacket, sweater, and jeans, and put on Lilly's clothes. The cargo pants and the sweater fit. Lilly's boots are half a size too big, but that's better than too small. The red fur-lined parka is nice but not the ideal choice for this weather. Lilly isn't a skier like me, or she'd know better.

Now comes the difficult task of dressing her in my own clothes. I wrestle Lilly's legs into my jeans, then get the jacket on, shoving her arms through the sleeves. I jam her feet into my suede boots. People pay attention to footprints, not feet. No one will notice her boots aren't the right size.

The last step is her wig. Pulling the hairpiece from her head reveals dark brown hair secured in a tight bun. Maybe a little darker than my current hair color, but similar enough. I use her ponytail holder and pins to secure my hair, then position the wig over it.

If only I could transfer my fake ID and matching credit cards into Lilly's pockets so whoever finds her will see the name Anna Winters, but I can't. All my IDs are in my missing purse.

When I finally step back, the resemblance is so uncanny it makes me dizzy. For a disorienting moment, I wonder if I actually died in that fight and this is some twisted afterlife where I'm forced to witness my corpse.

No, I'm not dead; my hands are shaking. But I almost was. If I hadn't fought back, if I hadn't gotten lucky with that kick, I would be the one lying dead in this cold room while Lilly walked away and reported back to Greytech. The margin between life and death came down to a single instant of desperation. I'm too wired with fear and adrenaline to feel grateful. That might come later, depending on how all this plays out.

Focus. Move. Get out of here.

The locker room remains empty. Everyone is inside staying warm and drinking, making the most of their time at the resort, just as I had been doing until Lilly ruined everything.

I need to cover the body. I don't want anyone to discover the corpse until morning, long after I'm gone.

Behind a stack of rental skis, I find several of those metallic silver blankets designed to retain body heat. Ironic, but they'll hide her.

I drag the body into the corner, then spread the reflective blankets over it.

I'm hurrying toward the main building when an ominous rumbling fills the air and shakes the ground. What the heck was that? I don't stop to find out. It doesn't last long.

Inside, the stairs offer more privacy than the elevators. I move with my head down, again touching my fingers to the tender area on my cheek because I can't stop assessing how bad it is. How will I explain it? Then I realize I won't have to. As soon as I get a ride, I'll be out of here.

FIFTY-THREE

Two days ago

My pulse races as I approach Room 340. Lilly's room. I tap the card against the sensor, holding my breath. I'm thinking about everything I need to do to pull this off.

When the light flashes green, I slip inside, quickly closing the door behind me. It looks barely occupied. She brought a single carry-on suitcase and a gray duffel bag.

Time to locate her car keys and get out of here.

After unzipping her suitcase, I tear through her belongings. Judging from the clothes she brought, she wasn't planning to stick around after she assassinated me. In a hidden compartment, I find exactly what I expected: fake passports, untraceable phones, cash, ammunition, and a compact pistol.

Like me, Lilly has several identities. Her passports are American, British, Polish, and Czech. I flip through them, studying the photos. She has brown eyes, and mine are blue. But that's easily fixed with my stash of colored contacts.

Behind the Czech passport is a photo of Lilly from before. She's younger, but her teeth are pre-veneer, and her hair looks like an at-home job. I'm surprised she kept her old prison ID card. Mine is long gone.

We first met at Danbury Correctional. I'd made the mistake of getting caught for selling my employer's data. The pharmaceutical industry wanted to make an example out of me. Lilly occupied a cell on the same block. I'd heard she embezzled from a tech millionaire's foundation. She was only a few weeks into a seven-year sentence, and then she was gone. I didn't understand why until the same thing happened to me a few months later. Greytech's recruiter showed up at my cell offering me freedom for service without an end date. The organization needs attractive, smart women. Desperate ones. I didn't want to spend the best years of my life in jail.

Later, I'll have to choose which version of Lilly to become. For now, Greytech has to think Lilly Childers did what she was told to do, then checked out of here. I have to take all her things with me as soon as I find her car keys. Where are they?

Finally, in the zippered pocket of her large duffel bag, I find a rental car key fob. Attached is a small plastic tag with the rental information: Black Hyundai, license plate XRJ-1831.

Perfect.

I catch sight of myself in the bathroom mirror and don't recognize the reflection. The blonde wig changes everything. My face looks harder, more angular. Except for the eye color, I look like Lilly.

A sound in the hallway makes me freeze. Voices. Getting closer. I zip up the suitcase and grab both bags.

Feeling like a criminal, which is appropriate, I wait behind the door until the voices pass, then slip out of the room and make my way down to the ground level.

The lobby is busy with guests warming themselves by the fire, drinks in hand. Again, I keep my head down and stride toward the exit, dragging the suitcase behind me.

Outside, wearing Lilly's coat, the wind slices through me like ice. Snow whips across the parking lot as I search through the snow-covered cars again, this time for the black Hyundai.

There's an empty spot beside the rabbit mural. The spot where Steve's SUV used to be. He left. He has my purse, and he's gone.

My heart pounds with urgency as I hurry toward the bear sign that marks the third floor. I click her key fob again and again, needing to leave this place behind before anyone finds her body. Before Greytech realizes no one has the algorithm and sends backup.

Finally, I hear a beep and spot Lilly's rental car buried under a thick layer of snow.

I brush off the driver's side of the windshield and window with frantic, clumsy movements that soak my gloves. After tossing my suitcase in the back, I climb into the driver's seat, my whole body shaking.

Come on, come on, start.

The engine turns over. I reverse out of the parking space and drive through the parking lot, my hands gripping the wheel so tightly my knuckles crack.

When my thoughts go to Steve, I stop myself from wondering what happened to him. I need to move on. I can't afford the luxury of worrying about anyone else.

A look in my rearview mirror makes me do a double take. Two snowmobiles are racing along in the same direction as me. That's strange.

As I round the bend toward the main road, I see a barricade I wasn't expecting. I slam on the brakes.

Beyond the barricade, the road is gone. A massive wall of snow and rocks lies where the paved highway should be. There's no way to cross it.

No one is getting out of Black Ridge. Not tonight. Maybe not for days.

I sit in the idling car, staring at the obstruction. Acid churns in my stomach as I grip the steering wheel. I'm supposed to be dead, but I can't escape. I'm held hostage at Black Ridge with Lilly's corpse.

FIFTY-FOUR

Two days ago

Time for Plan B. I need Greytech to think Anna Winters died, but I can't have anyone finding her body while I'm still here. Too much risk of exposure. The corpse has to disappear.

My hands won't stop shaking. Everything is spiraling out of control. The avalanche, being trapped here, Lilly's corpse waiting to be discovered. Breathe. Think. Hurry!

The note from Greytech flashes through my mind. Make it look like an accident. I still have the snowmobile key. And I have an idea. This can work. It has to work.

First, the champagne bottle. I park the Hyundai and race through the parking lot and the falling snow to the lodge. Inside, I go straight to Steve's room, taking the stairs two at a time. The bottle sits on the dresser where he left it. I fumble with the foil wrapper until it tears into pieces. The wire cage takes forever to untwist.

"Come on, come on," I mutter, my fingers slipping.

The cork explodes out of the bottle with a violent pop. It shoots across the room and smashes into the window. Champagne erupts over my hands, my jacket, the floor. I rush to the sink, liquid foaming over the sides. The smell fills the small bathroom as I pour it down the drain. The way I'm rushing, I can't hold anything steady, and liquid splashes onto the counter. When the bottle is empty, I wipe the glass with a hand towel and wedge the bottle between my coat and sweater. Lilly's sweater. The hard glass presses against my ribs, but it's secure there, hidden from view.

I need my things. Some of them at least. Lilly brought almost nothing, and I could be stuck here for days. I snatch what I can from the drawers. A soft cream-colored sweater, dark slacks, underwear, a pink bra from the floor, then the blue one because it's a favorite. I shove them into a plastic dry-cleaning bag until it's full. I need my toothbrush, too. I refuse to use Lilly's. Who knows where her mouth has been? I spin around, surveying the mess and the things I have to leave behind. I'm not moving fast enough. This is taking too long.

I burst outside and head to the equipment garage I saw earlier.

Turning on the lights and looking around isn't a good idea. Someone might see me. Instead, I squint through the darkness, searching the shadows until I find the machine with a number six decal on the front cowling.

Memories from my assignment in Alaska flood back to me. I can do this. I know how to drive these things.

The engine is loud. What if someone hears? What if they come to investigate?

I pull out my crumpled trail map. The paper keeps fluttering in the wind. Focus. Find a trail. Any trail.

It's not a location that catches my eye, but a name. Second Chance Trail. More irony. It's where I'll leave the woman whose death allows me a second chance to survive.

With a solid plan established, I park the snowmobile just outside the locker room, grateful for the storm that's shielded me from prying eyes.

Lilly's body is heavier than I imagined. Dragging her onto the snowmobile is a nightmare. She keeps slipping, and I have to haul her back up.

"Stay put," I pant, wrapping my arms around her torso from behind.

This is the definition of insane. I'm hauling a dead colleague through a blizzard. If I get caught—no, I won't get caught. I can't get caught.

The snowmobile lurches forward, and I have to lean around the dead body to reach the handlebars. The empty bottle jabs me with every movement. I want to yank it out and toss it into the snow, but it needs to be with Lilly's corpse when they find her. When they find "me."

The snowmobile struggles in the deep powder, sinking rather than gliding along.

Nothing looks right. The trails all look the same in this weather. White, white, everywhere white. Where is Second Chance Trail?

A single beam of light cuts through the snow ahead of me. Another snowmobile is coming.

I kill my headlight and veer off the trail, panic making me jerk the handlebars too hard. The snowmobile tilts dangerously. Behind me, the other machine changes course, following my tracks.

No, no, no, no, no.

I gun the engine, racing up a steep trail I don't recognize. Branches whip past my head. Lilly's body bounces against me with each bump, deadweight threatening to throw us both off.

My pursuer's headlights disappear, and I can no longer hear the engine. Maybe the person never spotted me at all. I allow myself one shaking breath, but now I'm lost.

Trail markers appear in my headlight beam. Red Fox Trail. Not Second Chance, but it doesn't matter anymore. I'm too far gone to entertain my whims.

I drag Lilly into the trees, arranging her arms to look natural beside the champagne bottle.

A drunk woman. Lost in a storm. Exactly what Greytech ordered.

By the time I make it back down the mountain, I'm shivering uncontrollably. I ditch the snowmobile outside the equipment garage, but pocket the keys, and slip into the lodge through a side entrance.

People crowd the lobby and the front desk. Everyone is talking about the avalanche. I keep my head down, the blonde wig hiding my face.

Near the reception desk, the general manager stands addressing a growing crowd of concerned guests. His voice carries across the lobby: "Please, everyone, we need you to remain in the main lodge building for now. Do not leave the property." He raises his hands, trying to maintain calm. "We're working with the Colorado authorities to assess the situation. For now, the safest place for everyone is right here."

They don't know I've just committed a murder.

My thoughts return to the present. Five minutes gone. Five minutes left.

That's how much time I have to decide what to do about Victoria Heslin. Five minutes to determine if she's another problem I need to eliminate, like the last guy who asked too many questions. The one I pushed down the stairs. This time I'll push harder.

Or I could try to leave. The Polaris keys are in my pocket.

FIFTY-FIVE

Maintaining her distance, Victoria followed behind the imposter as she strode from the spa.

Two women with identical prison ink, both at the same resort. Victoria would think it was the same person using different disguises if she hadn't already seen one of them dead.

Professional espionage made sense. Someone sent two operatives to go after Foster. One was dead, and the other was trying to hide.

Instead of following the path back to the lodge, the suspect headed toward the slopes, the area Peter had told them to avoid.

"Where are you going?" Victoria demanded.

She looked over her shoulder but kept moving. "I told you I'd meet you in my room. I have to get something." Her voice had changed to sharp and commanding. Her pace quickened as she headed toward the equipment garage.

She'd never intended to meet or show Victoria anything. She was running.

Victoria chased after her across the snow-packed ground, her boots sinking into the deep snow with each step.

She shot her weapon into the air as a warning.

A snowmobile roared behind Victoria, then cut between her and the fleeing woman. It was Alex. His machine kicked up a wall of snow, forcing her to shield her face and step back.

"Hey! What are you doing out here?" Alex pulled off his goggles, physically blocking her path.

The suspect used those critical seconds to sprint the remaining distance to the garage. She pulled keys from her pocket and mounted a Polaris snowmobile parked beneath the overhang.

Alex spotted her. "Neither of you should be out here!" He left his machine idling and ran toward the woman, limping and waving his arms. "Ma'am, stop!"

He was too late. The Polaris lurched forward, spraying snow as it accelerated toward a service trail.

Victoria moved toward Alex's idling machine. Every instinct told her this woman was Anna Winters—the key to what happened to Steve Foster and the victim. If she disappeared, the truth might vanish with her. "I have to go after her."

"No. Absolutely not." Alex shouted as he hurried back to Victoria. "Where she's headed isn't safe. You'll both get killed!"

"She's our only lead."

With every second, the woman was moving farther away. Victoria's muscle memory took over. She was already on the machine, twisting the throttle.

"Victoria, don't—"

The engine drowned out her brother's protests as she sped off, leaving him in a cloud of powder, his arm outstretched in futile warning.

FIFTY-SIX

The snowmobile vibrated beneath Victoria as she sped down the service trail. Letting a possible killer and thief escape wasn't an option.

Wind tore at her face, slipping beneath her collar despite her layers. She'd ridden snowmobiles before, but never at this speed or with so much at stake. She was risking the truth and her life. Alex had warned her, but Victoria couldn't think about that now. Justice didn't wait for perfect conditions. When she was working, fear was a luxury she couldn't afford.

The machine ahead flew over the white landscape and swerved right. When Victoria reached that point, a shiver rocked her body. The tracks came within inches of a drop-off that would guarantee death.

Victoria leaned forward and down, urging more speed from her vehicle. The gap between them narrowed. A hundred yards. Eighty. Sixty.

The suspect glanced back; her face a pale oval beneath her black hat. She jerked her machine hard to the right, veering onto a steeper route that cut between the pines.

Victoria followed. This terrain was more treacherous, the snow deeper, the path less defined. Branches whipped past her head as she navigated between the trees, narrowly missing a sharp turn. The machine's runners slid for excruciating seconds before she got them corrected.

Trees thinned, and she burst into a clearing. She was forty yards ahead now, heading toward another forested area. With a glance through the trees to her left, she caught sight of a plowed road. They weren't heading deeper into the wilderness but making a wide arc that had brought them parallel to the access road.

The snowmobile ahead drove over a rise and disappeared from view.

Victoria followed, catching air as she sailed over the hill. For an instant, she was weightless, then she hit the ground with a jarring impact that rattled her teeth.

The terrain opened up. They were approaching the outer perimeter of the resort property from the south. The other machine was less than thirty yards away. It cut hard to the right, breaking through the tree line along the main road, headed straight to the blocked area.

Trucks and machinery worked below, attempting to clear the first blockage about a half mile down the mountain.

Before she knew it, Victoria was following the other woman through the roadblocks and straight into the avalanche zone, riding over twenty feet of unstable snow and twisted metal that could collapse at any moment.

Victoria leaned lower over the handlebars and gunned the engine.

FIFTY-SEVEN

I lean forward on the snowmobile, following a path between the trees. The machine's engine screams beneath me, sinking into the deep powder. Acres upon acres of undisturbed snow, and I'm the only one out here. All I have to do is get to the nearest town, rent a car, and disappear. I should have done this two days ago rather than wasting so much time hiding out at that freezing cold resort. At least I dodged a bullet by avoiding the barbecue.

The rumble of another engine comes from behind me. I glance back.

Another snowmobile. A figure hunched down. Powder blue coat. Victoria Heslin. Did I make a huge mistake by running rather than facing my problem head-on?

The trees thin, and I burst into a clearing. It's difficult to tell where the path should lie. I try to stay in the middle.

The FBI agent's engine grows louder. She's gaining on me.

The access road lies to my left, leading to the avalanche blockage. To the right is a sheer drop—the reason we've had no other way out. There's no choice but to veer left. I tear through the deep powder until I reach the wooden sawhorses with reflective tape marking the danger zone. Moving beyond them is the only way out of Black Ridge.

I don't slow down. The snowmobile smashes through the sawhorses, splintering wood.

Ahead looms the massive pile of snow, rock, and broken trees cutting the resort off from civilization. The destruction looks like the aftermath of a war zone. Fresh snow has covered most of the debris. I can't see where the greatest dangers lie or where to cross. There's no way to know, and all the time in the world might not change that.

I hear more wood crack behind me. Victoria is close. She crossed the barriers but maybe she won't follow any further.

I gun the throttle, aiming for the slope to my left.

The snowmobile lurches upward through the loose snow. For a heart-stopping moment, I think I won't make it, then the machine crests the ridge. Cringing, I remember the giant trees and poles jutting out everywhere. Now they're hidden.

With no warning, the sled's front end dips, nearly sending me over the handlebars. I fight for control, using my body weight to keep the machine upright as it slides sideways, then straightens and plows through the deep powder.

I take a moment to orient myself. The road should emerge somewhere, leading toward the town. I stare, trying to make out the depression that represents the road, or the edge of a guardrail.

The front end of the machine suddenly drops, plunging nearly two feet into a hidden pocket in the snow. I jerk forward, and my chest hits the handlebars hard enough to knock the wind from my lungs. Pain explodes through my ribs. I gasp, tasting blood where I've bitten my lip.

I try to reverse. The treads spin uselessly, digging the machine deeper. I'm stuck.

When I get off the Polaris, my legs sink thigh-deep into the icy-cold snow. I stand behind the machine, pushing it with all my strength. Then I notice something. A strip of metal just beneath the snow. I squint and make out the curve of a vehicle's roof.

Silver. The same unusual shade as Steve's car.

But that can't be. He left before the avalanche.

My hands shake as I claw at the snow, scooping it off the vehicle.

The front windshield appears. It's a grainy mesh of ice-covered glass. Behind a deployed airbag, a dark figure slumps in the driver's seat. Head hanging sideways. Eyes closed. Motionless.

"Steve!" I scream, pounding on the window with my fists. The sound echoes, useless. "Steve!"

I keep clearing snow, searching for signs of life, though I know it's futile. He doesn't move or answer, because he's dead. Two days in single-digit temperatures will do that to a person. He'd almost made it. Almost escaped. Just like me. Both of us left too late.

I grab a chunk of ice and slam it against the glass. I hit it again, harder. My purse must be in there. If not, his laptop is. If I can just get inside, I'll have everything I need to complete the mission and get Greytech off my back.

The whine of another engine comes closer, then stops. The FBI agent shouts, "Don't move!"

Ignoring her, I grab a wrench from the snowmobile's toolkit and smash it against the glass.

In my peripheral vision, the agent approaches with her weapon. "Get up. Get on the back of my snowmobile now. This isn't safe!"

"I need to get in there." I slam the wrench into the window again. A few tiny cracks appear in the safety glass.

"Follow your tracks back to my snowmobile!" the agent screams. "Now!"

I don't stop. I keep hitting. A hole finally appears, but it's too little, too late. Victoria is behind me now.

I press my forehead against the ice-crusted glass. "I loved you. That wasn't a lie."

He's gone, frozen in his escape attempt, dead, just as I would have been if I'd left with him that night. So many close calls. Is it possible I'm the lucky one in all of this?

Finally, from my kneeling position on his shattered windshield, I turn. My face is wet with tears that have turned to ice, but my eyes feel empty. There's no way to get what I need until this FBI agent disappears.

I grip the wrench.

FIFTY-EIGHT

Hands on her hips, Victoria continued shouting at the woman to move.

A sound like thunder started up. Low, then gathering strength.

Both women froze. Their eyes met in shared horror. A massive sheet of snow detached and began sliding toward them with terrifying speed.

"Get on! Now!" Victoria grabbed the collapsible probe from Alex's snowmobile pack, gripping it tight in her left hand.

A massive, rumbling wave of white barreled toward them.

Victoria revved the engine. "Anna! Move!"

That name made her snap out of it. Eyes wide at the white tsunami rushing to engulf them, she leaped through the snow and jumped on the snowmobile behind Victoria.

Victoria took off, aiming for their recent tracks. Behind her, Anna screamed. "Faster! It's coming!"

The cleared road was just ahead—twenty yards, ten, five—

The avalanche caught them, swept them forward, lifting and hurling them into the air. Anna's grip tightened around Victoria's waist. They seemed suspended for seconds until gravity took over and the snowmobile's front end struck the ground with a sickening crunch. Like breaking ice, the surface gave way beneath them.

The machine pitched forward, then sideways. The impact tore Victoria from Anna's grip. She was flung clear of the vehicle, the probe still clutched in her fist as she tumbled, losing all sense of direction. The snow was everywhere, finding its way beneath her clothes, tearing off her hat and goggles. Sky became ground became sky again as she rolled until she stopped tu mbling... and began sinking. She kicked and grabbed for anything to stop herself, but it was like trying to swim through quicksand. As she sank, deep drifts of snow flowed in after her.

"Anna!" she called.

Light dimmed from brilliant white to gray, then disappeared entirely as more snow settled over her head.

Was Anna thrown clear? Was she buried somewhere nearby, fighting for air?

The roar of the avalanche had changed to an eerie, muffled silence.

Heart pounding, she clawed at the space around her face and chest, trying to create an air pocket before the snow set.

Which way is up?

Stay calm. Don't panic.

She remembered survival training. Spit to find the way up. When she spat, the saliva dripped down her chin. The sky was above her head. She tried to dig upward. The snow was already hardening around her. How deep was she buried? Five feet? Ten? Twenty?

Signal. You need to signal.

In her left hand, she gripped the probe she'd held onto through the crash. She worked it upward through the snow above her head, extending the telescoping segments to full length, praying that at least part of it would break the surface.

Please let someone see it.

Was Anna buried? Had she known to create an air pocket? Did she have anything to signal with?

Control your breathing. Slow, shallow breaths. Make the air last. Fifteen minutes, she remembered Alex saying. That's about all the time she had. If she were lucky.

Ice formed on her lips. Her fingers were already going numb inside her gloves as she kept digging, kept fighting for more space.

Claustrophobic panic clawed at her throat as she envisioned the crushing weight above. Maybe death had been stalking her since the plane crash, since she got shot in the side, or since criminals had dumped her into the ocean off the coast of Mexico.

But no, she'd survived the odds before.

Victoria pictured Ned's face. She'd told *him* not to do anything stupid that would get him maimed or killed. She remembered Alex shouting as she took off on his snowmobile. He'd been right about the danger. What had she been thinking? When would she learn to be more careful? Right now. This was the time. If she survived, she wouldn't put herself in another situation like this again. For Ned's sake, and for her own.

Alex had seen her go. He was probably racing into the destruction zone now, his life in danger because of her stupidity. She thought of her father, who'd already buried her mother and couldn't bear to bury a daughter, too.

Breathe. Think. Stay conscious.

She hated the helplessness. Somewhere nearby, Anna might be buried or lying broken on the surface, and Victoria couldn't help. She wasn't good at waiting and doing nothing. When she'd gotten dropped into the ocean in Mexico, miles from shore, she'd been able to swim, to fight, to move toward safety. Trapped under the snow, she could only endure and prevent panic from consuming her remaining oxygen.

She pushed against the walls of her snow prison, but they held firm. Her shoulders ached from the cramped position.

Focus.

Biting down hard on her tongue, she used pain to fight the drowsiness creeping in. Her eyelids felt heavy. She forced them open, even in the darkness. Each breath was work now.

Her thoughts started to fragment. Alex and Minka, together at their wedding. Ned's handsome, hopeful face when he'd proposed. Her dogs. Her mother's wedding dress hanging in her closet.

The probe slipped from her numb fingers. She heard her own heartbeat slowing, felt her body giving up the fight against the cold.

Then nothing.

FIFTY-NINE

Darkness all around. My arm is bent wrong. The pain is excruciating, but I can't feel my legs. Am I paralyzed? Does it even matter?

I'm going to die.

This is how it happens. Thirty years old. Buried alive under tons of snow. I've imagined different ways before. Some fast, some torturous. Bullets. Strangulation. Car crash. Poison. But not this random act of nature. How many people die this way? There can't be many.

I have no choices to make. No moves to play except trying to guess how long before my heart stops beating. Seconds or minutes? How should I spend them?

I see Steve's face. The way he looked at me when we whispered about being stuck for an extra day or two. He never said he loved me, but I think he did. He thought Anna Winters was worth loving. If he'd known who I really am... but he didn't know. For a few weeks, I was a normal person who deserved happiness. Not someone whose job is to seduce and steal.

When he was freezing to death in his car, did he think of me? Or his wife?

Stop. Stop thinking about him. He's dead. So is Lilly. I killed her. And for what? A few extra days of life in the resort from hell? The privilege of dying slowly instead of quickly?

I was stupid. Look where it got me. But this could have happened to anyone. Wrong place, wrong time. That's all it takes.

I'm laughing. Why? This isn't funny. None of it's funny, but I can't stop, and it's using up my air. I need to stop.

Should have quit Greytech as soon as I discovered what they'd really hired me for.

Each breath is harder than the last. Can't dig. Can't even move.

Getting colder. Is this what dying is like?

But I don't want to die. Not like this. Not at all.

Fight it. But how? What can I do? My good arm won't move more than an inch. Can't push up. Can't dig sideways. The snow is like cement now.

No. No, this can't be how it ends. I survived prison and Greytech training. Survived assignments in Moscow and Alaska. Three years of this dangerous job. I can't die because of the stupid snow.

But I can't move. Can't breathe right. Getting weaker.

Greytech doesn't care. They won't miss Lilly or me. They'll move on to the next target with new assets.

Hey, Grandma Gigi, we're both dead now. Throw out your chocolate chip banana bread.

I laugh again. Or maybe I'm crying.

It's so quiet. But not peaceful. It feels like nothing.

Like floating away. Fading.

My arm has stopped screaming. Nothing hurts.

What happens next? Is there anything after this?

At least I won't have to explain myself to anyone. I don't have to lie anymore.

SIXTY

"What is she doing?" Alex yelled, staring after his sister.

He waited for Ned to jump on behind him, then twisted the throttle, following Victoria's tracks toward the blocked access road. "I told her not to go."

She never listened. Not when they were kids, not now. Once Victoria set her sights on a goal, she couldn't let go. It was who she was, and who she'd always been. Usually, that drive led her toward causes he admired. Helping others. Pursuing justice. Rescuing animals. But now, that same stubborn focus might get her killed.

The anger that had flared when Victoria ignored his warning had already dissolved into a powerful fear for her life.

If anything happened to her, it would be his fault. He'd invited her to Black Ridge. Then, he'd pulled her into this investigation because they needed her expertise. He knew that if anyone could get the job done, it was his sister.

The tracks ahead cut a straight line toward the avalanche zone. With a steep cliff on one side, there was no way around the debris field. He prayed Victoria hadn't tried to cross it.

The rumble came first as a vibration through the snowmobile's handlebars, then as sound rolling down the valley like thunder. Alex's fear intensified.

Ned shouted into his ear. "Was that..." The rest of the words were lost to the wind and the thundering sound of moving snow.

Alex couldn't find his voice. He could only nod.

When they reached the avalanche zone, everything was still again.

The snowmobile tracks he'd followed led directly into the debris field, then vanished. With adrenaline flooding his body, Alex scanned the jumble of snow and trees, desperate for a splash of color, movement, any sign of her. Where were they? Maybe they'd made it across the wreckage before that slide and were out of sight.

He killed the engine and looked around in desperation. The sun glinted off a shiny object about ten yards into the zone. A snowmobile. Part of the tunnel—the metal housing that covered the track. But which snowmobile? Who had been riding it, his sister or the woman she chased?

Ned saw it too. "Victoria!" He shouted as he ran toward the debris field.

"Stop!" Alex grabbed Ned's arm. This time, Alex would make sure Ned listened. He would not let him run out there and die. "It's not safe. There might be another slide any second. I'll go. Stay here."

Ned opened his mouth to protest. Alex cut him off. "Someone has to stay here in case one of us doesn't make it. You'll have to tell them where to dig. If we both get buried, no one will know Victoria is even out here."

Alex moved fast, opening his rescue pack with trembling hands, suppressing the terror that threatened to paralyze him. He'd done this before. But never with his sister's life at stake. He couldn't lose her.

The battery in his radio had been dying for days. He'd tried to conserve some power for a situation just like this one. He only needed to get one call through, provided someone on the other end also had a working radio.

"It's Alex. There's a fresh avalanche on the access road. One or two people on snowmobiles got buried. I need immediate backup with shovels and stretchers."

Static. Nothing but static.

He tried again, adjusting the frequency. "Ski patrol at Black Ridge calling any unit. Emergency. Avalanche burial, access road point seven. Repeat, emergency."

Dead air.

Still moving through the deep snow, aware every step might send him plunging to an icy burial, Alex slammed the radio against his palm, then tried once more. "Mayday, mayday. Fresh slide, people buried."

The radio buzzed with white noise, then fell silent. The display screen turned black.

Of all times for the equipment to fail. They were on their own now, unless someone back at the lodge had heard the avalanche and knew it *wasn't* a controlled detonation. Help would come eventually. But would they arrive in time?

Alex glanced over his shoulder to make sure Ned hadn't followed.

Ned was still at the edge of the debris field, pacing, shielding his eyes from the sun as he scanned the debris. Behind him, Elspeth raced to catch up.

"Elspeth!" Alex called, though she was already bounding toward him, following his tracks as he'd taught her to do. He directed her to search around the partially buried snowmobile. She moved through the powder, her nose and tail down, investigating in widening circles.

Minutes had already passed since the slide. Every second, the snow was hardening. What little oxygen they had was disappearing, replaced by carbon dioxide.

Fifteen yards from the buried snowmobile, Elspeth stopped moving. Her body grew rigid. She sniffed with renewed intensity, then began barking. Alex's heart pounded faster. His dog's alert was strong and confident. She'd detected carbon dioxide under the snow.

At almost the same moment, Ned hollered, "Look!" He pointed to a rod sticking up from the snow about twenty yards in the opposite direction.

Probably just the end of a tree. Alex looked closer and saw yellow paint. The top of a probe.

Two signals. Two people buried. Every second mattered. Which one was Victoria?

"We have to split up," Alex shouted. "Go to Elspeth. Follow her tracks. Test the snow with each step before you put all your weight down. If you hear a creak when you step, freeze. Don't move. Do you understand me?"

"I understand. If that's her under the probe, how deep is she?" Ned asked, his focus on saving Victoria and not the dangers he faced.

"Up to ten feet." Alex didn't mention cases with victims buried deeper than that. Those were body recoveries, not rescues. "Just get there in one piece and start digging. We're running out of time."

They moved to their respective locations slowly, Alex eyeing the visible cracks in the snow. He trudged past Elspeth, who was already digging with her paws. "Good girl. Good girl."

He dropped to his knees. The probe protruded a few inches above the surface. If the person beneath had extended her arms and moved the probe over her head, then she was buried deep. Possibly too deep for him to reach in time.

He began removing mounds of snow with his gloves. Hand over hand, working furiously. He dug as if Victoria's life depended on it, because it did.

A few more minutes gone.

Yards away, Ned grunted and gasped as he tore through the snow in the same manner at a relentless pace.

"Alex!" The call came from behind him. He looked up but didn't stop digging. Corey and Jordan. They'd driven from the resort and brought equipment. Shovels.

"Jordan, help Ned," Alex commanded. "Corey, get over here with me." They were all risking their lives now. "Listen for signs of instability. This slope could move again at any moment."

The additional men and the shovels made a difference. They dug faster, turning the snow over in furious arcs, careful not to dig too deep at once and injure anyone awaiting rescue under the snow.

The burn in his lungs was constant, each breath like drowning in the thin mountain air. Sweat froze on his forehead.

"Contact!" Jordan shouted from the probe site, then swore. "Never mind. It's a tree branch."

Fifteen yards away, Elspeth let out sharp, urgent barks.

"She hears something," Alex said, every muscle strung tight with hope and fear. "Keep digging."

The dog's barks became more frantic. From somewhere below them, a faint sound traveled up through the snow.

"We're here! Hang on! We're going to get you out!" Ned shouted into the hole they'd created.

"Conserve her air," Alex warned. "Don't make her talk. Just dig." He wanted to know who they'd found, but he didn't dare ask. He increased his pace. His shoulders burned, his lungs screamed, but he kept digging. "I see something," he called, but kept his voice controlled. Too many false alarms already.

Possibly blue fabric. Victoria had been wearing a light blue jacket.

"Please," he whispered, not caring who heard him. "Please, please, please."

He dropped the shovel and switched to digging with his hands, tearing his gloves on the sharp edges of compressed snow. His fingers tingled, then lost all sensation.

More blue appeared. Definitely fabric, not rock this time. He worked faster, his scraped knuckles bleeding.

Too many minutes had passed.

Please let this be Victoria. Please let her be alive.

A weak cough came from beneath them, followed by a voice he knew as well as anyone's.

Alex sucked in a shuddering breath and kept digging. "We're getting you out. Just hold on. Don't say another word. Just relax."

Together, Alex and Corey clawed snow away from her face and torso. Victoria's lips were blue.

Alex grinned through his tears. "We've got you."

It took another five minutes to dig both women out.

Alex sat back on his heels, sagging under the full weight of what had almost happened. His stubborn, brilliant, irreplaceable sister had come close to dying.

He stared at his hands, at the blood on his torn knuckles under his ripped gloves. Then he looked at Ned as he held Victoria, his face still etched with fear he'd never forget.

This was what Ned dealt with every day, loving a woman who ran toward danger. He probably lived with constant worry Victoria might not come home, that each case might be her last.

Alex thought about Minka waiting for him to call when he returned to the lodge at the end of every long day. She was aware an avalanche might shift course or equipment might fail. How many nights had she lain awake during storms, worried about him?

His job was necessary work that he loved. But seeing Victoria's blue face beneath the snow, he finally understood that choosing safety over adrenaline was a kindness to the people who loved you.

For the first time, a desk job didn't seem like giving up. It seemed like growing up.

SIXTY-ONE

Outside the avalanche zone, Alex and Ned were on all fours in the snow with a ski patrol medical kit spread around them. Both women were wrapped in silver blankets, their faces deathly pale.

As he checked Victoria's pulse, Ned's hands shook from the residual terror of almost losing her.

Alex was tending to the other woman. Her injuries appeared worse.

Jordan and Corey worked nearby, pushing the barricades back into place and coordinating with the incoming helicopter crew via radio.

As Ned adjusted a portable oxygen mask over Victoria's nose and mouth, her eyes fluttered open, unfocused at first, then finding Ned's face.

"Victoria," he said.

She pushed the oxygen mask aside. Her lips moved, but no words came out. She turned her head toward the woman lying unconscious with a cervical collar around her neck. "Her name is Anna Winters."

"Chasing her almost got you killed," Ned said.

"I know. I'm so sorry. How is she?"

"Unconscious, but alive. You're both headed to the hospital to get assessed for internal trauma. There's a medivac helicopter on the way."

"She and Jane Doe were trying to steal an algorithm from Steve Foster. They're professional thieves, and I still don't know their real names. I couldn't let her get away. I had to go after her or we'd never find her."

"No, you didn't have to chase her. You didn't have to do anything." Anger flared in Ned's voice. "You could have waited. You should have listened to Alex. Do you think either of us cares more about her getting away than losing you?"

Blinking, Victoria fought to keep her eyes open. "I'm sorry. I couldn't stop myself. Don't be mad at me," she whispered. "Please."

"I'm not angry." Ned drew a deep breath through his nose and exhaled. "I mean, I'm beyond furious, but I'm also so grateful you're alive that I can hardly think straight." Tears glistened in his eyes. "You were both buried. We didn't know which one was you..." His voice broke. "I've never been so terrified in my life."

He'd almost lost the woman he loved, the person he wanted to share everything with.

Victoria shivered so violently, it looked like she was seizing.

"Those tremors are normal," Alex said. "Her body's trying to generate heat."

The thrum of rotor blades echoed off the valley walls, growing steadily louder.

"Thank God you had that probe," Ned said. "And Elspeth deserves the biggest steak ever." Despite everything, he almost managed a smile.

The helicopter circled once then lowered toward a cleared section of road.

Victoria squeezed Ned's hand as the downdraft stirred up snow around them.

"Promise me," Ned said. "Never again."

"Promise," she whispered, though they both knew Victoria's promises about staying out of danger had a poor track record.

SIXTY-TWO

In a private room at Denver General, Victoria's bruised ribs ached with each breath, but she was alive and otherwise well. That was more than she'd expected twenty-four hours ago when the snow closed over her head.

Ned appeared in the doorway carrying a cup of hot tea. Despite the mental and physical stress he'd endured, his body had recovered, just like it did after a triathlon. His cough was gone. He looked healthy, handsome, and alert. Much better than she felt.

Victoria accepted the cup with gratitude. "As soon as the doctor gives the okay, I can leave. Any word on Anna?"

"Not since she came out of surgery." Ned sat beside the bed. "She has fractures in her left arm and leg, and an injury to her spleen. She's supposed to be okay once those heal."

"I spoke with Sheriff Wilson while you were gone," Victoria said. "Brought him up to speed on everything we uncovered. He'll work with the Denver FBI office to build a case against Anna and move it forward."

"Good. I'm glad they're taking over. What happens now? Is your involvement over?"

"I'll have to write a report and do some debriefing. And I'm waiting for Anna to wake up to see if she'll cooperate." Victoria sipped her tea and appreciated the warmth.

Ned kissed her forehead, his lips warm against her skin. "I need to call the clinic. I'll be in that room at the end of the hall. Try to get some rest."

After Ned left, Alex appeared in the doorway. "How are you feeling?"

"Like I got hit by a bus." Victoria managed a weak smile. "How about you?"

"Better now that I know you're okay." He took the chair Ned had vacated.

Victoria looked over at him. "I'm sorry about what I did. I should have listened when you told me not to go after Anna."

"You've already apologized enough. You did what you had to do. That's who you are. But maybe you can do me a favor."

"What?" she asked.

"It's about Jordan."

The serious tone in his voice put her on alert. "What about him?"

"When you write your report, do you have to mention that he took the DNA swabs? I know he screwed up, but he was scared. He's a good guy who made a terrible decision."

Victoria studied her brother's concerned expression. "He tampered with evidence in a homicide case."

"He didn't kill anyone. You know that. And he gave the evidence back, still sealed."

"After I confronted him about it."

Alex leaned forward, his elbows on his knees. "He's got a record from when he was eighteen. Stupid kid stuff, but it's there. If he gets arrested, it will destroy his future. The guy saves lives, Victoria. Can you help him?"

The plea in her brother's voice made Victoria's chest tight. She understood the loyalty that developed between people who trusted each other with their lives. But she also understood the law.

"I'm sorry, Alex. I have to report the facts. Everything that happened is part of the official record." She reached out and touched his arm. "But I'll make sure my report reflects that he cooperated fully once confronted, and that his actions didn't impede the investigation's ultimate resolution. That should help."

Alex nodded, disappointment lining his face. "I understand. I had to ask."

A knock at the door interrupted them. A uniformed deputy stepped inside.

"Agent Heslin? Anna Winters is conscious."

Victoria looked at Alex. "Help me up. This should be interesting."

Anna was down the hall, with a deputy stationed outside the door. In her bed, she looked small surrounded by the medical equipment. A cast encircled her left arm, and pulleys kept her left leg elevated.

The blonde wig was gone, revealing brown hair matted against her scalp. Without the disguise, she possessed the same malleable beauty as the victim—unremarkable features that could transform into anything with the right styling and conviction. An ideal face for deception, and confidence that made her dangerous. Victoria knew better than to underestimate her now.

"Five minutes," a nurse told Victoria.

"I heard you were okay," Anna said, watching Victoria approach. "I wondered when you'd show up."

Victoria pulled a chair close to the bed. "Tell me who sent you to steal Foster's algorithm."

Anna's expression didn't change. "I don't know anything about that."

"The FBI has your phones, Anna. Both of them. The messages from 'Grandma Gigi.' We know you're employed by a corporate espionage operation. We know they targeted Foster's company."

"Good luck proving that."

Victoria leaned back in her chair, studying Anna's face. "Your cooperation will go a long way in determining how you're treated in custody. Help us understand who you work for, and I'll make sure the prosecutor knows you assisted the investigation."

Anna laughed, a bitter sound that dissolved into a cough that made her grip the bedsheets. "You think I'm afraid of prison? Prison would be a vacation compared to what they'll do if they think I talked."

"We can protect you."

Anna scoffed. "No, you can't."

"Who runs it? Give us names, locations, data we can work with."

Anna turned her head toward the window, staring at the afternoon sky. "I've already said too much."

"Then give us your real name at least. Your family deserves to know what happened to you."

Anna turned around. For an instant, her mask slipped, and a vulnerable look crossed her features. Then the walls returned. She closed her eyes, and the conversation was over.

Frustrated but not surprised, Victoria stood. "The offer stands," she said from the doorway. "When you're ready to talk, I'll be ready to listen."

Anna's eyes remained closed, but Victoria caught the slight nod before she looked away.

Out in the hallway, Alex was waiting, leaning against the wall.

"Any luck?" he asked.

Victoria shook her head. "Professional criminals fear their employers more than law enforcement. Whoever Anna works for is powerful enough to inspire that level of terror."

SIXTY-THREE

Two days after checking out of the hospital, Victoria entered the Denver FBI field office for her debrief on the Black Ridge case. Though there might be more questions, and plenty of ongoing paperwork, the meeting signaled the end of her direct involvement.

Agent Bruce Rork waited for her inside a conference room. He was bald, lean, strong, and younger than she'd expected.

"Agent Heslin," he said, extending his hand. "It's great to meet you in person."

"You too," Victoria replied, settling into a chair across from him.

SSA Coleman was older, with jet-black hair to her shoulders. She looked up from the tablet in her hands to greet Victoria. "We wanted to thank you before we take over the investigation from here. I just finished reading your preliminary report. Very interesting."

Victoria glanced down at the crime scene photos on the table. One of them included a coroner's photo of Steve Foster. Rork slid it toward her. "We have Foster's autopsy results. The likely cause of death is hypothermia, after suffering internal injuries from the avalanche. No signs of foul play. Just terrible timing."

"And his decision to move the barricades and drive through them," Coleman added. "He'd tried to escape, and ended up in a worse trap."

"What about our victim? Jane Doe?" Victoria asked.

"Cause of death was an internal brain injury," Rork answered.

"Do you know who she is?"

"Yes. The medical examiner used dental records. Her real name was Misty Lemming. Twenty-nine years old. Born and raised in Connecticut. She was in prison for corporate theft but got released long before completing her sentence. No one ever heard from her again."

Victoria clasped her hands together. "I knew she'd been in prison, yet her prints weren't in the system."

Coleman nodded. "That's right. Her employer must have recruited her from jail, changed her name, and erased her prints from the Federal databases. They have serious resources and capabilities. Security audits of Foster's company reveal months of failed cyberattacks. When those didn't work, the thieves sent someone to seduce Foster."

Victoria looked over the photos again. The frozen corpse in the silver sweater seemed like a lifetime ago, though it had been less than a week. So much death and deception, all for an algorithm that would probably be obsolete within a few years.

"Did they get what they were after from Foster?"

"We recovered a thumb drive from a small purse in Foster's vehicle." Rork tapped another photo. "The purse belonged to Anna. The information never made it to whomever she worked for."

Coleman set her tablet down. "We formally charged Ms. Winters, for lack of her real name, with corporate espionage, conspiracy to commit theft, and felony murder. We agree with your assessment that she and Misty Lemming were colleagues. Two operatives, and one became expendable."

"Any leads on their employer?"

"Dead ends everywhere. Burner phones, high-quality fake IDs. But we're not giving up."

The resolution felt incomplete. Without Anna's cooperation, they might never know the full story. Anna faced trial and would most likely go back to prison, but the shadowy organization she worked for would continue operating, finding new assets and targets. The FBI might chase individual cases forever without making a dent in the larger machine.

"You did good work at Black Ridge with no backup and improvised equipment," Coleman said when the debrief was wrapping up. "That's going in your file."

"Thank you for helping me when I was there," Victoria said. "I'm grateful."

"That's what we're here for," Coleman said.

"It was great to work with you," Rork added.

After a bit of small talk and questions about The Numbers Killer case she'd worked years ago, they shook hands and said their goodbyes. Victoria left them to continue their investigation.

As she walked toward the elevator, her phone rang. A call from Ned.

"Hey. You're finished with your FBI meeting?"

"Just leaving."

"Good. I picked up our stuff from Black Ridge, and I'm on my way back to the city."

"Thank you for getting everything. How was the resort?" she asked as she pressed the down button.

"Power is back, but everyone wanted to get out. Including me. I'll meet you at Alex and Minka's condo."

"See you soon. I love you."

The elevator doors opened to carry her away from case files and crime scene photos for a short while.

SIXTY-FOUR

Five days ago

E verything is going great with Anna at Black Ridge. She's not as good a skier as my wife, but she's a lot better in bed. She's exactly what I need to get my mind off my work stress. Now that I'm ready to sell the algorithm, things are getting crazy.

I can't wait to go back to our room, drink the champagne I bought, and have fun with Anna.

A text comes in from an unknown number.

She's a liar. She isn't who you think she is.

My first thought is—who? But the pictures of Anna that follow make the subject clear.

Fear rises inside me as I scroll through the images. Anna and me at dinner last week, holding hands across the table. Walking through the resort yesterday. Laughing over breakfast. Someone has been watching us and taking pictures. Believing my wife must have hired a private investigator, I feel sick with shame.

The next photos make me think this isn't about my affair. At first, I don't recognize the woman with black hair in the photos. She's dressed so differently than the Anna I'm with now. She's with a man I've never seen, and she seems to know him very well. Their hands are all over each other.

Is he a former boyfriend? A husband she never mentioned? Is he the one behind this?

I keep scrolling, my world collapsing as I stare at more photos of Anna. Blonde hair now, and a different man she's equally *friendly* with.

I've been played.

Did someone set me up to have an affair? Is this a blackmail scheme? Nausea wracks my body.

Anna reaches for me, and I move away. I can't even look at her.

I throw cash on the bar and storm toward the elevator, my mind racing. Anna tricked me. She made me believe every lie.

I've built a multi-million-dollar company, and I'm about to sell an algorithm I created for an insane amount of money. How could I have been so stupid?

That thought makes me freeze. The algorithm. Two women from my company disappeared while working on the project. Vanished without a trace. I didn't tell the police my suspicions. It sounded crazy, for one. And I didn't want anyone to know what we'd created.

Is this related? Did Anna copy files from my laptop while I was sleeping? My phone? She's never once asked me about my work or what I do. Was that part of the scheme?

In my room, I lock the bolt and chain behind me and tear through her things until I find a small black purse. There's a tiny thumb drive hidden in a makeup holder. Another wave of sickness hits me.

Calm the hell down, I tell myself. The thumb drive might be her address book. Her poetry. It could be anything. As soon as I get out of here, I'm going to find out. I pocket the drive and grab her purse in case it has something else I've missed.

Somewhere in my emails is the number for a company that handles security and investigations. After a quick search through my phone, I jot the number on the resort's notepad, then tear off the top sheet. I'll call from the car so that I can get out of here before I have to face Anna again. I'd like to confront her, but why bother when I can't believe a word she says?

Out of habit, I leave tip money on the console, then curse myself for the automatic courtesy. I don't trust Anna anymore. She'll probably steal the cash before housekeeping gets here.

When I step outside, the storm's ferocity shocks me. Snow stings my face like the worst micro-needling procedure I've ever had.

Fresh powder has buried my SUV. I brush the windshield with the back of my arm, then throw everything into the back seat.

At 9:08, I call Jewell Security and leave a voicemail. "This is Steve Foster. Start a background check on a lady called Anna Winters immediately. I'm sending a photo. I want to know everything about her."

While I'm on the phone with them, I text Elaine: "Just left the hotel. On my way home. Road conditions are bad. It's going to take a lot longer than usual."

Then I remember Elaine is in Aspen with her girlfriend. Or girlfriends. That will give me more time to figure things out. Like how to explain that I fell for the oldest con in the book, and I can't tell the difference between attraction and manipulation. And the lady who tricked me might have stolen the algorithm.

I've made a mistake. The biggest mistake of my life.

I'm almost half a mile down the road when I remember my skis are still in the equipment room. I may be upset, but there's no way I'm leaving them behind. I turn my SUV around and drive back to the lodge, banging my hand against the steering wheel and cursing out loud.

The ski storage area is behind the main building. My shortcut has me struggling through knee-deep drifts and slipping on the ice beneath. My phone rings. First, the burner, which has to be Anna because she's the only one with that number. Then, my personal phone. I ignore both.

As I'm leaving the equipment shed with my skis, I see her stumbling through the snow about fifty yards away. Behind her, another figure moves through the darkness, following her path. Neither of them sees me.

Part of me wants to go after Anna, to demand answers, to confront her about the photos and the thumb drive. But what's the point? She's a liar, and a small part of me is afraid. I don't want to be the next person from my company to disappear. If I'm right about that part, I'm lucky to be leaving here alive.

I turn away and trudge back to my SUV. After loading my equipment, I leave for the second time tonight.

This time, when I'm almost to the point where I turned around earlier, two figures in ski patrol gear are hauling wooden sawhorses across the road. They stop when they see me. I roll my window partway down as one approaches.

"Road's closed," he says as the wind rushes in. "Avalanche risk. Trust me on this. You need to turn around."

"I have to get home."

"Not tonight. The roads aren't safe. Head back to the lodge."

He just stands there, blocking my path, and I wonder if this is part of Anna's plan to trap me.

I return to the parking lot and remain in the idling car, heater blasting, watching the snow accumulate on my windshield. Maybe they're right. Maybe I should wait until morning. But not when Anna and whoever took those photos are here, too.

When I check the weather, it shows the snow is going to stop soon. We have a lull before the next storm hits.

Time crawls. I look at the photos again and get angrier than before. I leave another message for Jewell Security and tell them it's urgent.

When they finish positioning the blockades, ski patrol drives past me on their snowmobiles.

At 10:15, when the snow is definitely letting up, I get out and drag the first sawhorse aside, ignoring the giant Danger sign attached to it. The wind nearly knocks me over, but I create a gap wide enough for my SUV.

I'm back in the car, creeping forward through the gap, when I hear a sound I've never heard before. Like a massive freight train bearing down at full speed, or the earth ripping apart at the seams.

When I look left, the entire mountain is moving. A torrent of snow rushes down the slope above me, devouring trees and boulders in its path.

I floor the accelerator, but it's too late. The avalanche catches my SUV like a toy, lifting it, spinning it, carrying me forward in a maelstrom of ice and broken trees. The airbag explodes in my face.

Before everything goes black, I realize this mistake was bigger than my last.

SIXTY-FIVE

Peter sat in his empty office, watching the last of the guests load into shuttle buses headed for the airport. Corporate was preparing for an onslaught of lawsuits, and insurance investigators were digging into the resort's "management protocols."

Through his office window, three maintenance men heaved the charred remains of the lobby's Christmas tree into a garbage truck. Peter cringed, remembering the men fighting over blankets. He hadn't seen that coming.

He turned back to his computer screen, where his cursor blinked at the top of a blank document. After letting out a long sigh, Peter typed a single line: I submit my resignation as General Manager of Black Ridge Resort, effective immediately.

The avalanche that blocked the road wasn't his fault. That section of the access road wasn't resort property, he'd tried to remind everyone. The city crews had dropped the ball, not his team. But no one else seemed to get that distinction. In the court of public opinion, Black Ridge was responsible for everything that had gone wrong: getting stranded by the storm, a murder, the power outage, panic, the failed generators, the food poisoning. It all happened on his watch.

Scrubbing and scraping sounds reached him from the lodge, coming from the new cleaning crew Corporate had hired. They'd dressed in hazmat suits, ridiculous in his opinion. They were treating every surface in the lobby, sterilizing and disinfecting everything from the bathrooms to the kitchen.

The ordeal had unleashed a media circus. Every network picked up the story of the resort's deteriorating conditions. The kid with the purple mohawk posted that he'd sold his footage for a small fortune and mentioned plans for a movie called the Black Ridge Nightmare. Not to mention the story of the already famous FBI agent who got buried in an avalanche while pursuing a murder suspect.

Peter had spent fifteen years climbing the hospitality ladder, building his reputation one successful season at a time. Now, unfortunately for him, his legacy would be the manager of the Black Ridge disaster.

SIXTY-SIX

Victoria knocked once below the Christmas wreath before pushing open the door to the condo. When she walked into the kitchen, the scent stopped her in her tracks.

"Come in, come in." Minka rushed forward to hug her.

"It smells so good in here. It smells like..." Victoria paused, inhaling deeply as memories flooded back. She spotted the ceramic bowl on the kitchen counter, filled with fresh oranges studded with whole cloves. "Oh, my mother made those every Christmas."

Minka's face lit up with a knowing smile. "That's why Alex wanted to do it."

Victoria's throat tightened with unexpected emotion. She could still picture her mother pressing cloves into oranges, filling their childhood home with the same warm, spicy fragrance. Alex was only twelve that last Christmas. "He remembered that?"

Alex emerged from the living room, Elspeth trotting beside him. "Course I remembered. I used to pull out the cloves and eat the oranges."

Victoria looked at the holiday cards taped to the fridge. She recognized some of Alex's classmates from high school and college, now in photos with spouses and babies. She pointed to a card featuring a man in a tuxedo next to a bride. "Is that Tommy from our old neighborhood?"

"That's him. He got married last winter. Had a small ceremony in Vail."

Victoria studied another card showing a family of four on a beach. "This is Sarah from your college team, right?"

"Yeah. Can you believe it? She has two kids now. Lives in California."

Ned entered the kitchen from the living room and embraced her. "I beat you here."

"Let's go sit," Minka said.

She led them into the living room, where a tall Christmas tree stood in the corner. Lights twinkled around ornaments that looked collected over the years rather than bought as a set. Evergreen garland draped the fireplace mantel, accented with simple red velvet bows. The Denver skyline was visible through the windows.

The hosts had arranged crackers, cheese, fruits, and vegetables on a serving board, and Victoria helped herself.

"Were you at Black Ridge today?" she asked Alex as she spread cheese and a peppery jam onto a cracker.

"Nope. The resort is going to close for the next three weeks, maybe longer. Insurance investigations, safety reviews, repairs, the whole thing. Your report helped Jordan, by the way. He got suspended pending internal review, but the issue is getting handled in house. Figured you would want to know."

Victoria nodded, grateful for how that had worked out. Jordan's mistakes had been born of panic, not malice. He deserved a second chance.

Alex cleared his throat. "On another topic, I keep thinking about you under all that snow."

"Alex—" Victoria began.

"Let me finish. I've taken risks before, just like you, and it's not fair to Minka. Seeing you buried made me realize what I put her through. So now... I'm not certain I want to go back to Black Ridge. I'm considering a change. More of a desk job."

Victoria's eyes widened as the corners of her mouth rose. She could hardly believe what she was hearing. "Really?"

Minka curled up beside him. "We've been talking about it. Elspeth stays with Alex, of course. She's earned her retirement."

Minka had been unusually quiet, a small smile playing at her lips as she watched the three of them. She glanced at Alex, who nodded.

"We asked you here because it's been a while since we were together, and we wanted to share some good news in person," she said, her hand resting on her stomach.

Alex was grinning. They stretched the suspense for seconds before he blurted, "We're having a baby."

Tears sprang to Victoria's eyes for the second time that evening. "Oh! Yes! I knew it! I knew it!"

"Due mid-May." Alex's grin widened as he pulled Minka closer. "We're just through the first trimester."

Victoria jumped up to embrace them, and Ned was close behind with congratulations.

"This is the best news." Victoria squeezed Minka's hands. "I'm so happy for you both and so excited to be an aunt. Oh, does Dad know? Have you told him yet?"

"We did," Alex said. "He's excited, too."

As they relaxed on the couch, snow was falling outside, but it was peaceful, even beautiful. Just weather, not a threat.

Victoria tucked her legs beneath her. "When we were in your office that first night at Black Ridge, before the avalanche, I was thinking I wanted us to be close again, like when we were kids."

Alex laughed. "Careful what you wish for."

"No, I mean it. I'm so glad we came." She paused, glancing at Ned, then back to her brother. "And I understand what you said earlier. About taking risks and what that means for the people who love us." She squeezed Ned's hand. "I have some things to think about, too."

They'd survived another ordeal. The experience had stripped away the polite distance that had grown between the siblings over the years and returned them to the closeness and protectiveness they'd shared as children.

Victoria would carry the memories of Black Ridge forever, but she'd also carry the comfort of Ned's arm around her, the sound of Alex's laughter, the warmth of Minka's smile, Elspeth's contented sighs as she dozed by the tree, and the promise of new beginnings.

NOTE FROM THE AUTHOR

Hello, this is Jenifer Ruff, the author. Thank you for choosing LIES IN THE SNOW. Black Ridge is entirely fictional. I hope you pictured your own version of the ski resort as you read.

I wrote this novel so it could be enjoyed as a standalone. It's also book ten in a series featuring Agent Victoria.

I love putting my characters in dire situations, forcing them to make difficult decisions where true character emerges. Victoria's ordeal at Black Ridge is one of many harrowing trials she's survived with courage and determination.

Throughout this story, there were mentions of her other investigations: Victoria and Ned's survival after a plane crash, the time she was dumped in the ocean and left for dead, her first confrontation with a serial killer, and when Ned's best friend went missing at his own wedding. If you're curious about those cases, all of Victoria's stories are available in print, ebook, and audiobook. They always include the villain's point of view. Book one is THE NUMBERS KILLER.

If you enjoyed LIES IN THE SNOW, I would be deeply grateful if you'd consider leaving a review or telling a friend. Word of mouth means everything to authors like me, and I'm thankful for every reader who takes the time to share their thoughts.

All the best,
Jenifer Ruff

ALSO BY JENIFER RUFF

The Agent Victoria Heslin Thriller Series

The Numbers Killer
Pretty Little Girls
When They Find Us
Ripple of Doubt
The Groom Went Missing
Vanished on Vacation
The Atonement Murders
The Ones They Buried
The Bad Neighbor
Lies in the Snow

THE FBI & CDC Thriller Series

Only Wrong Once, Only One Cure, Only One Wave

The Brooke Walton Series

Everett, Rothaker, The Intern

Psychological Thrillers

When She Escaped
Lauren's Secret

Made in United States
Cleveland, OH
18 December 2025

28559564R00166